# Cat & Cat

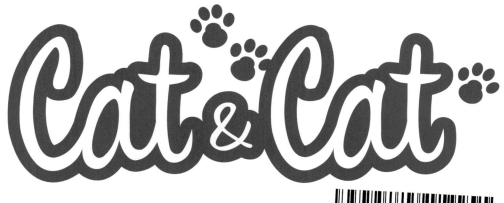

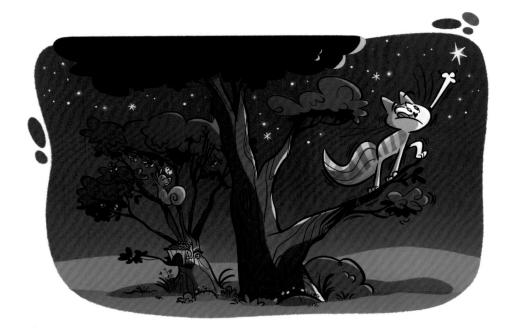

PAPERCUTZ

# MORE GREAT GRAPHIC NOVEL SERIES AVAILABLE FROM
# PAPERCUT Z™

THE SMURFS TALES

BRINA THE CAT

CAT & CAT

THE SISTERS

ATTACK OF THE STUFF

LOLA'S SUPER CLUB

SCHOOL FOR EXTRATERRESTRIAL GIRLS

GERONIMO STILTON REPORTER

THE MYTHICS

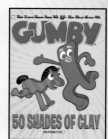

GUMBY

MELOWY

BLUEBEARD

GILLBERT

ASTERIX

FUZZY BASEBALL

THE CASAGRANDES

THE LOUD HOUSE

MANOSAURS

GEEKY F@B 5

THE ONLY LIVING GIRL

## papercutz.com
Also available where ebooks are sold.

Melowy, Geronimo Stilton; © 2018 Atlantyca S.p.A; The Sisters, Cat & Cat © 2018 BAMBOO ÉDITION; Brina the Cat © 2021 TUNUÉ (Tunué s.r.l.); Attack of the Stuff © 2021 Jim Benton; Lola's Super Club © Christine Beigel + Pierre Fouillet, 2010, Bang. Ediciones, 2011, 2013; School for Extraterrestrial Girls © 2021 Jeremy Whitley and Jamie Noguchi; Mythics © 2021 Éditions Delcourt; GUMBY ©2018 Prema Toy Co., Inc.; Bluebeard © 2018 Metaphrog; Gillbert © 2021 Art Baltazar; ASTERIX® - OBELIX® - IDEFIX® -DOGMATIX ®© 2021 HACHETTE LIVRE; Fuzzy Baseball © 2018 by John Steven Gurney; The Loud House and The Casagrandes © 2018 Viacom International Inc.; Manosaurs © 2018 Stuart Fischer and Papercutz; Geeky Fab Five ©2021 Geeky Fab Five LLC.; The Only Living Girl © 2018-2019 Bottled Lightening LLC.

© Peyo - 2021 - Licensed through I.M.P.S. (Brussels) - www.smurf.com

# 4. SCAREDY CAT

CHRISTOPHE CAZENOVE
HERVÉ RICHEZ
SCRIPT

YRGANE RAMON
ART

YRGANE RAMON
JOÃO MOURA
COLOR

New York

*To my parents,*

*To Shadow, Tsatsiki, Lotus, and Pixel.*
*To the late Toudougras AKA Zigouingouin.*
*To La grisette, Jeannot, Villard & Minette.*
*To friends, readers, and all the cats who bring this series to life.*
*To Pierre.*
*Thanks.*

*— Thanks to Pierre Leloup for the preparation for colorization of the first half of this book.*
*A huge thanks to João Moura for the coloring of the characters in the second half of this volume.*

*www.joaomouraart.com*

*— Yrgane*

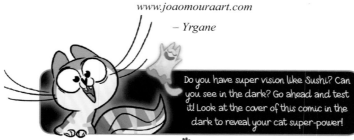

Do you have super vision like Sushi? Can you see in the dark? Go ahead and test it! Look at the cover of this comic in the dark to reveal your cat super-power!

# Cat & Cat

#4 "Scaredy Cat"
Christophe Cazenove &
Hervé Richez — Writers
Yrgane Ramon — Artist, Colorist
João Moura — Colorist
Joe Johnson — Translator
Wilson Ramos Jr.  —  Letterer

Special thanks to Catherine Loiselet

Production — Mark McNabb
Managing Editor — Jeff Whitman
Jim Salicrup
Editor-in-Chief

© 2017. 2018-2021 Bamboo Édition.
English translation and all other material © 2021 Papercutz.

Papercutz books may be purchased for business or promotional use. For information on bulk purchases please contact Macmillan Corporate and Premium Sales Department at
(800) 221-7945 x5442.

Hardcover ISBN: 978-1-5458-0700-2
Paperback ISBN: 978-1-5458-0701-9

Printed in Turkey
Elma Basım
July 2021

Distributed by Macmillan
First Papercutz Printing

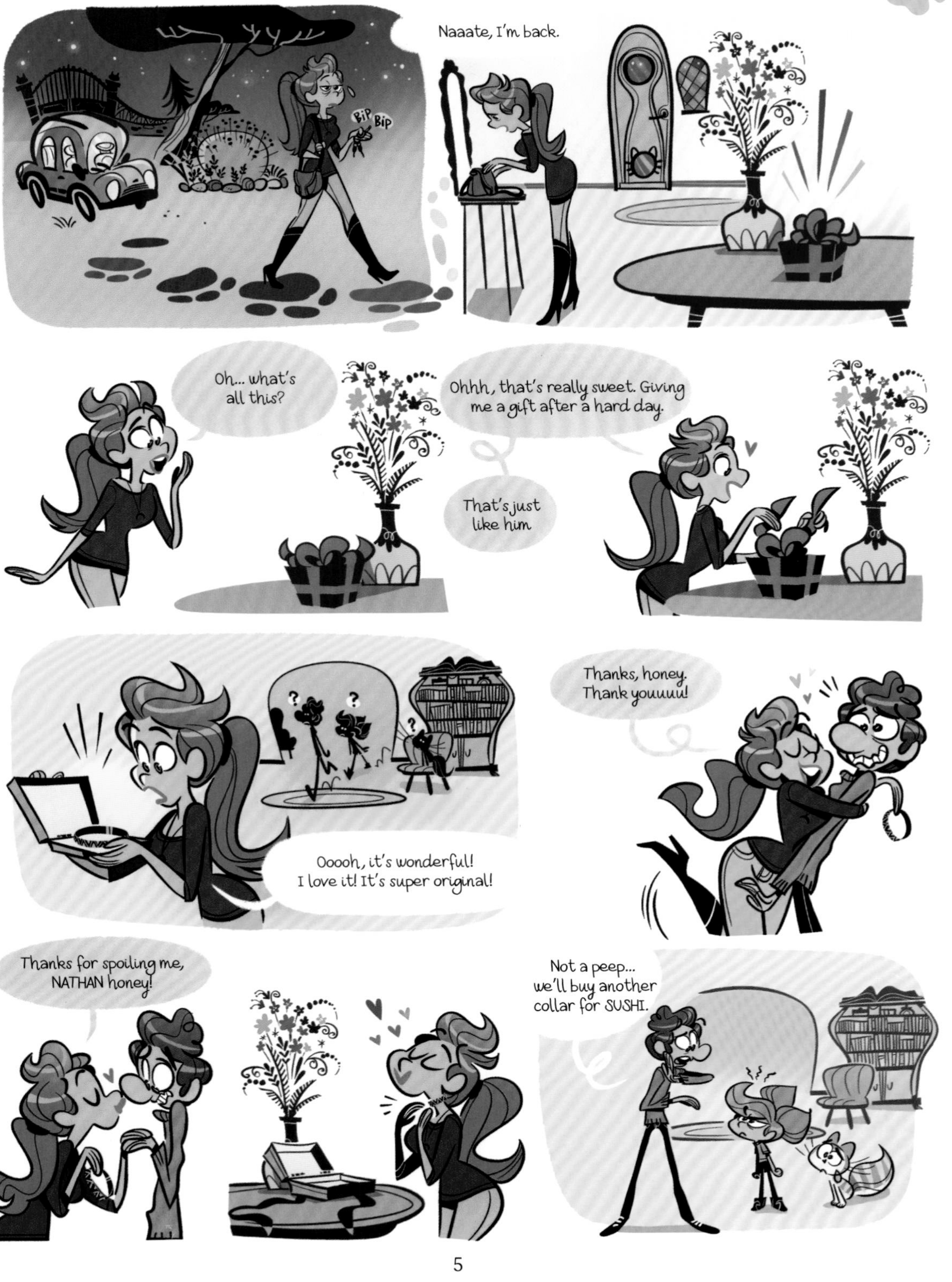
BIP BIP
Naaate, I'm back.
Oh... what's all this?
Ohhh, that's really sweet. Giving me a gift after a hard day.
That's just like him
Ooooh, it's wonderful! I love it! It's super original!
Thanks, honey. Thank youuuu!
Thanks for spoiling me, NATHAN honey!
Not a peep... we'll buy another collar for SUSHI.

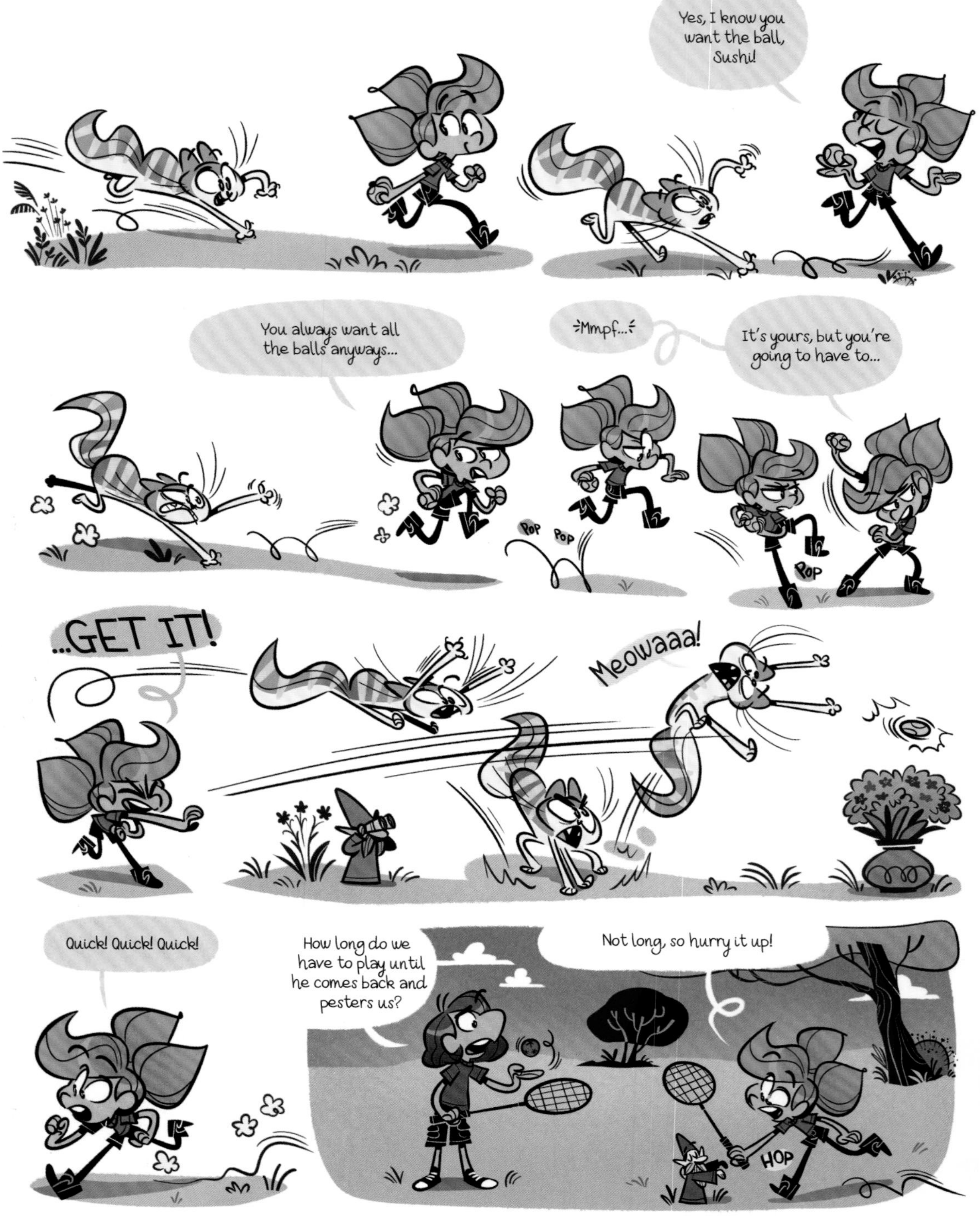
Yes, I know you want the ball, Sushi!
You always want all the balls anyways...
Mmpf...
It's yours, but you're going to have to...
POP POP
POP
...GET IT!
Meowaaa!
Quick! Quick! Quick!
How long do we have to play until he comes back and pesters us?
Not long, so hurry it up!
HOP

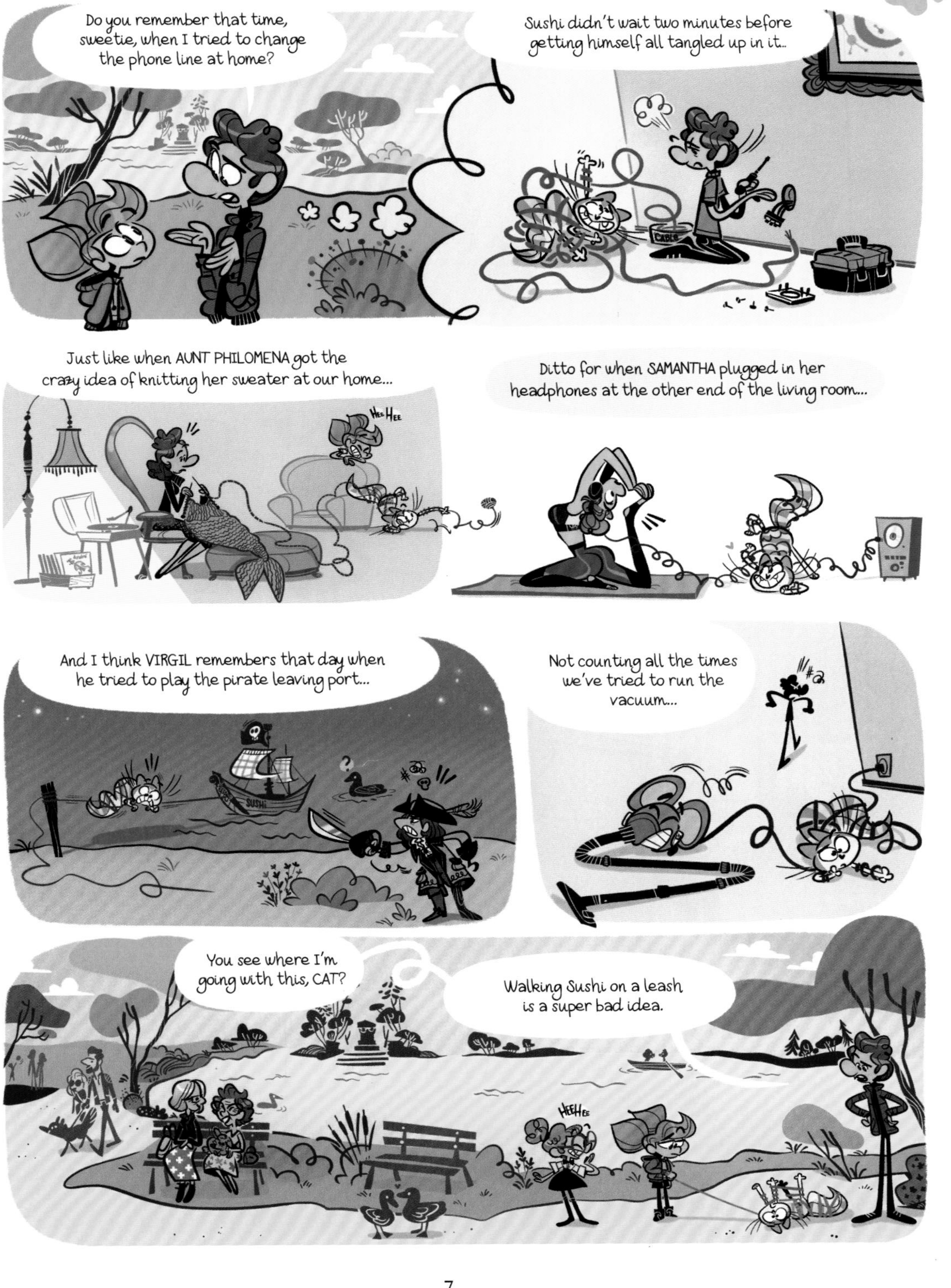
Do you remember that time, sweetie, when I tried to change the phone line at home?
Sushi didn't wait two minutes before getting himself all tangled up in it...
Just like when AUNT PHILOMENA got the crazy idea of knitting her sweater at our home...
Ditto for when SAMANTHA plugged in her headphones at the other end of the living room...
And I think VIRGIL remembers that day when he tried to play the pirate leaving port...
SUSHI
Not counting all the times we've tried to run the vacuum...
You see where I'm going with this, CAT?
Walking Sushi on a leash is a super bad idea.
HEEHEE

Stop, Miss Cat! STOP!

You can't go to school dressed like that!

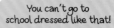

Oh, why not?

You're too old to be wearing a t-shirt with Sushi on it!

Huh?

Besides, you're in a strict school. No, you can't wear that!

But I love my Sushi. I want him always to be with me. Even as a photo on my t-shirt.

Go change, I said!

≥Sniff≥... Come on, Sushi, we'll choose something else... ≥Sniff...≥

Zwipp

HMF

And you're going to the office like that?

Like what?

?!

Tap Tap

8

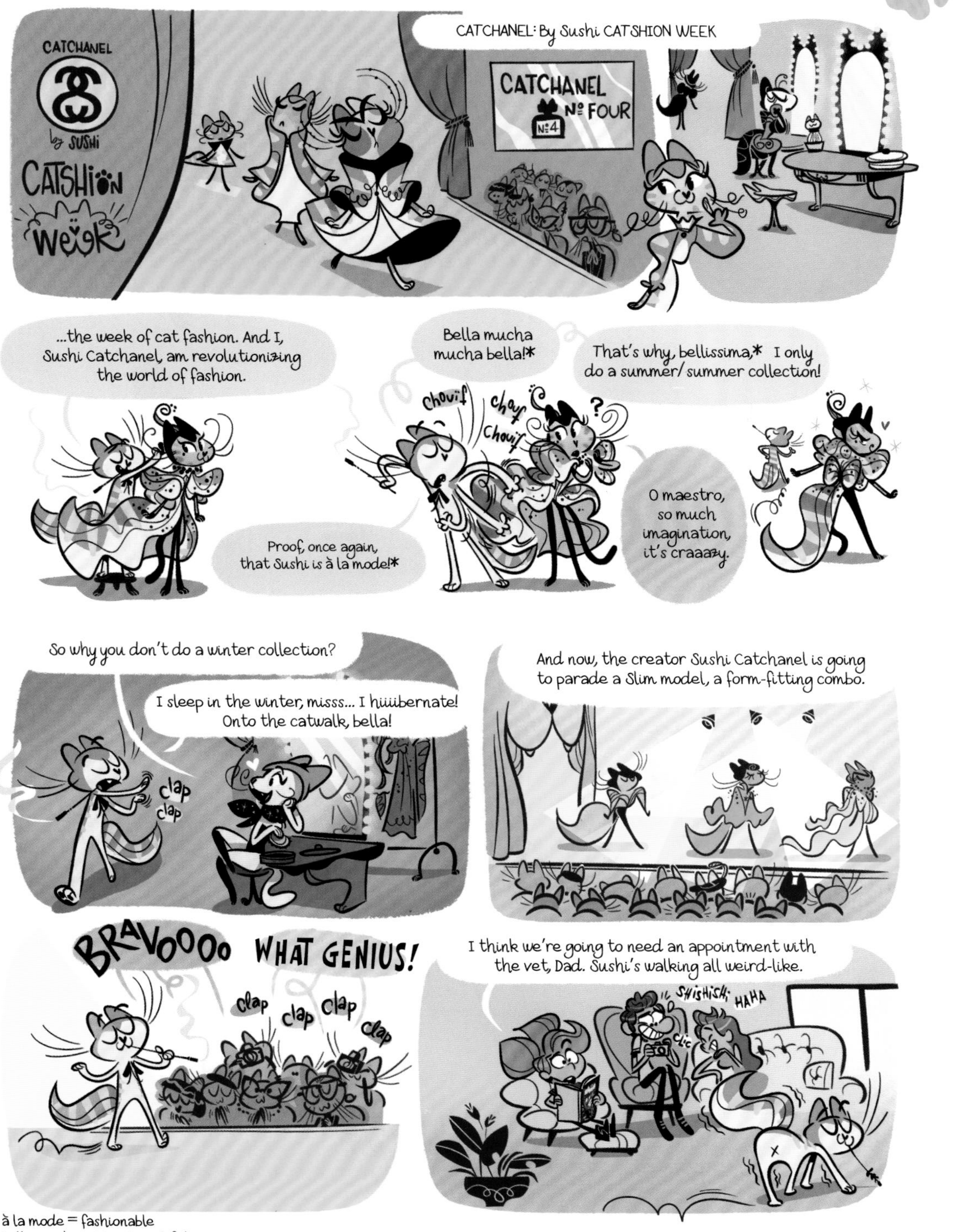
CATCHANEL
by SUSHi
CATSHiON
WEEK
CATCHANEL: By Sushi CATSHION WEEK
CATCHANEL
Nº FOUR
Nº4
...the week of cat fashion. And I, Sushi Catchanel, am revolutionizing the world of fashion.
Proof, once again, that Sushi is à la mode!*
Bella mucha mucha bella!*
Chouif
Chouf
Chouif
That's why, bellissima,* I only do a summer/summer collection!
O maestro, so much imagination, it's craaazy.
So why you don't do a winter collection?
I sleep in the winter, misss... I hiiiibernate! Onto the catwalk, bella!
clap
clap
And now, the creator Sushi Catchanel is going to parade a Slim model, a form-fitting combo.
BRAVOOOO
WHAT GENIUS!
clap
clap
clap
clap
I think we're going to need an appointment with the vet, Dad. Sushi's walking all weird-like.
SHISHISHi
HAHA
Clic

* à la mode = fashionable
Bella mucha = Very Beautiful
Bellissima = Gorgeous.

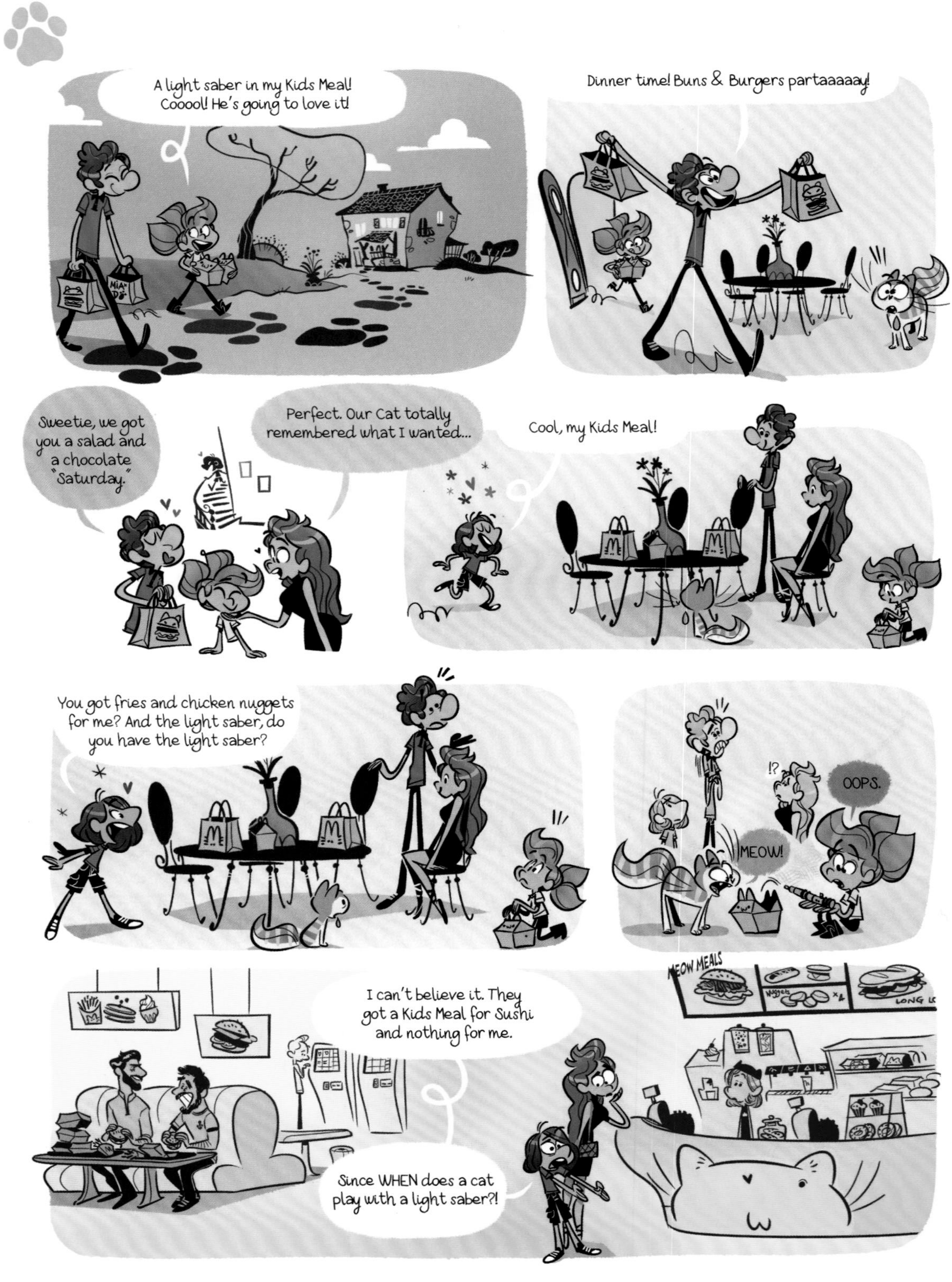
A light saber in my Kids Meal! Cooool! He's going to love it!
MIA DÖ
Dinner time! Buns & Burgers partaaaaay!
Sweetie, we got you a salad and a chocolate "Saturday."
Perfect. Our Cat totally remembered what I wanted...
Cool, my Kids Meal!
You got fries and chicken nuggets for me? And the light saber, do you have the light saber?
!?
OOPS.
MEOW!
MEOW MEALS
Nuggets
LONG
I can't believe it. They got a Kids Meal for Sushi and nothing for me.
Since WHEN does a cat play with a light saber?!

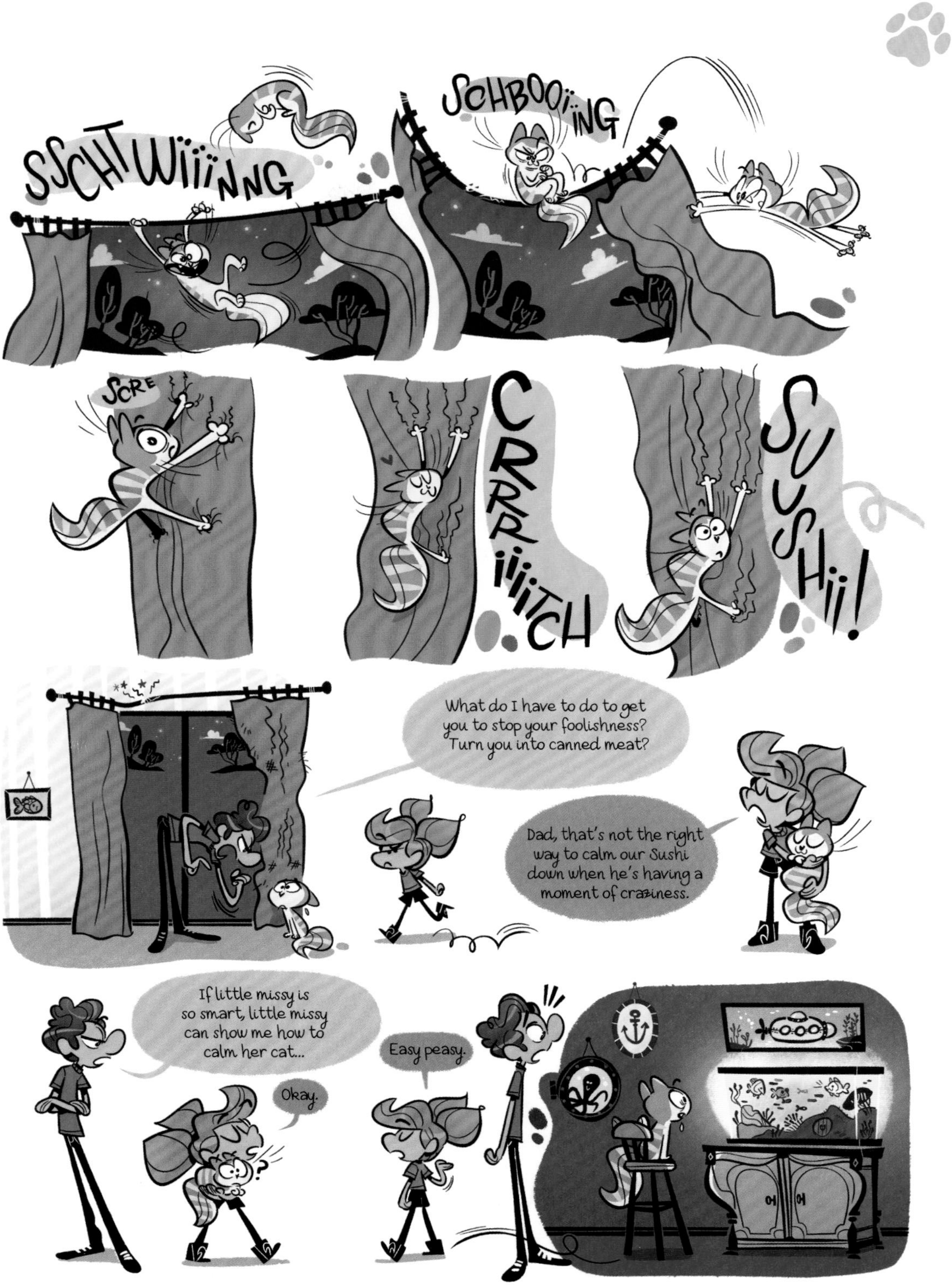
SSCHTWIIIINNG
SCHBOOÏING
SCRE
CRRRIIIITCH
SUUSHII!
What do I have to do to get you to stop your foolishness? Turn you into canned meat?
Dad, that's not the right way to calm our Sushi down when he's having a moment of craziness.
If little missy is so smart, little missy can show me how to calm her cat...
Okay.
Easy peasy.

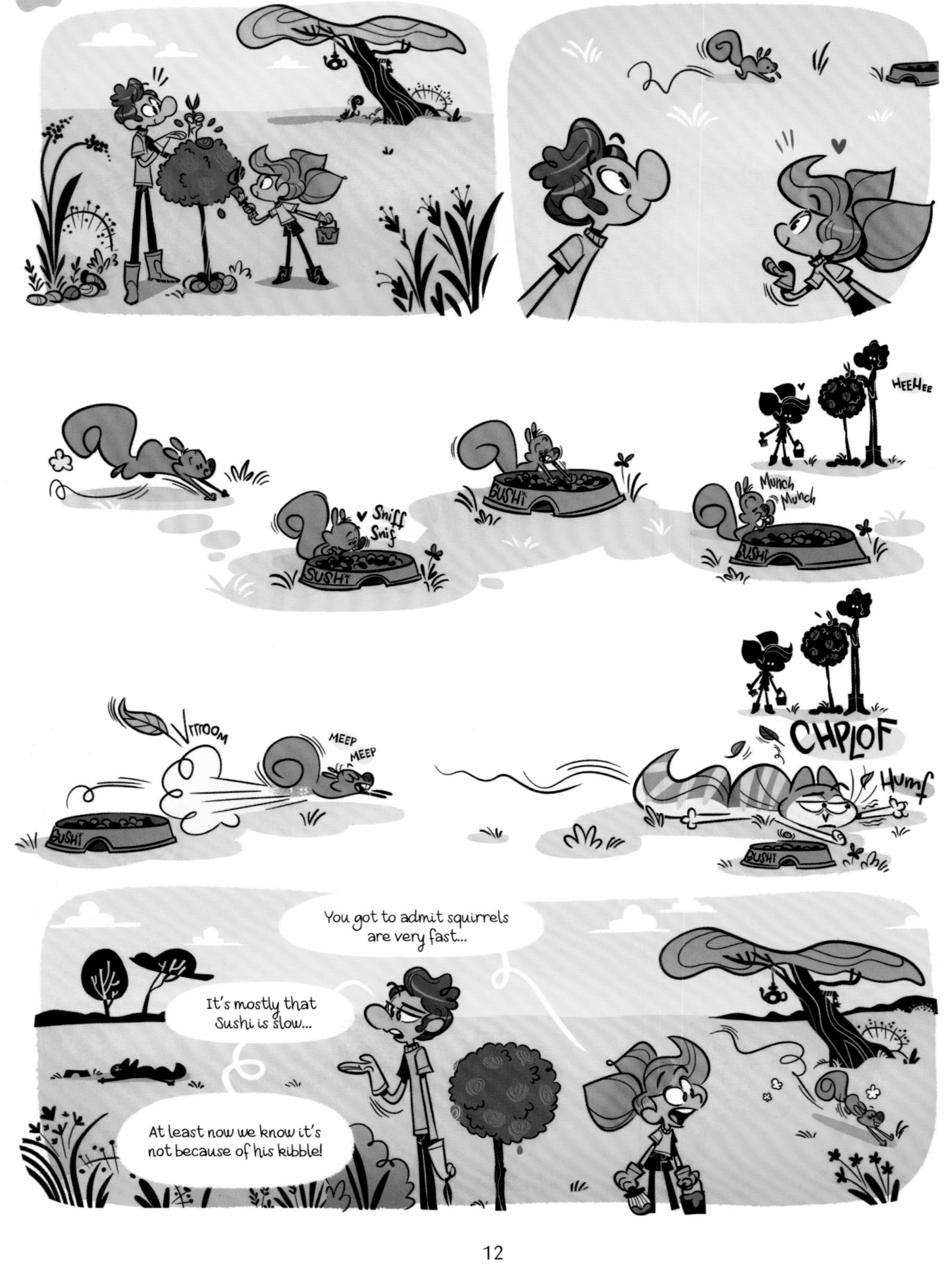
SUSHI
Sniff
Snif
SUSHI
HEEHEE
Munch
Munch
SUSHI
Vrrroom
MEEP
MEEP
SUSHI
CHPLOF
Humf
SUSHI
You got to admit squirrels are very fast...
It's mostly that Sushi is slow...
At least now we know it's not because of his kibble!

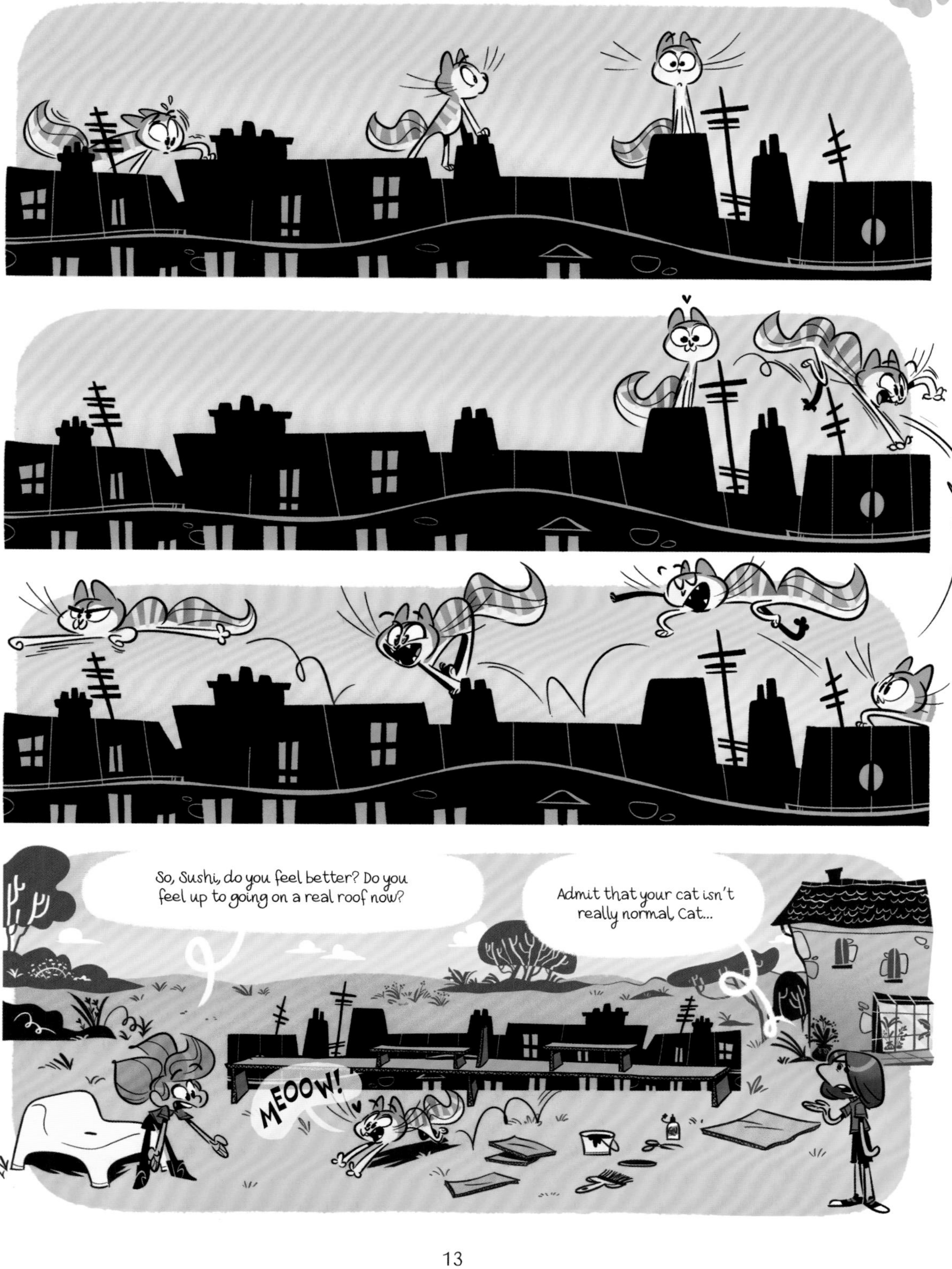
So, Sushi, do you feel better? Do you feel up to going on a real roof now?
Admit that your cat isn't really normal, Cat...
MEOOW!

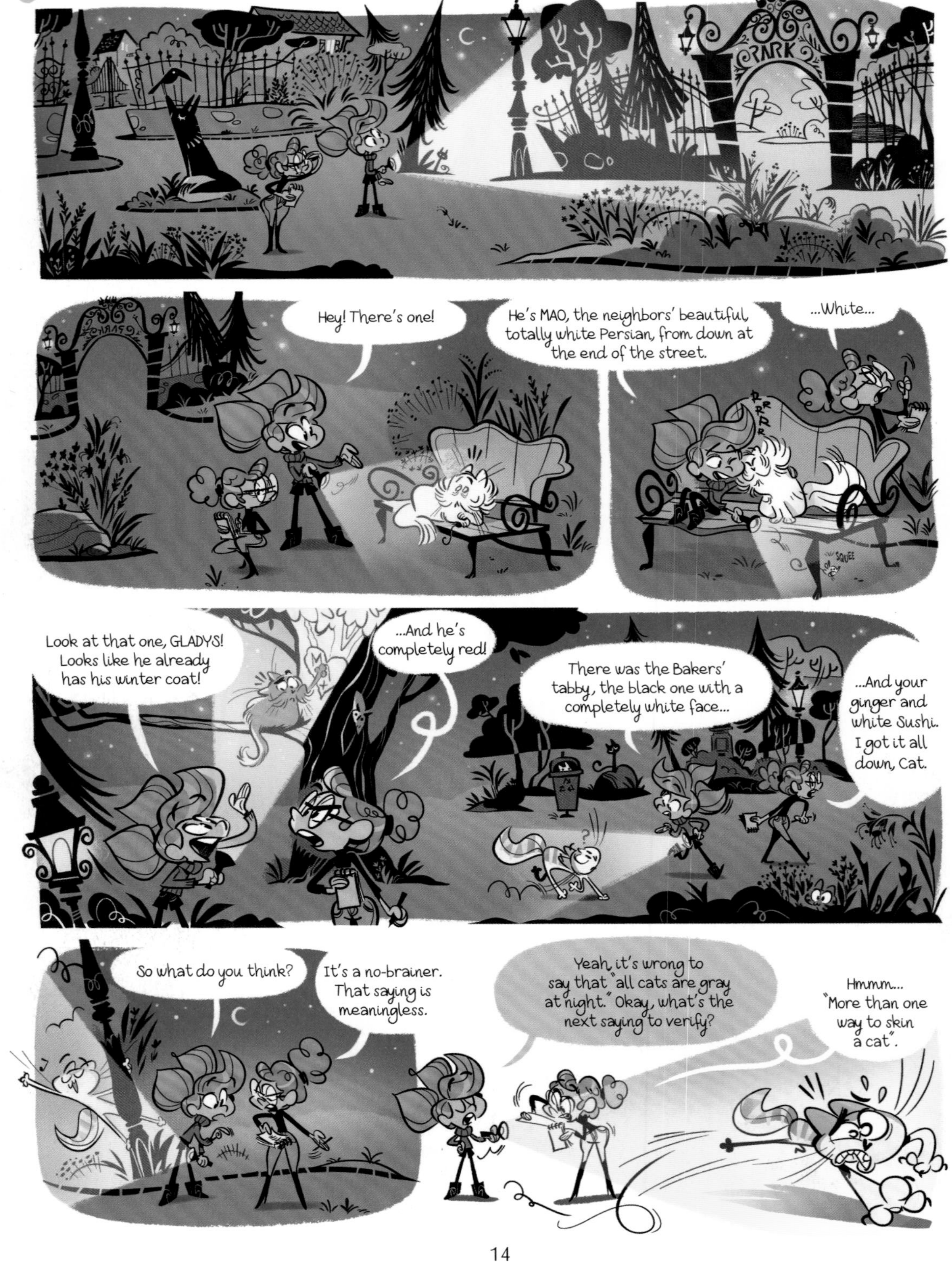
PARK
Hey! There's one!
He's MAO, the neighbors' beautiful, totally white Persian, from down at the end of the street.
...White...
SQUEE
Look at that one, GLADYS! Looks like he already has his winter coat!
...And he's completely red!
There was the Bakers' tabby, the black one with a completely white face...
...And your ginger and white Sushi. I got it all down, Cat.
So what do you think?
It's a no-brainer. That saying is meaningless.
Yeah, it's wrong to say that "all cats are gray at night." Okay, what's the next saying to verify?
Hmmm... "More than one way to skin a cat".

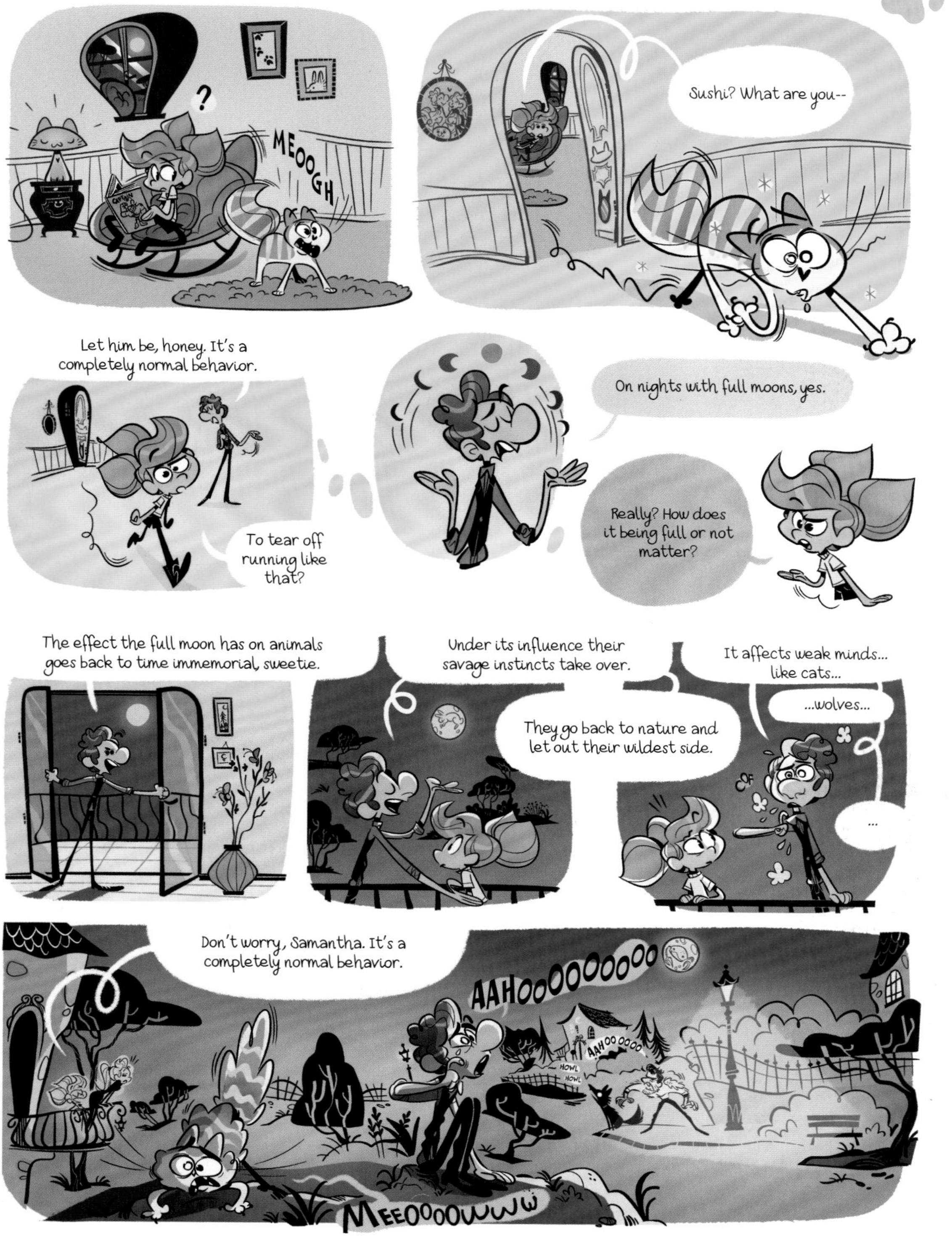
?
MEOOGH
Sushi? What are you--
Let him be, honey. It's a completely normal behavior.
To tear off running like that?
On nights with full moons, yes.
Really? How does it being full or not matter?
The effect the full moon has on animals goes back to time immemorial, sweetie.
Under its influence their savage instincts take over.
They go back to nature and let out their wildest side.
It affects weak minds... like cats...
...wolves...
COF
...
Don't worry, Samantha. It's a completely normal behavior.
AAHOOOOOOOOOO
AAHOO OOOO
HOWL
HOWL
MEEOOOOWWW

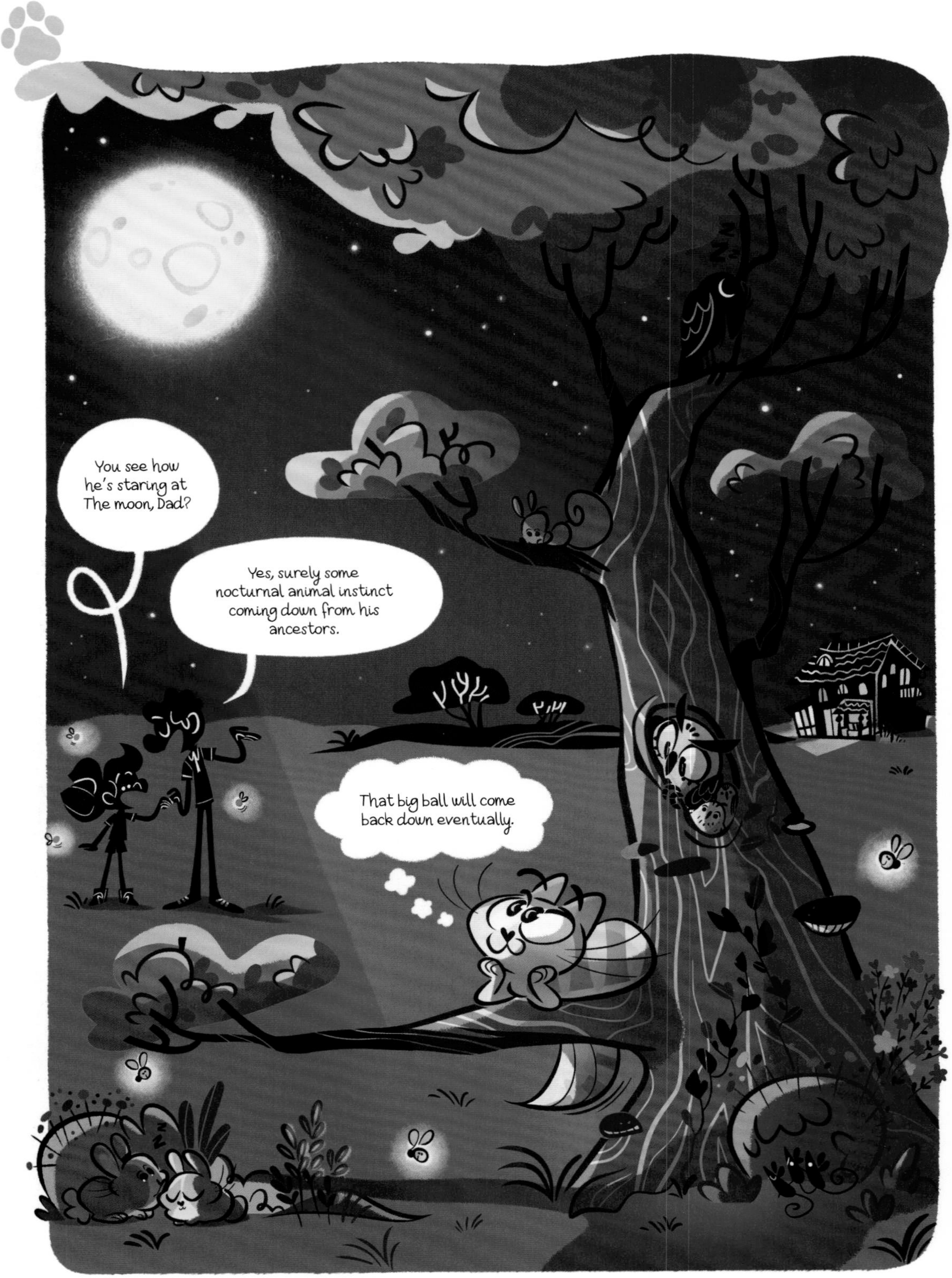
You see how he's staring at The moon, Dad?
Yes, surely some nocturnal animal instinct coming down from his ancestors.
That big ball will come back down eventually.

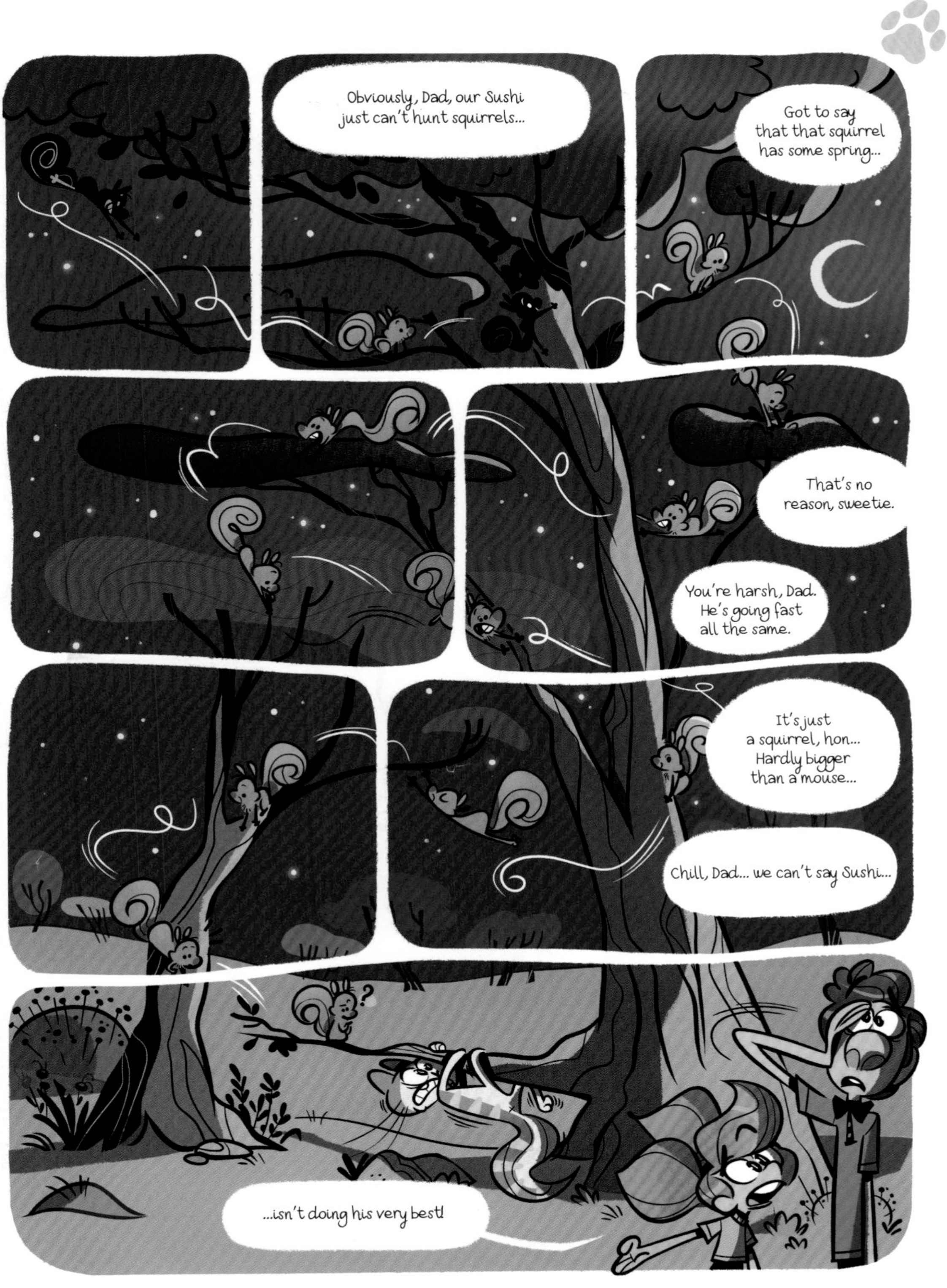
Obviously, Dad, our Sushi just can't hunt squirrels...
Got to say that that squirrel has some spring...
That's no reason, sweetie.
You're harsh, Dad. He's going fast all the same.
It's just a squirrel, hon... Hardly bigger than a mouse...
Chill, Dad... we can't say Sushi...
...isn't doing his very best!

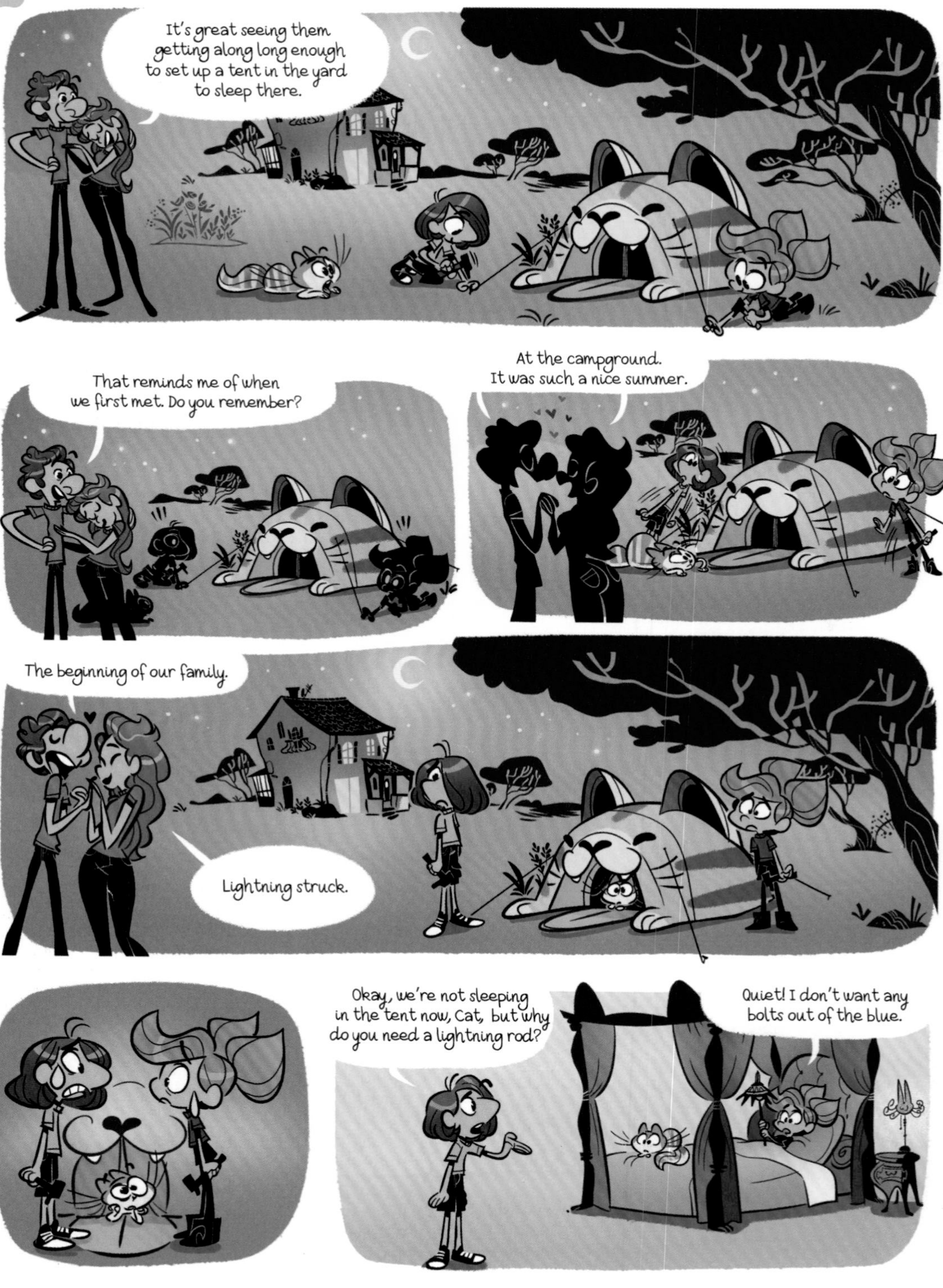
It's great seeing them getting along long enough to set up a tent in the yard to sleep there.
That reminds me of when we first met. Do you remember?
At the campground. It was such a nice summer.
The beginning of our family.
Lightning struck.
Okay, we're not sleeping in the tent now, Cat, but why do you need a lightning rod?
Quiet! I don't want any bolts out of the blue.

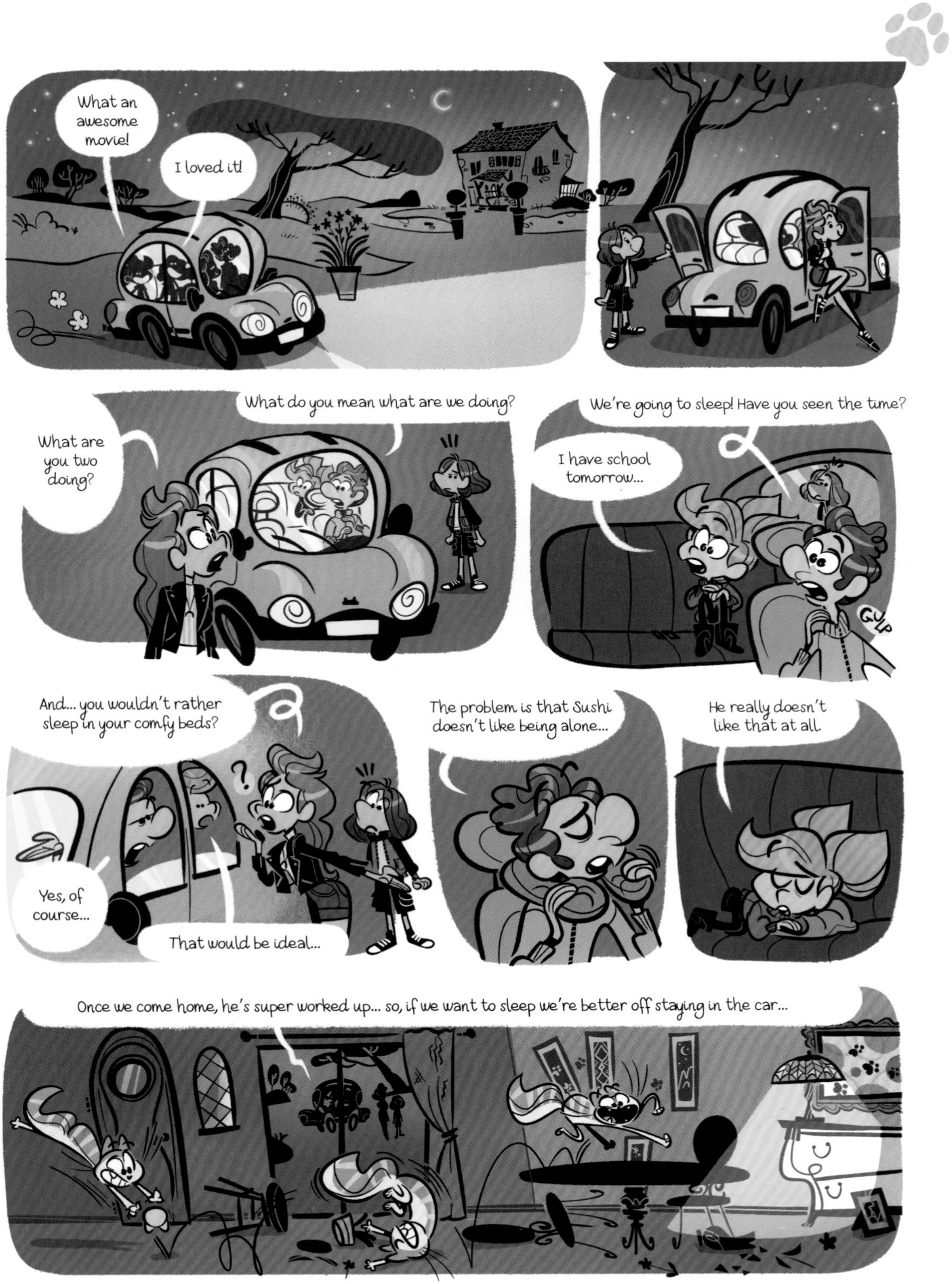
What an awesome movie!
I loved it!
What are you two doing?
What do you mean what are we doing?
We're going to sleep! Have you seen the time?
I have school tomorrow...
GULP
And... you wouldn't rather sleep in your comfy beds?
?
Yes, of course...
That would be ideal...
The problem is that Sushi doesn't like being alone...
He really doesn't like that at all.
Once we come home, he's super worked up... so, if we want to sleep we're better off staying in the car...

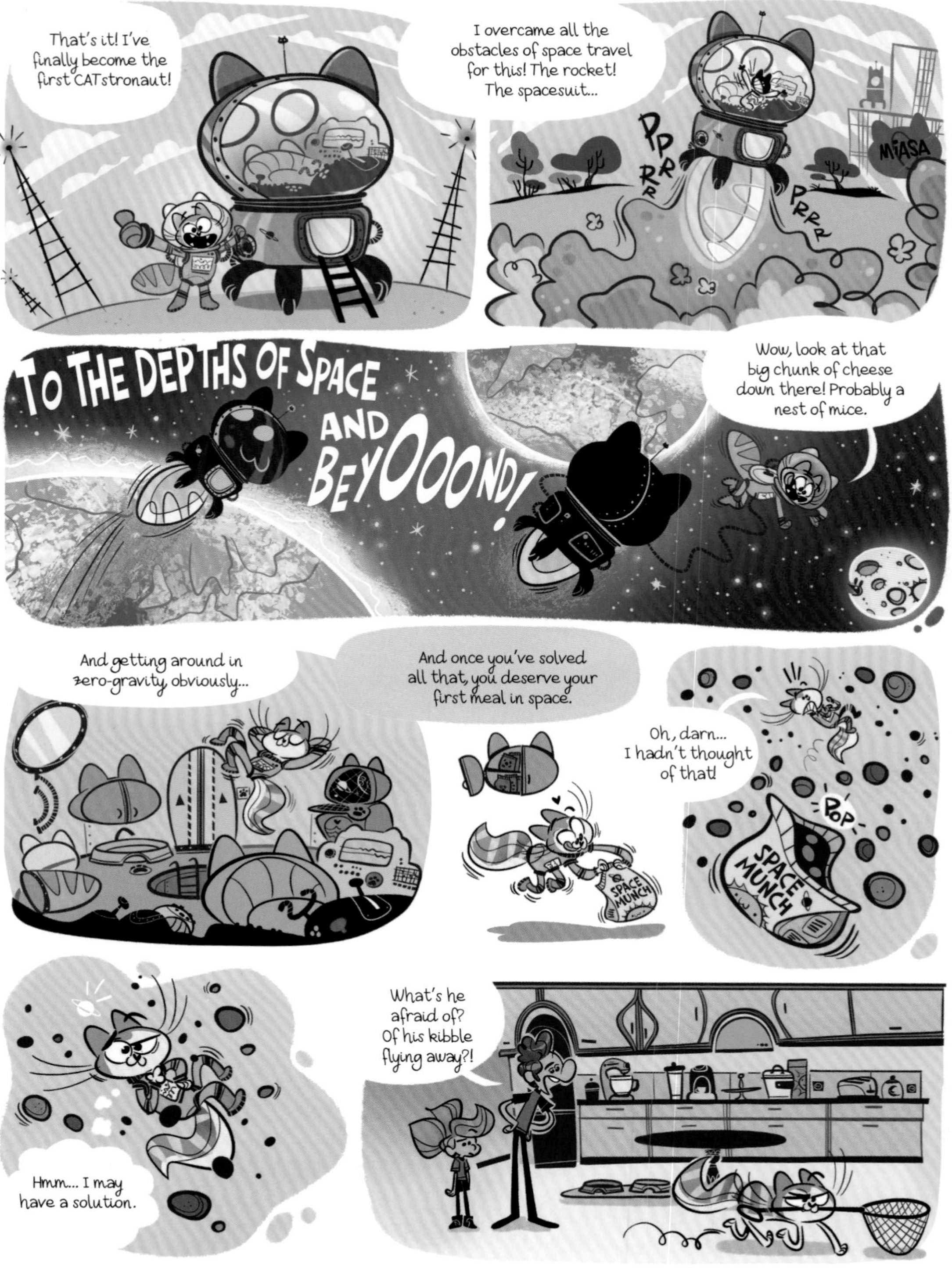
That's it! I've finally become the first CATstronaut!
I overcame all the obstacles of space travel for this! The rocket! The spacesuit...
PPRRR
PRRRR
MIASA
TO THE DEPTHS OF SPACE AND BEYOOOND!
Wow, look at that big chunk of cheese down there! Probably a nest of mice.
And getting around in zero-gravity, obviously...
And once you've solved all that, you deserve your first meal in space.
Oh, darn... I hadn't thought of that!
SPACE MUNCH
POP
SPACE MUNCH
Hmm... I may have a solution.
What's he afraid of? Of his kibble flying away?!

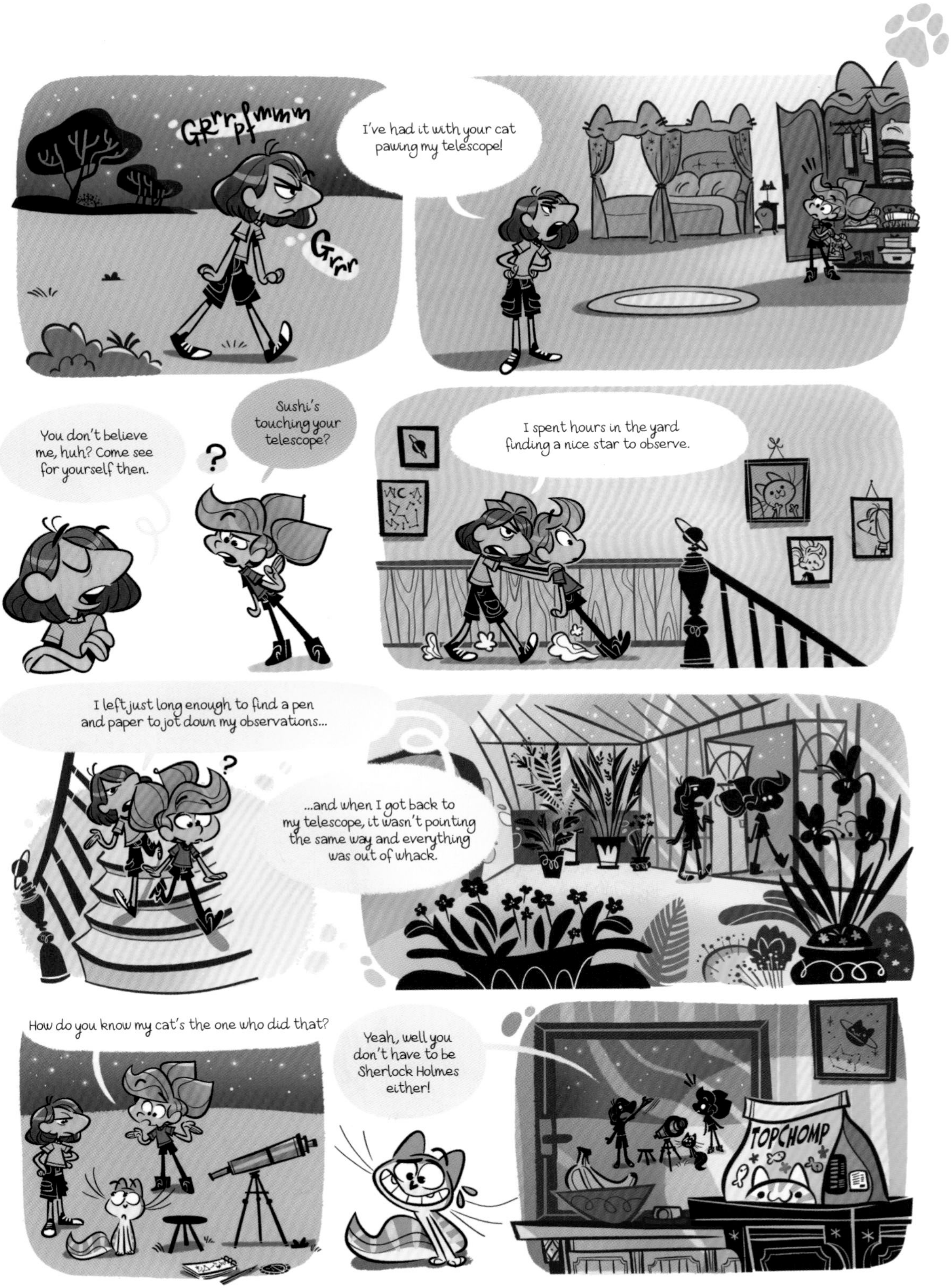
GRrrpfmmm
Grrr
I've had it with your cat pawing my telescope!
Sushi's touching your telescope?
You don't believe me, huh? Come see for yourself then.
?
I spent hours in the yard finding a nice star to observe.
I left just long enough to find a pen and paper to jot down my observations...
?
...and when I got back to my telescope, it wasn't pointing the same way and everything was out of whack.
How do you know my cat's the one who did that?
Yeah, well you don't have to be Sherlock Holmes either!
TOPCHOMP

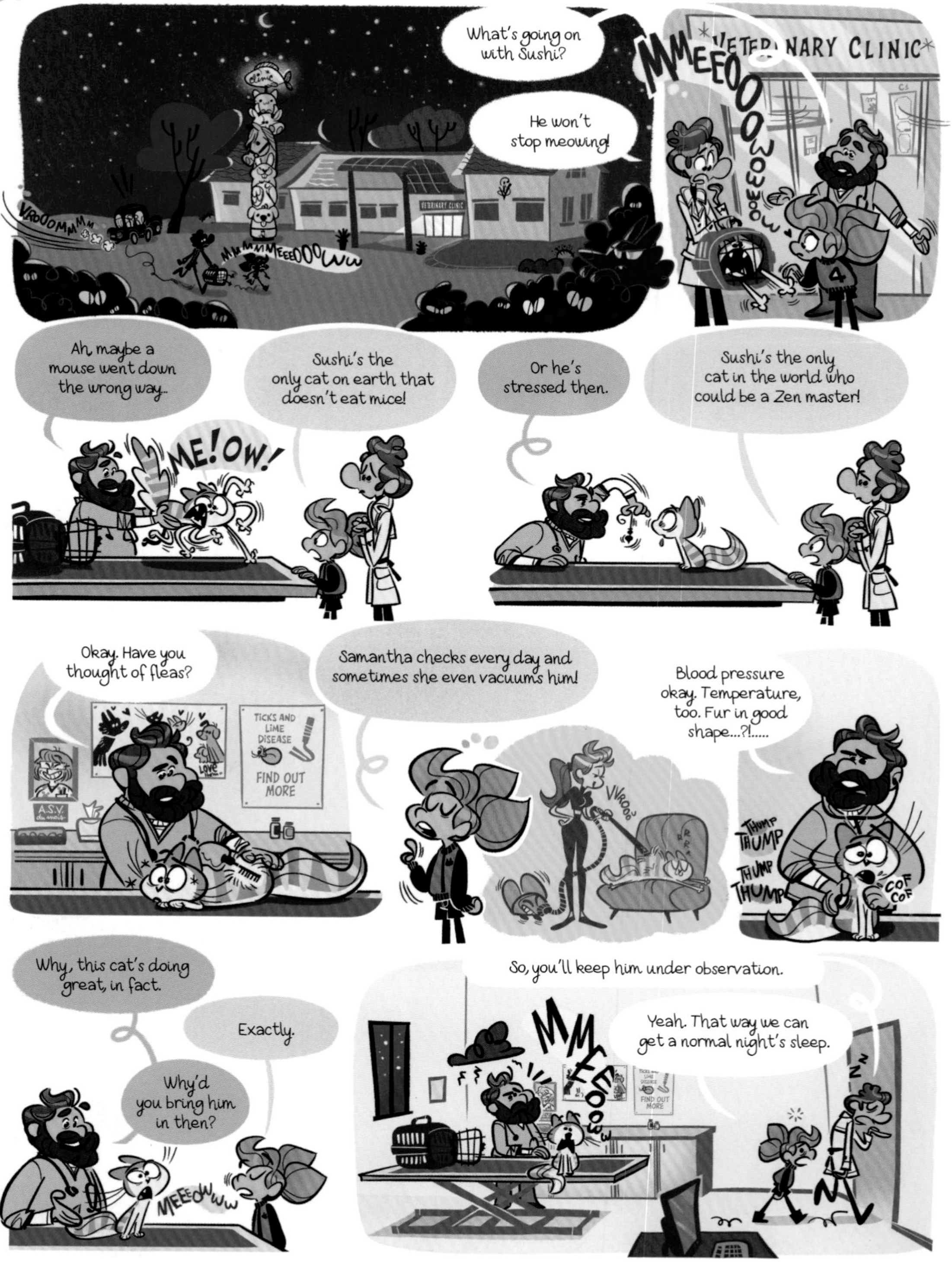

What's going on with Sushi?
He won't stop meowing!
VETERINARY CLINIC
MMEEOOOOOWWOWWOWW
Ah, maybe a mouse went down the wrong way...
ME!OW!
Sushi's the only cat on earth that doesn't eat mice!
Or he's stressed then.
Sushi's the only cat in the world who could be a Zen master!
Okay. Have you thought of fleas?
TICKS AND LIME DISEASE
FIND OUT MORE
Samantha checks every day and sometimes she even vacuums him!
Blood pressure okay. Temperature, too. Fur in good shape...?!.....
THUMP THUMP THUMP THUMP
COF COF
Why, this cat's doing great, in fact.
Exactly.
Why'd you bring him in then?
MEEEOWWW
So, you'll keep him under observation.
Yeah. That way we can get a normal night's sleep.
MMYEOOOW

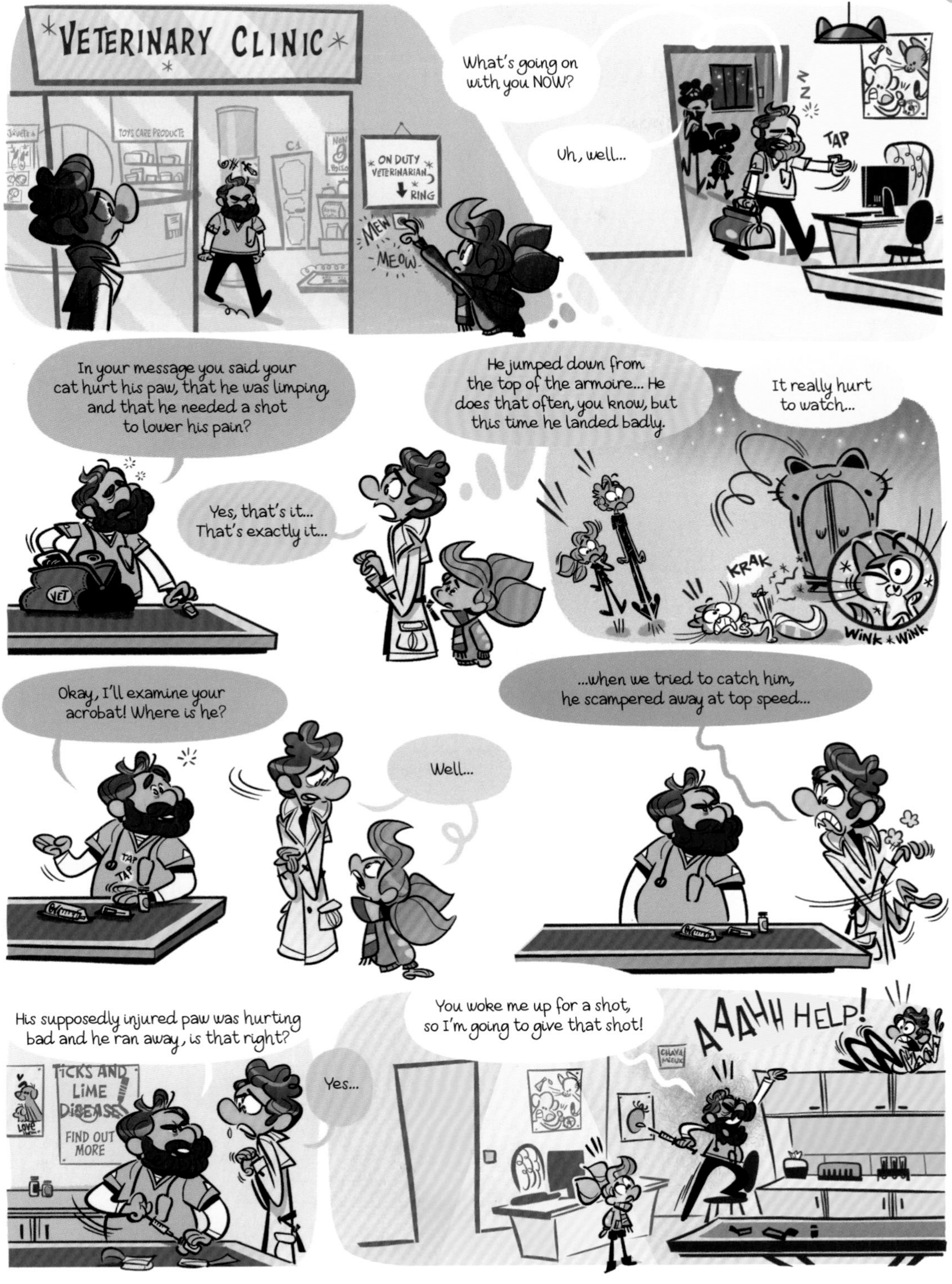
VETERINARY CLINIC
TOYS CARE PRODUCTS
ON DUTY VETERINARIAN RING
MEW
MEOW
What's going on with you NOW?
Uh, well...
TAP
In your message you said your cat hurt his paw, that he was limping and that he needed a shot to lower his pain?
Yes, that's it... That's exactly it...
He jumped down from the top of the armoire... He does that often, you know, but this time he landed badly.
It really hurt to watch...
KRAK
WINK WINK
Okay, I'll examine your acrobat! Where is he?
TAP TAP
Well...
...when we tried to catch him, he scampered away at top speed...
His supposedly injured paw was hurting bad and he ran away, is that right?
TICKS AND LIME DISEASE FIND OUT MORE
Yes...
You woke me up for a shot, so I'm going to give that shot!
AAAHH HELP!

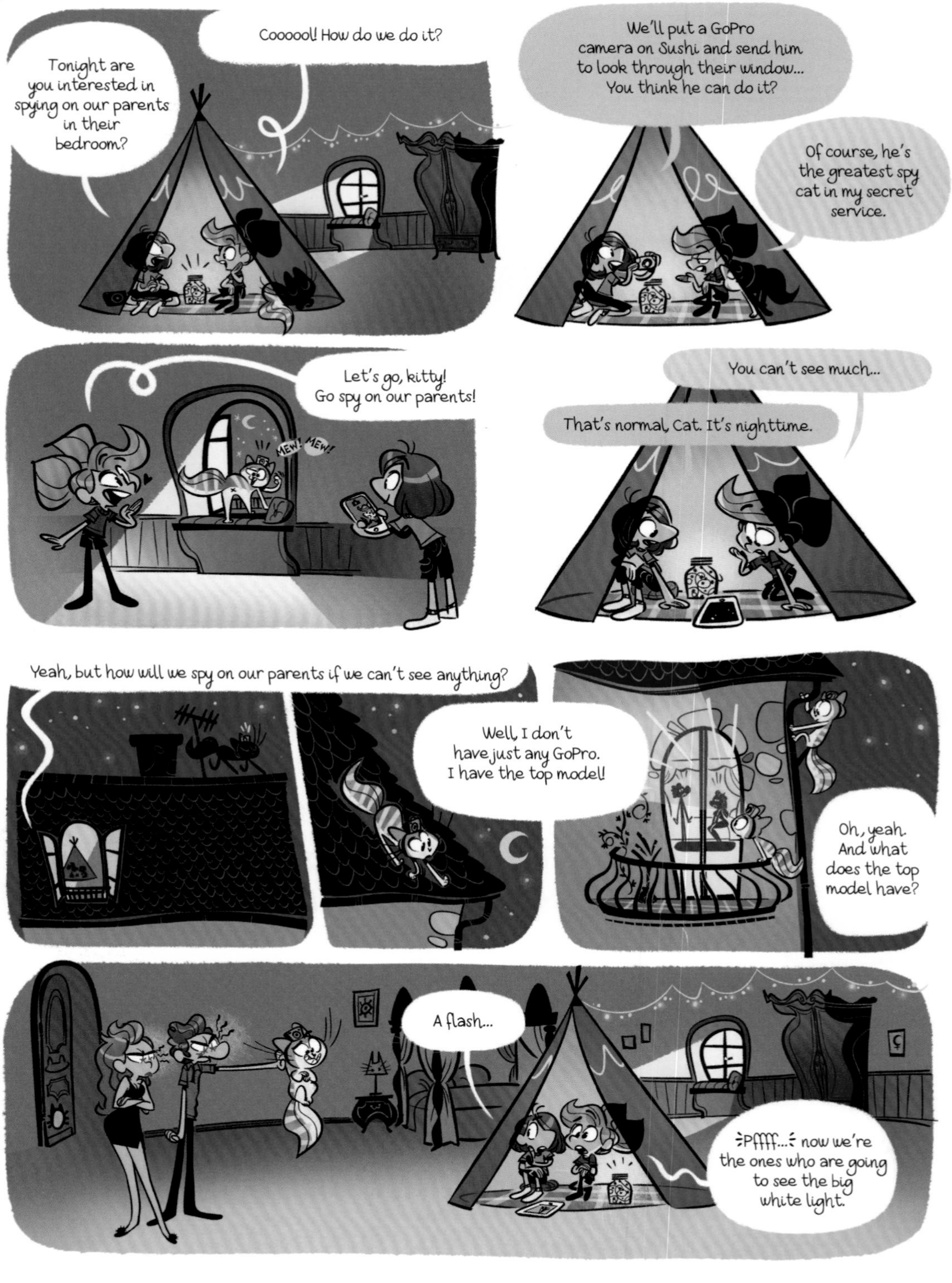
Tonight are you interested in spying on our parents in their bedroom?
Coooool! How do we do it?
We'll put a GoPro camera on Sushi and send him to look through their window... You think he can do it?
Of course, he's the greatest spy cat in my secret service.
Let's go, kitty! Go spy on our parents!
MEW! MEW!
You can't see much...
That's normal, Cat. It's nighttime.
Yeah, but how will we spy on our parents if we can't see anything?
Well, I don't have just any GoPro. I have the top model!
Oh, yeah. And what does the top model have?
A flash...
Pffff... now we're the ones who are going to see the big white light.

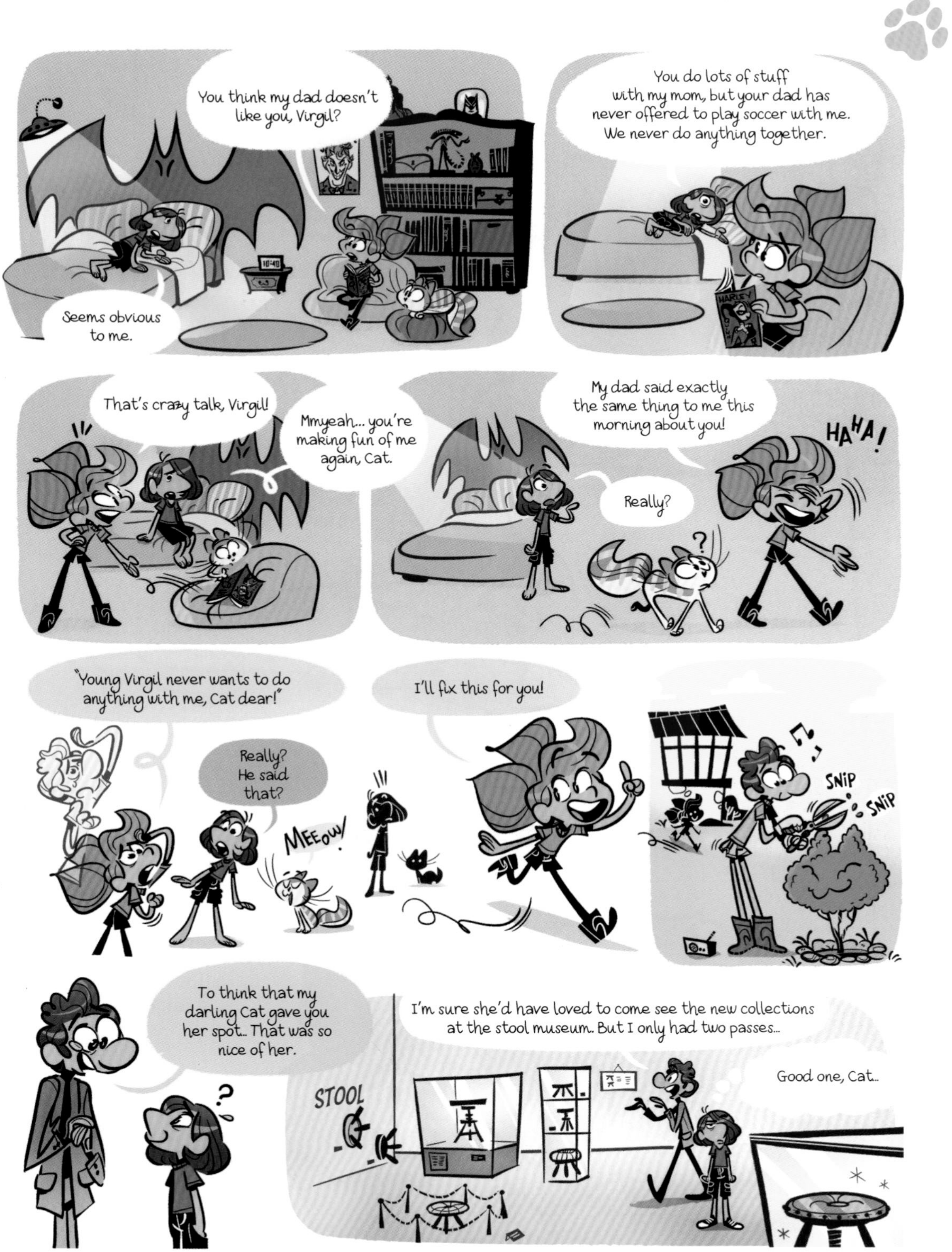

You think my dad doesn't like you, Virgil?
Seems obvious to me.
You do lots of stuff with my mom, but your dad has never offered to play soccer with me. We never do anything together.
That's crazy talk, Virgil!
Mmyeah... you're making fun of me again, Cat.
My dad said exactly the same thing to me this morning about you!
HAHA!
Really?
"Young Virgil never wants to do anything with me, Cat dear!"
Really? He said that?
MEEOW!
I'll fix this for you!
SNIP
SNIP
To think that my darling Cat gave you her spot... That was so nice of her.
I'm sure she'd have loved to come see the new collections at the stool museum. But I only had two passes...
STOOL
Good one, Cat...

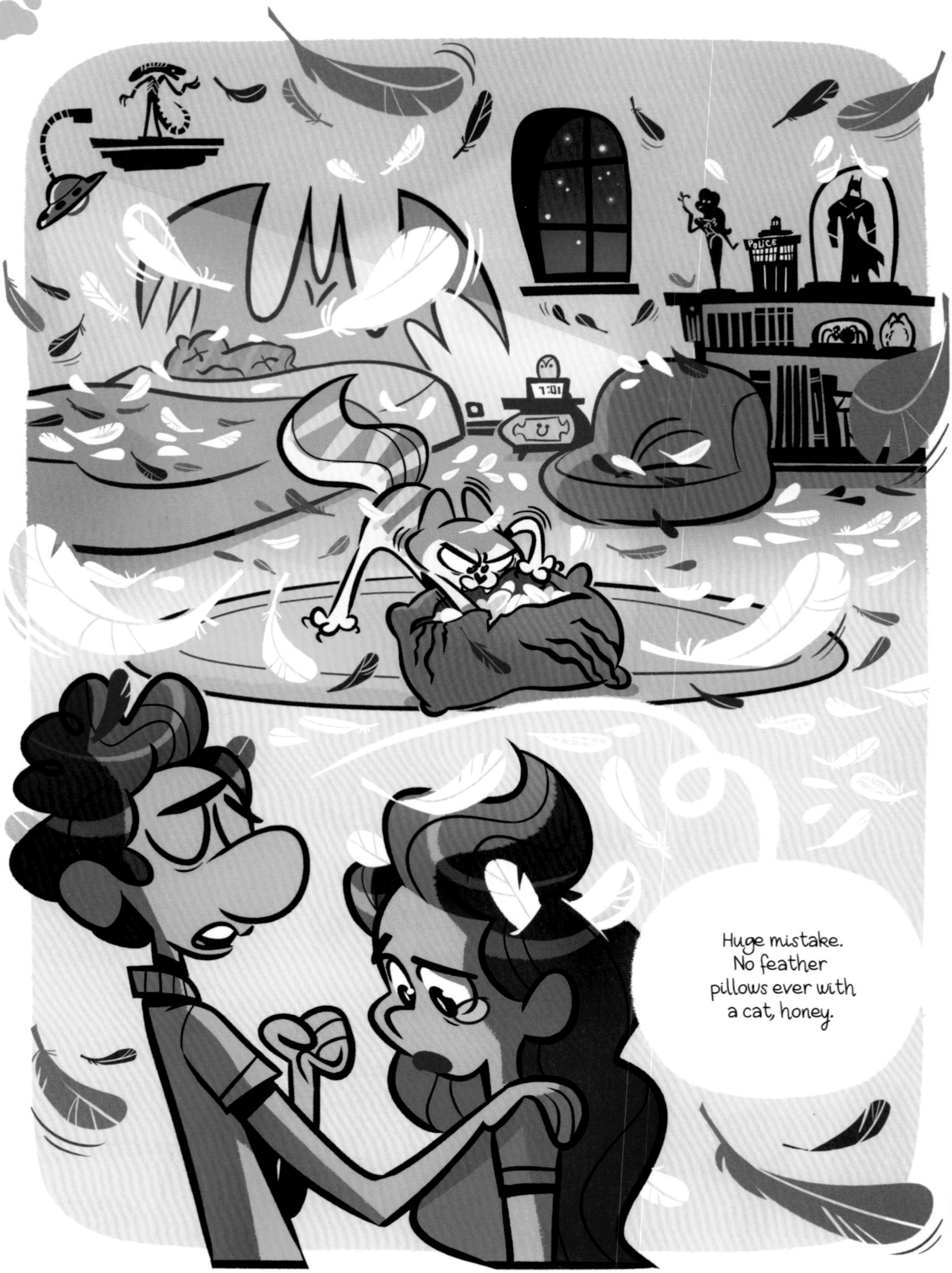
7:01
POLICE
Huge mistake. No feather pillows ever with a cat, honey.

Dad, is it true there's no cat constellation in space?

Hmm?

Because we saw there was one once...

cat + constellation

...but it got eliminated since then. So, there isn't one anymore, right?

Hmmm, yes, I remember such a constellation got created, in 1779 in fact, but it no longer exists, yes, there it is...

Constellations Fa

Okay, thanks, Dad!

MEOW!

Did you see how our kids are developing their scientific minds? I'm blown away, Sam.

The CATsonauts!

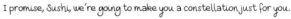

Maybe they're two little geniuses!

I promise, Sushi, we're going to make you a constellation just for you.

...or not!

This ladder has to be tall enough to stick up a few stars!

GLUE

The CAT

27

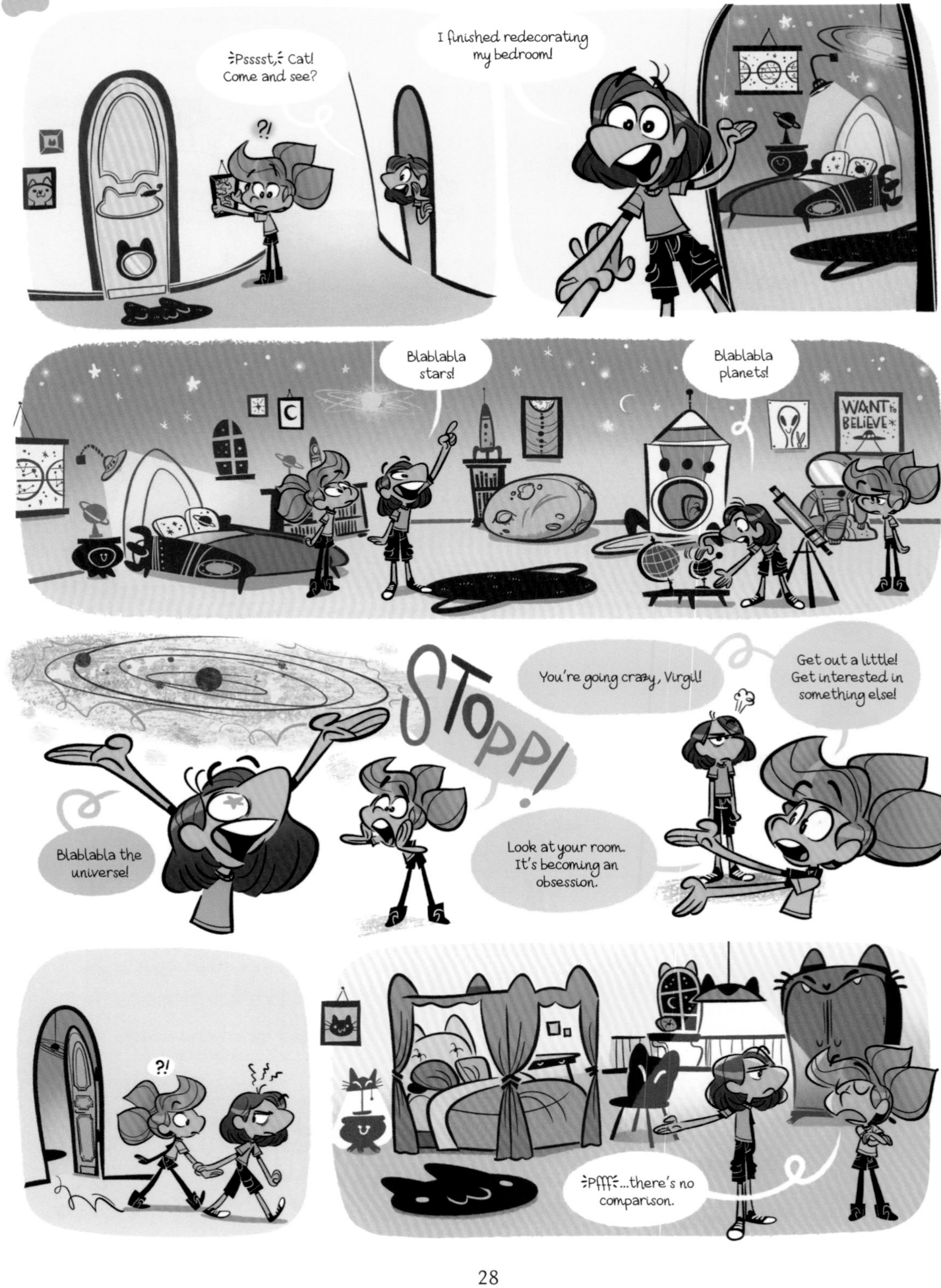
Psssst, Cat! Come and see?
?!
I finished redecorating my bedroom!
Blablabla stars!
Blablabla planets!
WANT to BELIEVE
Blablabla the universe!
STOPP!
You're going crazy, Virgil!
Look at your room. It's becoming an obsession.
Get out a little! Get interested in something else!
?!
Pfff... there's no comparison.

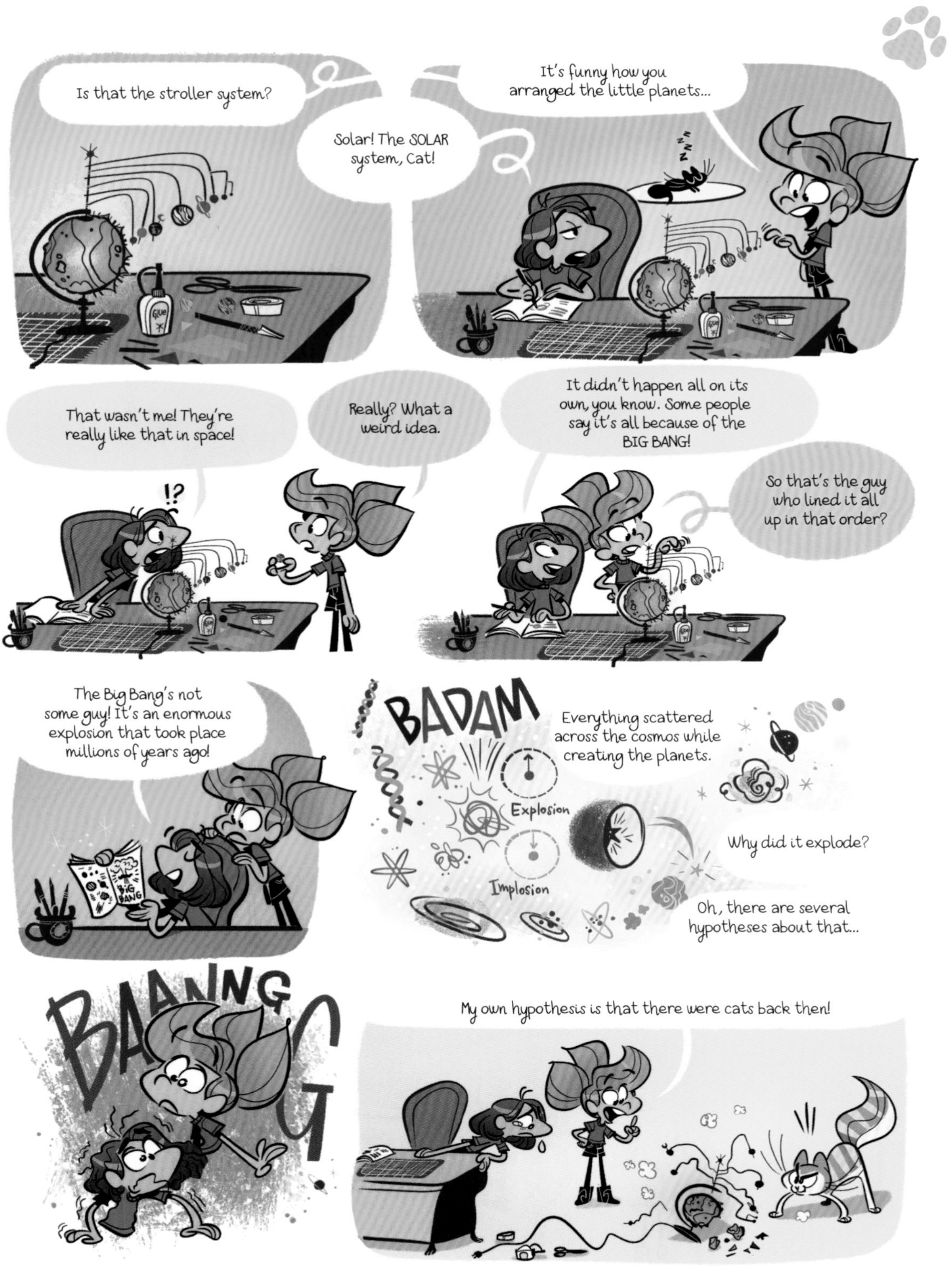
Is that the stroller system?
Solar! The SOLAR system, Cat!
It's funny how you arranged the little planets...
That wasn't me! They're really like that in space!
!?
Really? What a weird idea.
It didn't happen all on its own, you know. Some people say it's all because of the BIG BANG!
So that's the guy who lined it all up in that order?
The Big Bang's not some guy! It's an enormous explosion that took place millions of years ago!
BIG BANG
BADAM
Everything scattered across the cosmos while creating the planets.
Explosion
Implosion
Why did it explode?
Oh, there are several hypotheses about that...
BAANNG
My own hypothesis is that there were cats back then!

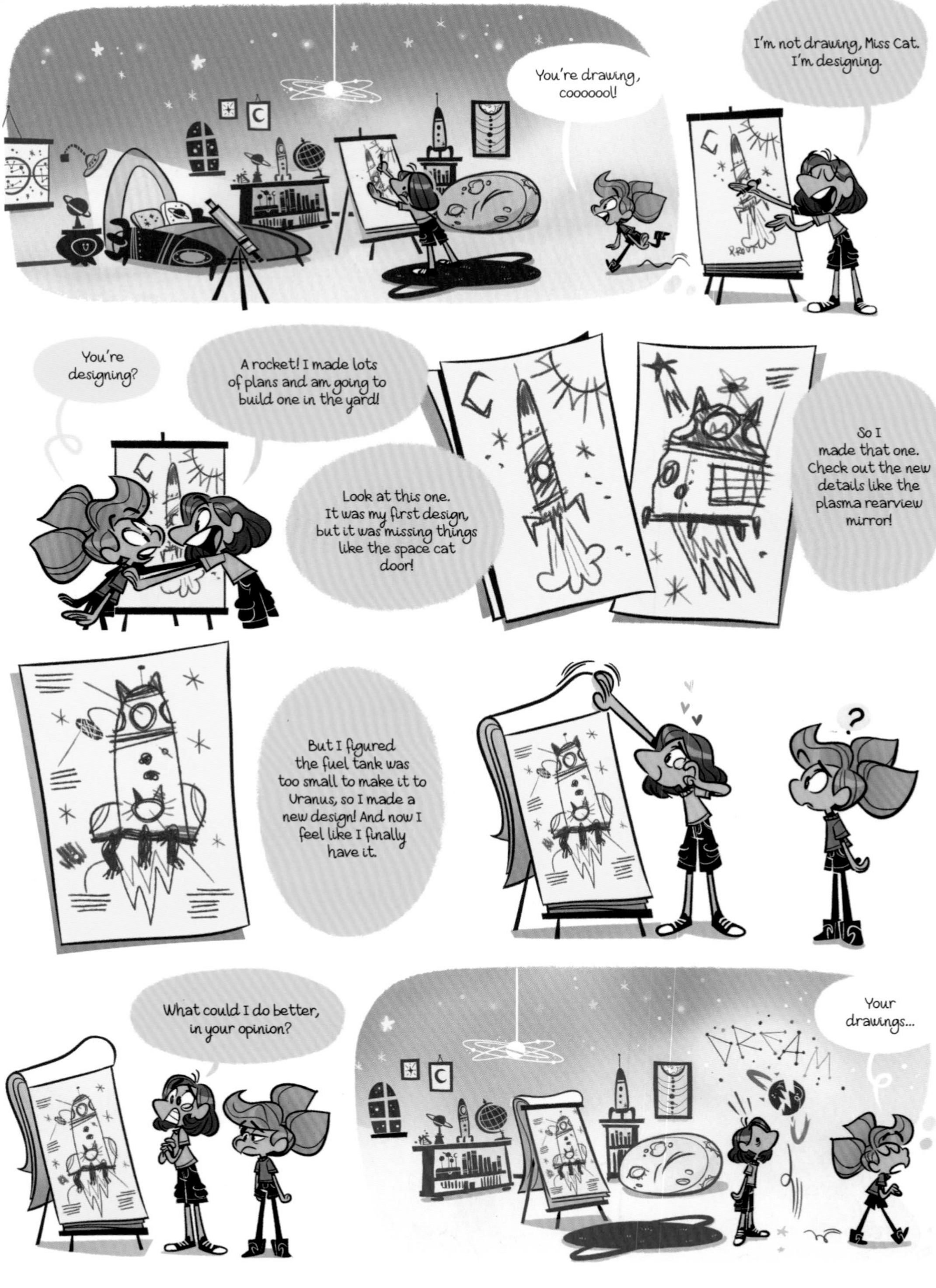
You're drawing, coooooool!
I'm not drawing, Miss Cat. I'm designing.
You're designing?
A rocket! I made lots of plans and am going to build one in the yard!
Look at this one. It was my first design, but it was missing things like the space cat door!
So I made that one. Check out the new details like the plasma rearview mirror!
But I figured the fuel tank was too small to make it to Uranus, so I made a new design! And now I feel like I finally have it.
What could I do better, in your opinion?
Your drawings...
DREAM

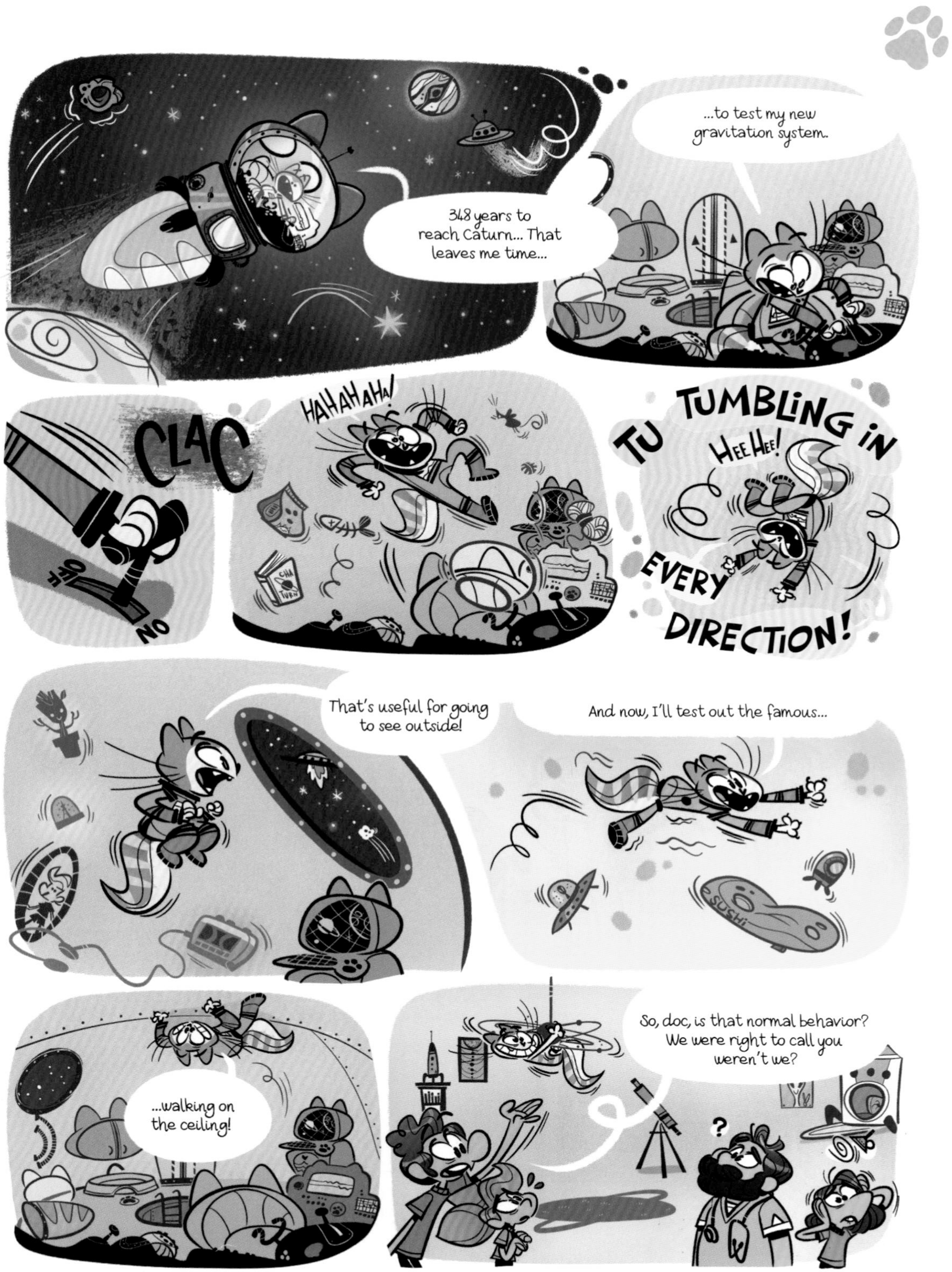
348 years to reach Caturn... That leaves me time...
...to test my new gravitation system.
CLAC
OFF
NO
HAHAHAHA!
CHA TURN
TUMBLING IN EVERY DIRECTION!
HEE HEE!
That's useful for going to see outside!
And now, I'll test out the famous...
SUSHI
...walking on the ceiling!
So, doc, is that normal behavior? We were right to call you weren't we?
?

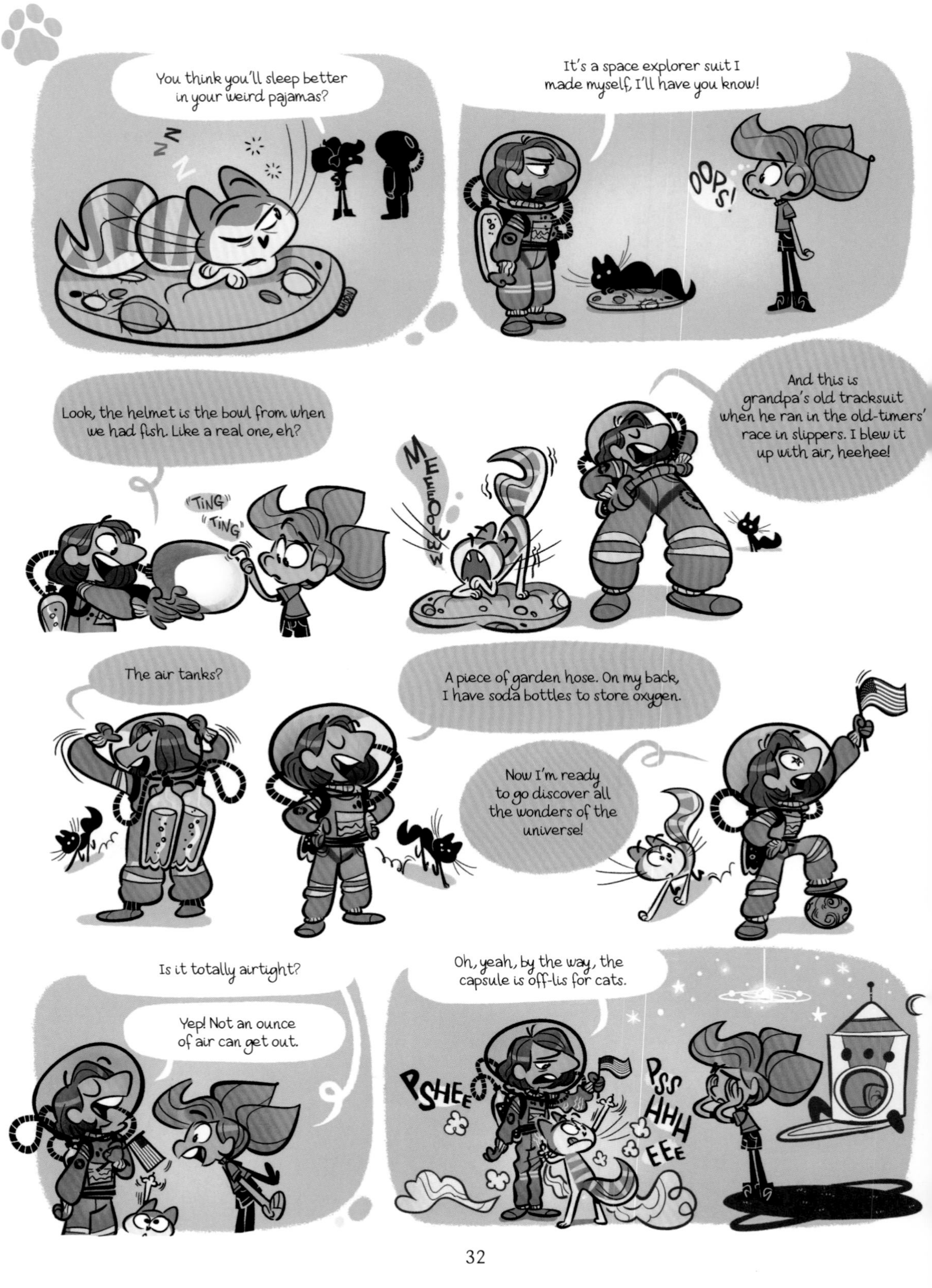

You think you'll sleep better in your weird pajamas?
It's a space explorer suit I made myself, I'll have you know!
OOPS!
Look, the helmet is the bowl from when we had fish. Like a real one, eh?
"TING" "TING"
MEEEOOWW
And this is grandpa's old tracksuit when he ran in the old-timers' race in slippers. I blew it up with air, heehee!
The air tanks?
A piece of garden hose. On my back, I have soda bottles to store oxygen.
Now I'm ready to go discover all the wonders of the universe!
Is it totally airtight?
Yep! Not an ounce of air can get out.
Oh, yeah, by the way, the capsule is off-lis for cats.
PSHEEE
PSSHHHEEE

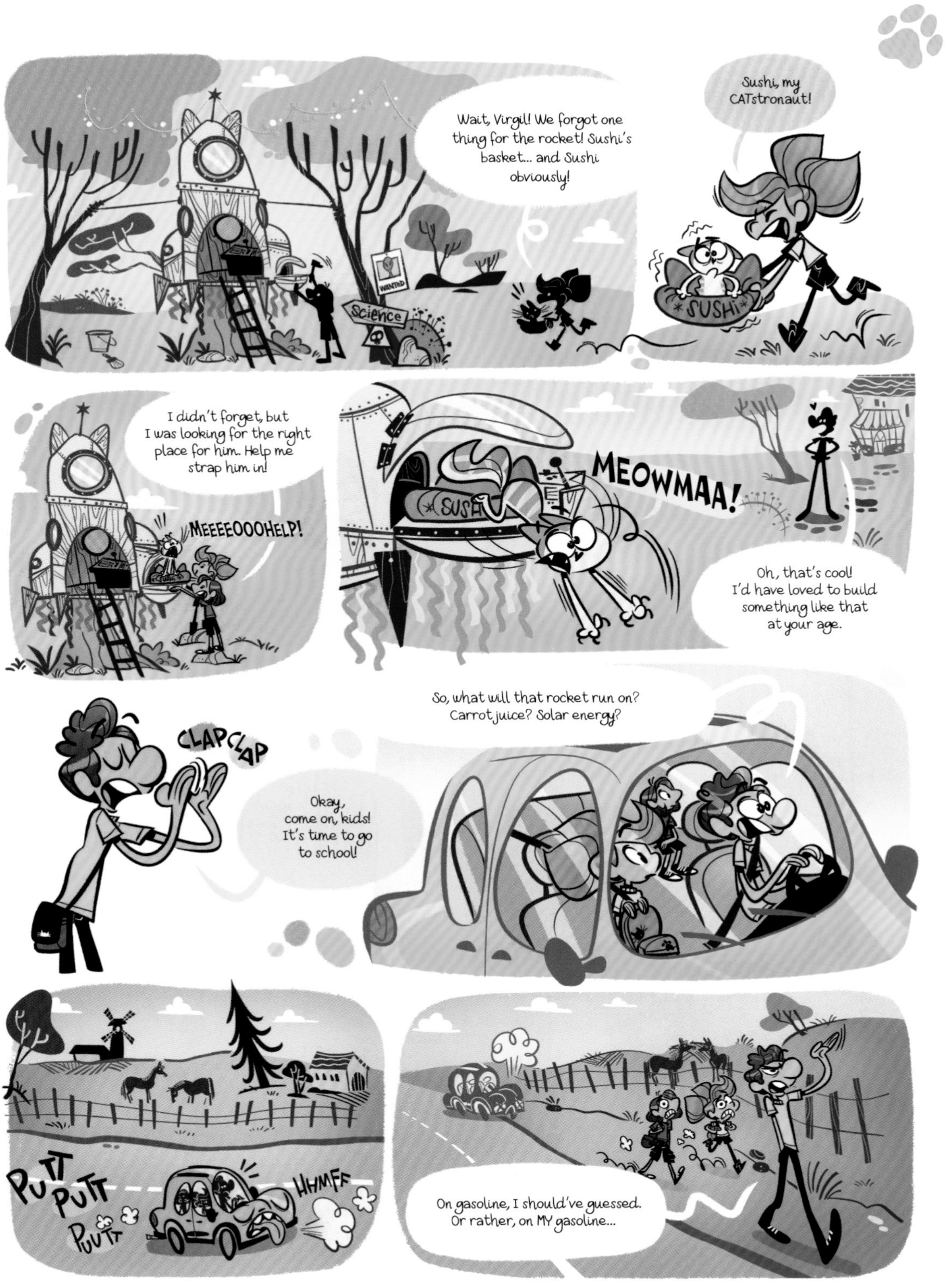

WANTED
Science
Wait, Virgil! We forgot one thing for the rocket! Sushi's basket... and Sushi obviously!
Sushi, my CATstronaut!
SUSHI
I didn't forget, but I was looking for the right place for him. Help me strap him in!
MEEEEOOOHELP!
MEOWMAA!
Oh, that's cool! I'd have loved to build something like that at your age.
CLAPCLAP
Okay, come on, kids! It's time to go to school!
So, what will that rocket run on? Carrot juice? Solar energy?
PUTT PUTT PUTT
HHMFF
On gasoline, I should've guessed. Or rather, on MY gasoline...

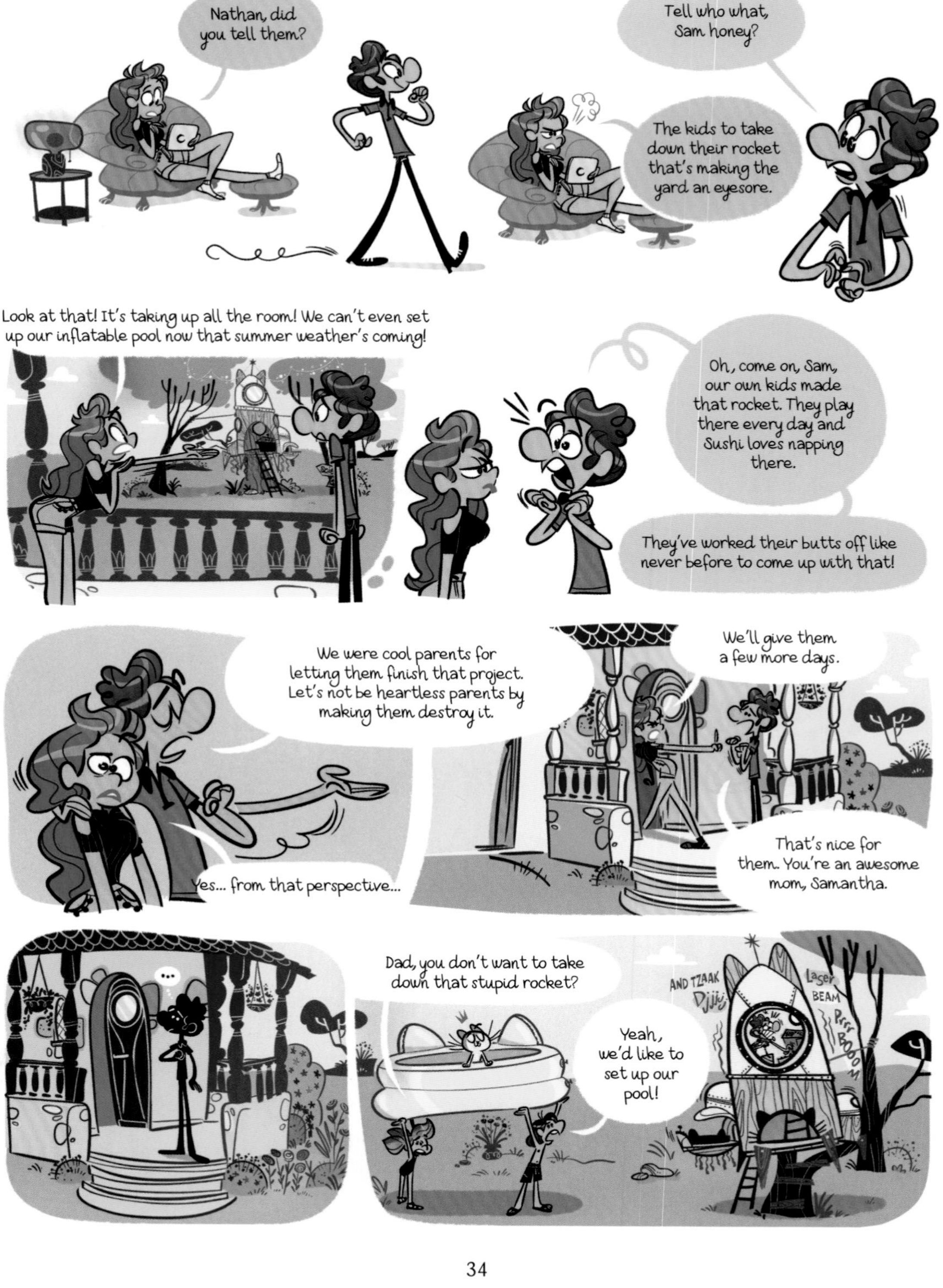

Nathan, did you tell them?
Tell who what, Sam honey?
The kids to take down their rocket that's making the yard an eyesore.
Look at that! It's taking up all the room! We can't even set up our inflatable pool now that summer weather's coming!
Oh, come on, Sam, our own kids made that rocket. They play there every day and Sushi loves napping there.
They've worked their butts off like never before to come up with that!
We were cool parents for letting them finish that project. Let's not be heartless parents by making them destroy it.
Yes... from that perspective...
We'll give them a few more days.
That's nice for them. You're an awesome mom, Samantha.
...
Dad, you don't want to take down that stupid rocket?
Yeah, we'd like to set up our pool!
AND TZAAK
Djjj
Laser BEAM
Prrr
BOOOOM

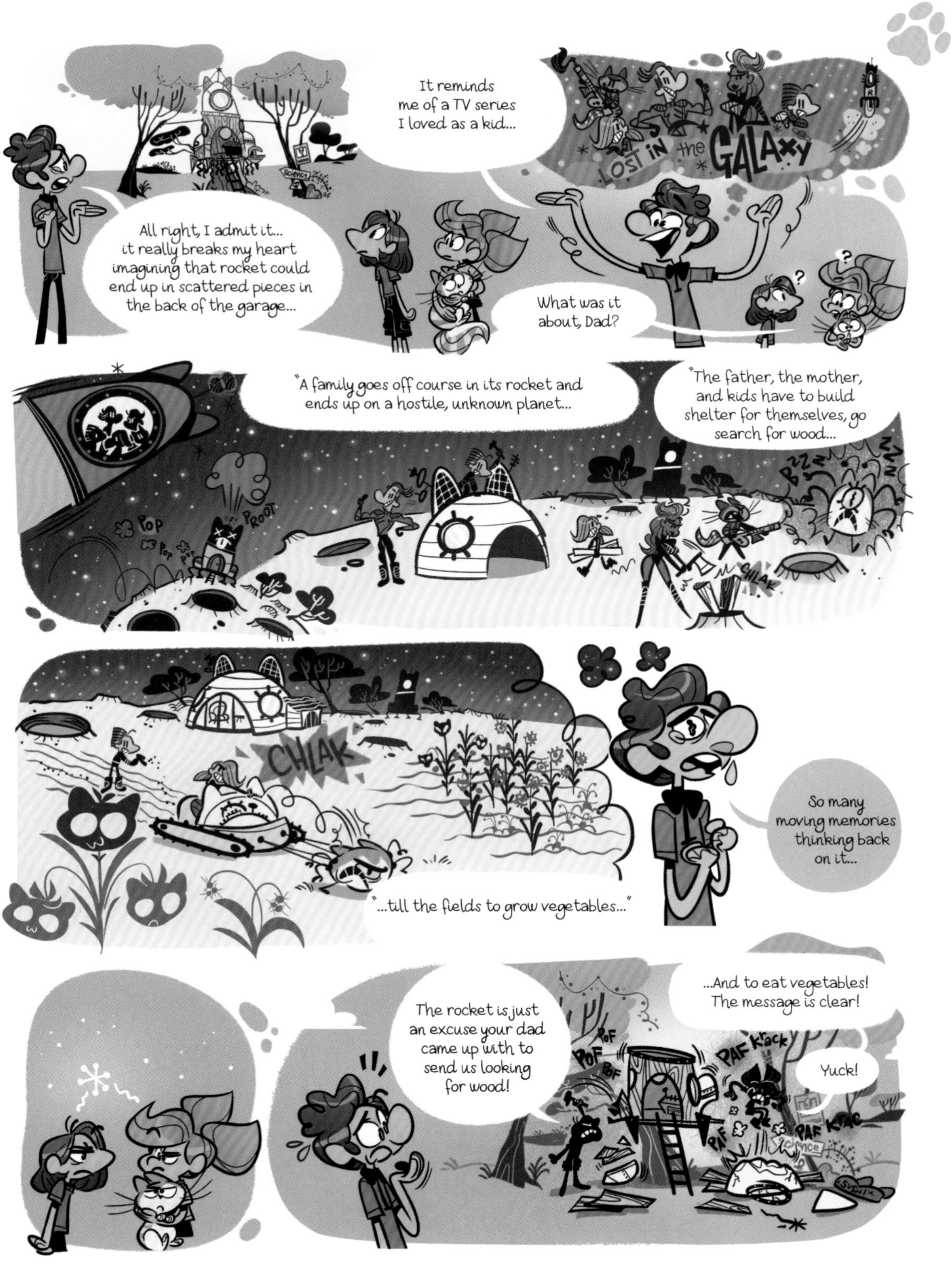
All right, I admit it... it really breaks my heart imagining that rocket could end up in scattered pieces in the back of the garage...
It reminds me of a TV series I loved as a kid...
LOST IN the GALAXY
What was it about, Dad?
"A family goes off course in its rocket and ends up on a hostile, unknown planet...
"The father, the mother, and kids have to build shelter for themselves, go search for wood...
POP
POP
PROOT
CHLAK
CHLAK
...till the fields to grow vegetables..."
So many moving memories thinking back on it...
The rocket is just an excuse your dad came up with to send us looking for wood!
...And to eat vegetables! The message is clear!
Yuck!
POF
POF
PAF
KRACK
PAF
KRAC

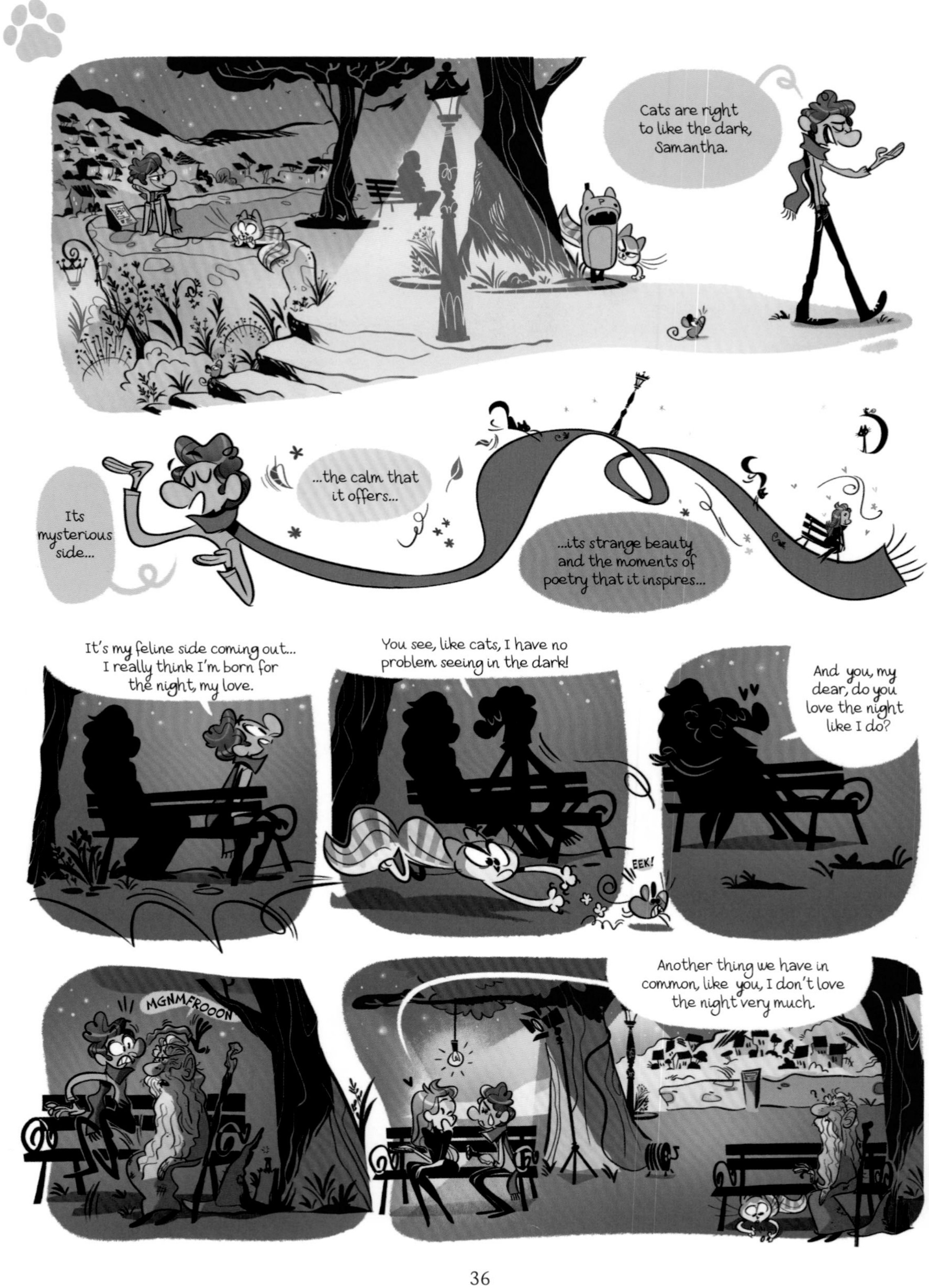

Cats are right to like the dark, Samantha.
Its mysterious side...
...the calm that it offers...
...its strange beauty and the moments of poetry that it inspires...
It's my feline side coming out... I really think I'm born for the night, my love.
You see, like cats, I have no problem seeing in the dark!
EEK!
And you, my dear, do you love the night like I do?
MGNMFROOON
Another thing we have in common, like you, I don't love the night very much.

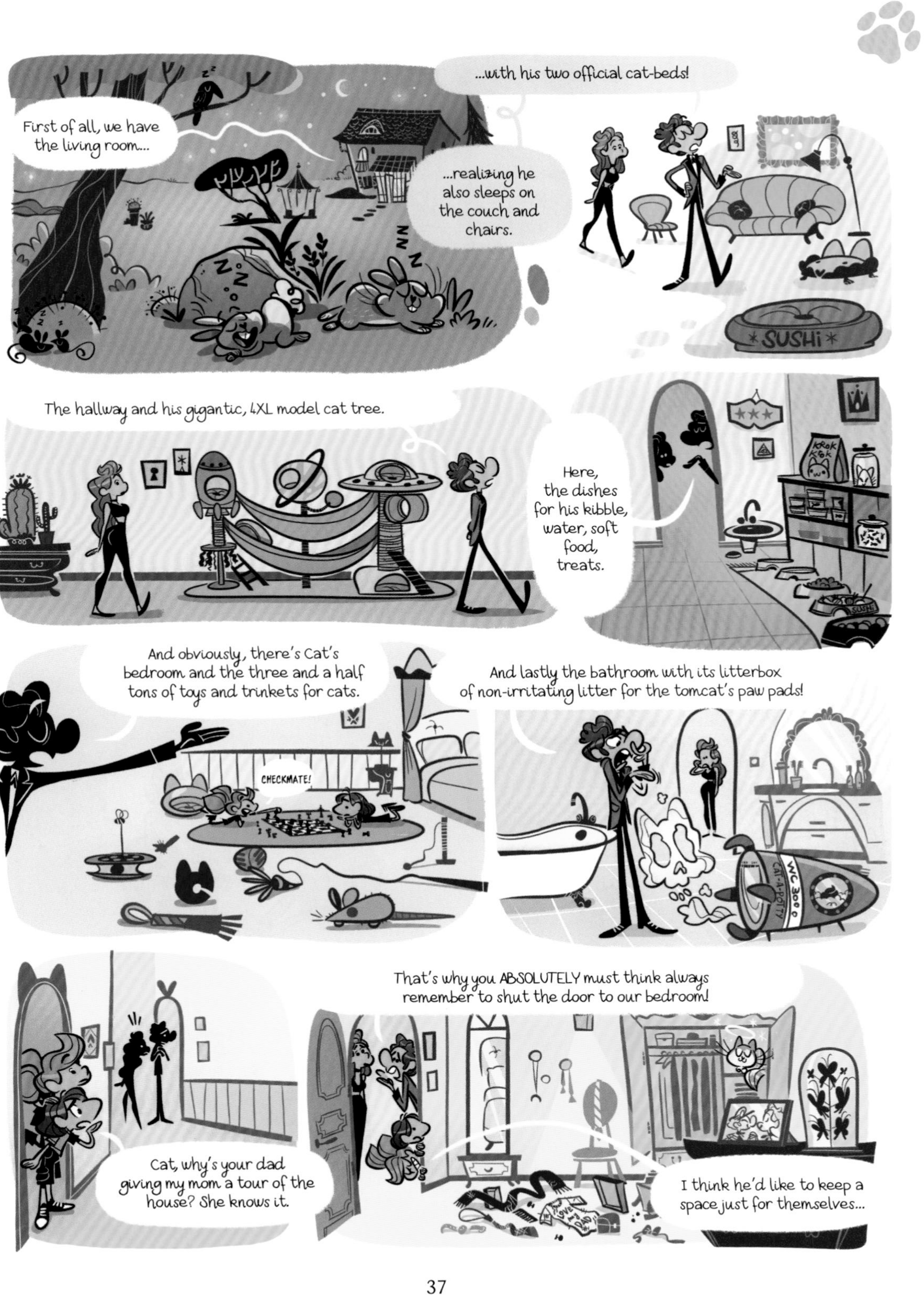
First of all, we have the living room...
...realizing he also sleeps on the couch and chairs.
...with his two official cat-beds!
*SUSHi*
The hallway and his gigantic, 4XL model cat tree.
Here, the dishes for his kibble, water, soft food, treats.
KROK KROK
And obviously, there's Cat's bedroom and the three and a half tons of toys and trinkets for cats.
CHECKMATE!
And lastly the bathroom with its litterbox of non-irritating litter for the tomcat's paw pads!
WC 3000
CAT-A-POTTY
Cat, why's your dad giving my mom a tour of the house? She knows it.
That's why you ABSOLUTELY must think always remember to shut the door to our bedroom!
I think he'd like to keep a space just for themselves...

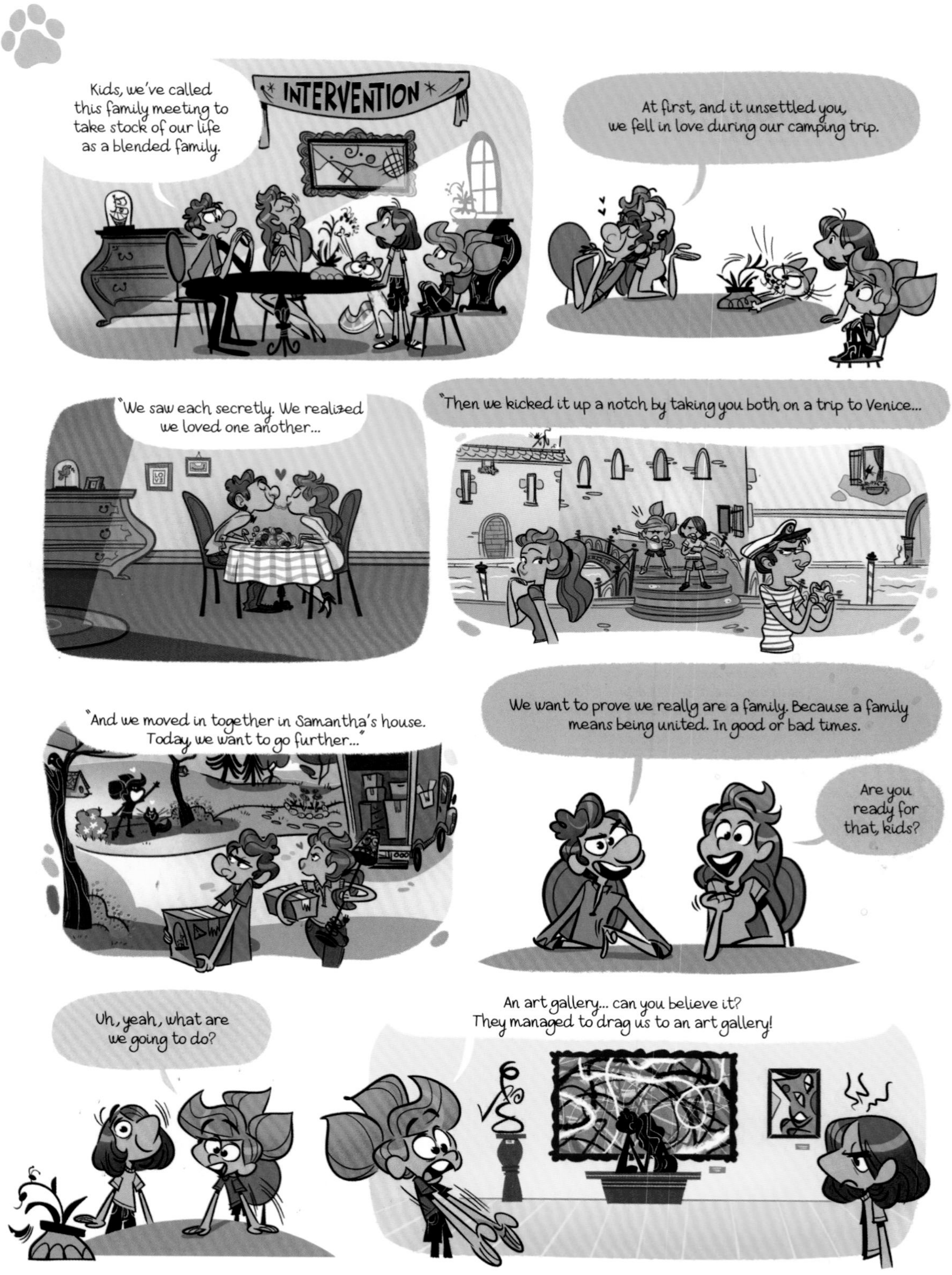

Kids, we've called this family meeting to take stock of our life as a blended family.
INTERVENTION
At first, and it unsettled you, we fell in love during our camping trip.
"We saw each secretly. We realized we loved one another...
"Then we kicked it up a notch by taking you both on a trip to Venice...
"And we moved in together in Samantha's house. Today, we want to go further..."
We want to prove we really are a family. Because a family means being united. In good or bad times.
Are you ready for that, kids?
Uh, yeah, what are we going to do?
An art gallery... can you believe it? They managed to drag us to an art gallery!

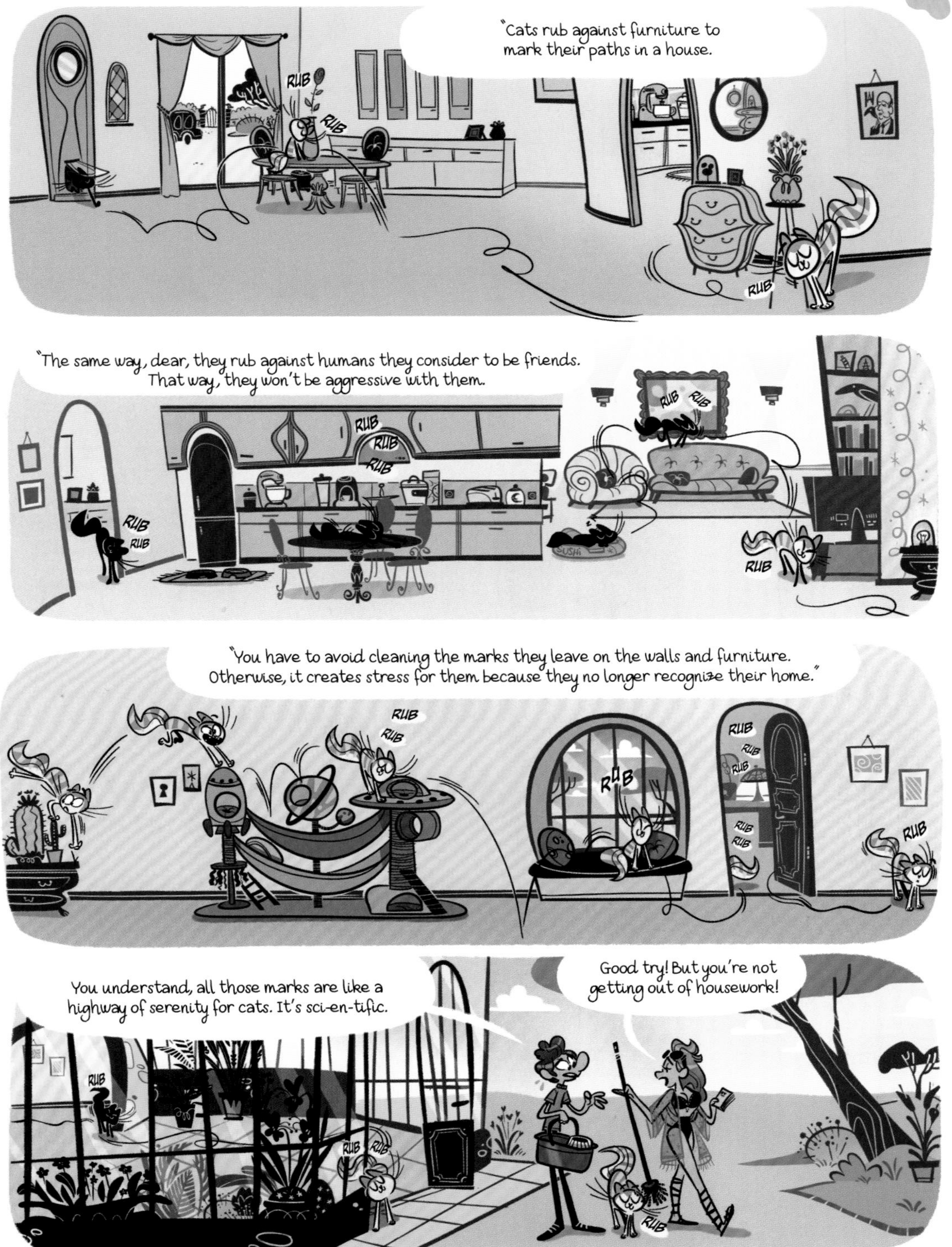
"Cats rub against furniture to mark their paths in a house.
RUB
RUB
RUB
"The same way, dear, they rub against humans they consider to be friends. That way, they won't be aggressive with them.
RUB
RUB
RUB
RUB
RUB
RUB
RUB
RUB
RUB
"You have to avoid cleaning the marks they leave on the walls and furniture. Otherwise, it creates stress for them because they no longer recognize their home."
RUB
RUB
RUB
RUB
RUB
RUB
RUB
RUB
RUB
You understand, all those marks are like a highway of serenity for cats. It's sci-en-tific.
Good try! But you're not getting out of housework!
RUB
RUB
RUB
RUB

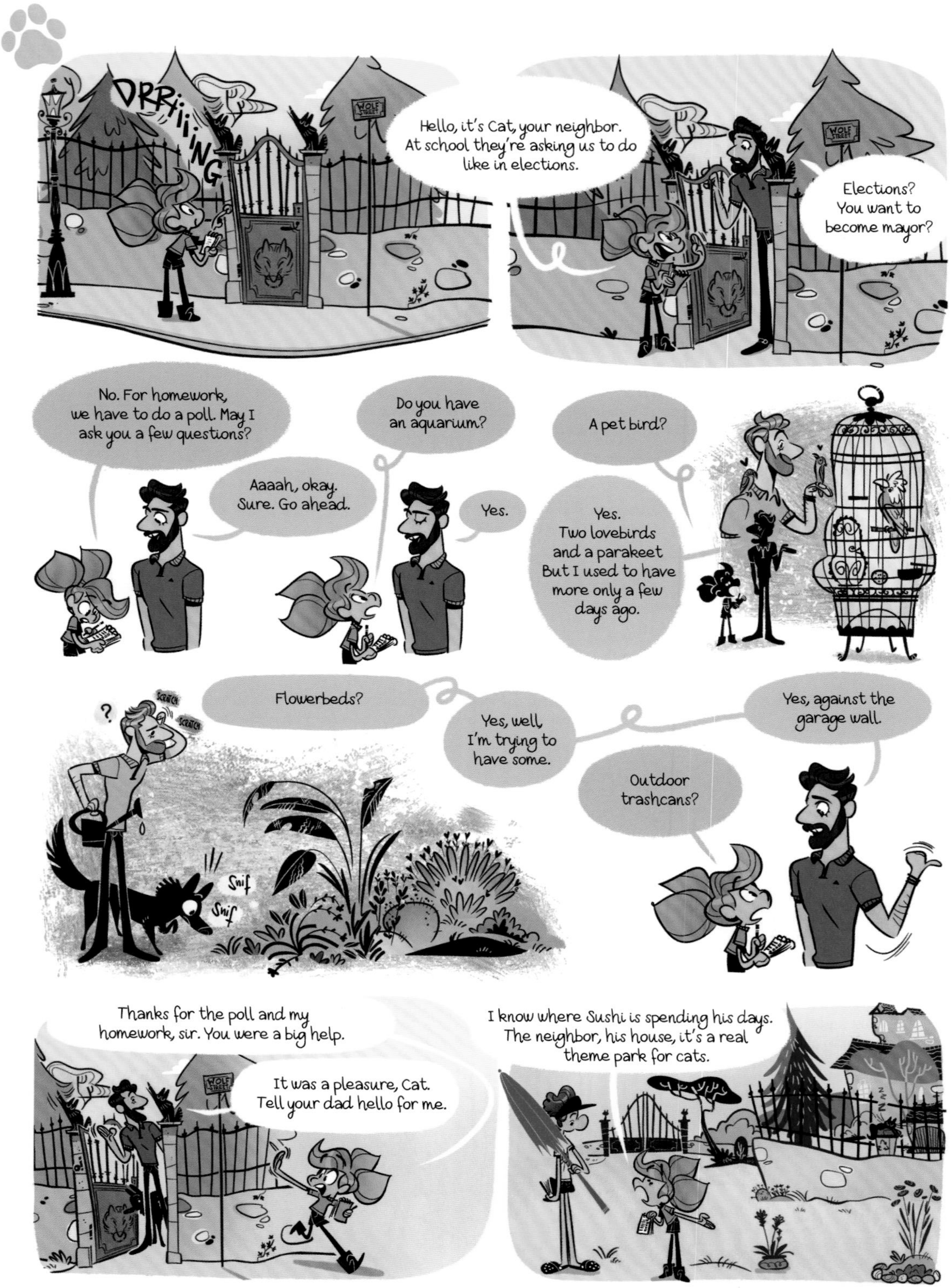
DRRriiiiNG
WOLF STREET
Hello, it's Cat, your neighbor. At school they're asking us to do like in elections.
Elections? You want to become mayor?
No. For homework, we have to do a poll. May I ask you a few questions?
Aaaah, okay. Sure. Go ahead.
Do you have an aquarium?
Yes.
A pet bird?
Yes. Two lovebirds and a parakeet But I used to have more only a few days ago.
Flowerbeds?
SCRATCH
SCRATCH
?
Yes, well, I'm trying to have some.
Snif
Snif
Outdoor trashcans?
Yes, against the garage wall.
Thanks for the poll and my homework, sir. You were a big help.
It was a pleasure, Cat. Tell your dad hello for me.
I know where Sushi is spending his days. The neighbor, his house, it's a real theme park for cats.

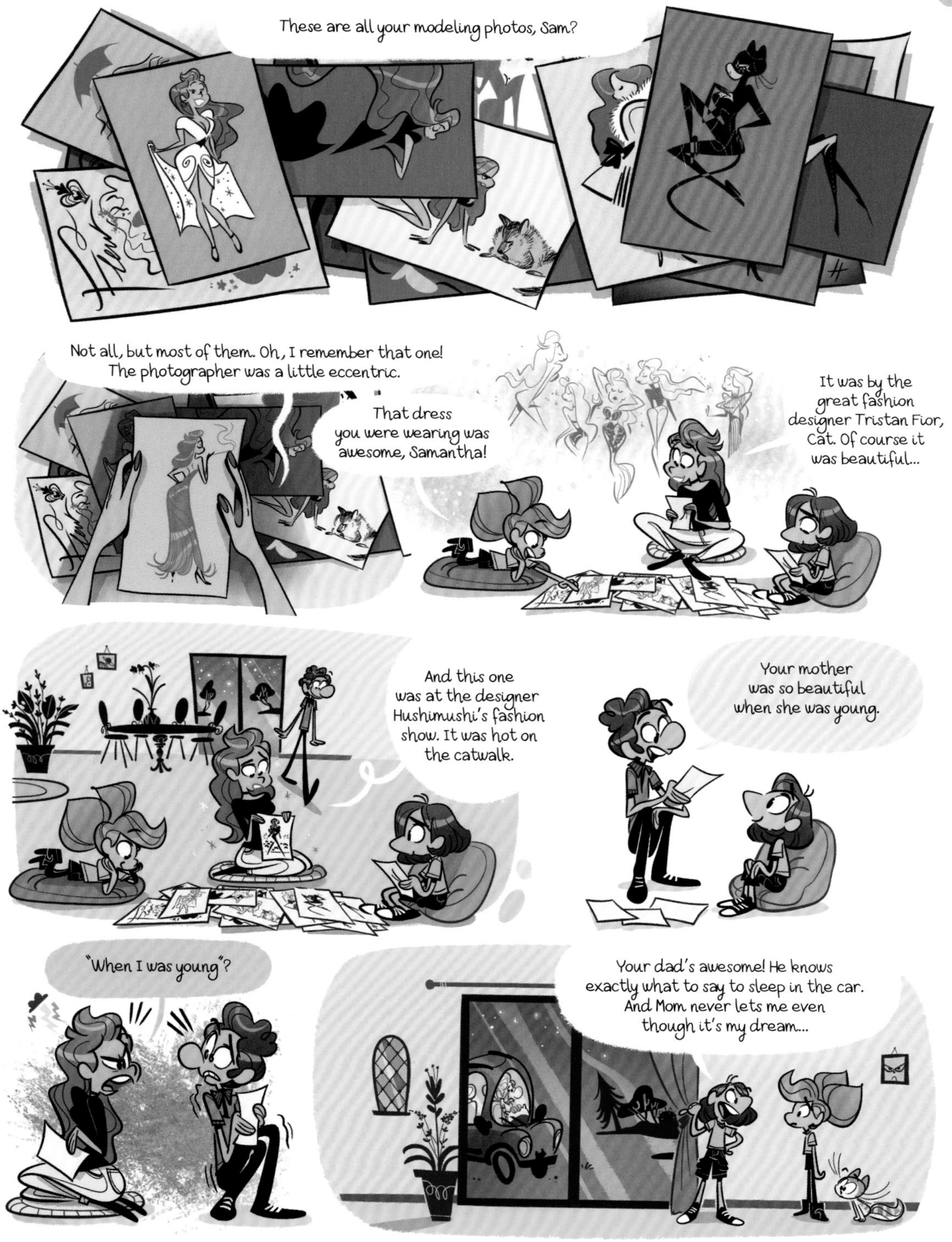

These are all your modeling photos, Sam?
Not all, but most of them. Oh, I remember that one! The photographer was a little eccentric.
That dress you were wearing was awesome, Samantha!
It was by the great fashion designer Tristan Fior, Cat. Of course it was beautiful...
And this one was at the designer Hushimushi's fashion show. It was hot on the catwalk.
Your mother was so beautiful when she was young.
"When I was young"?
Your dad's awesome! He knows exactly what to say to sleep in the car. And Mom never lets me even though it's my dream...

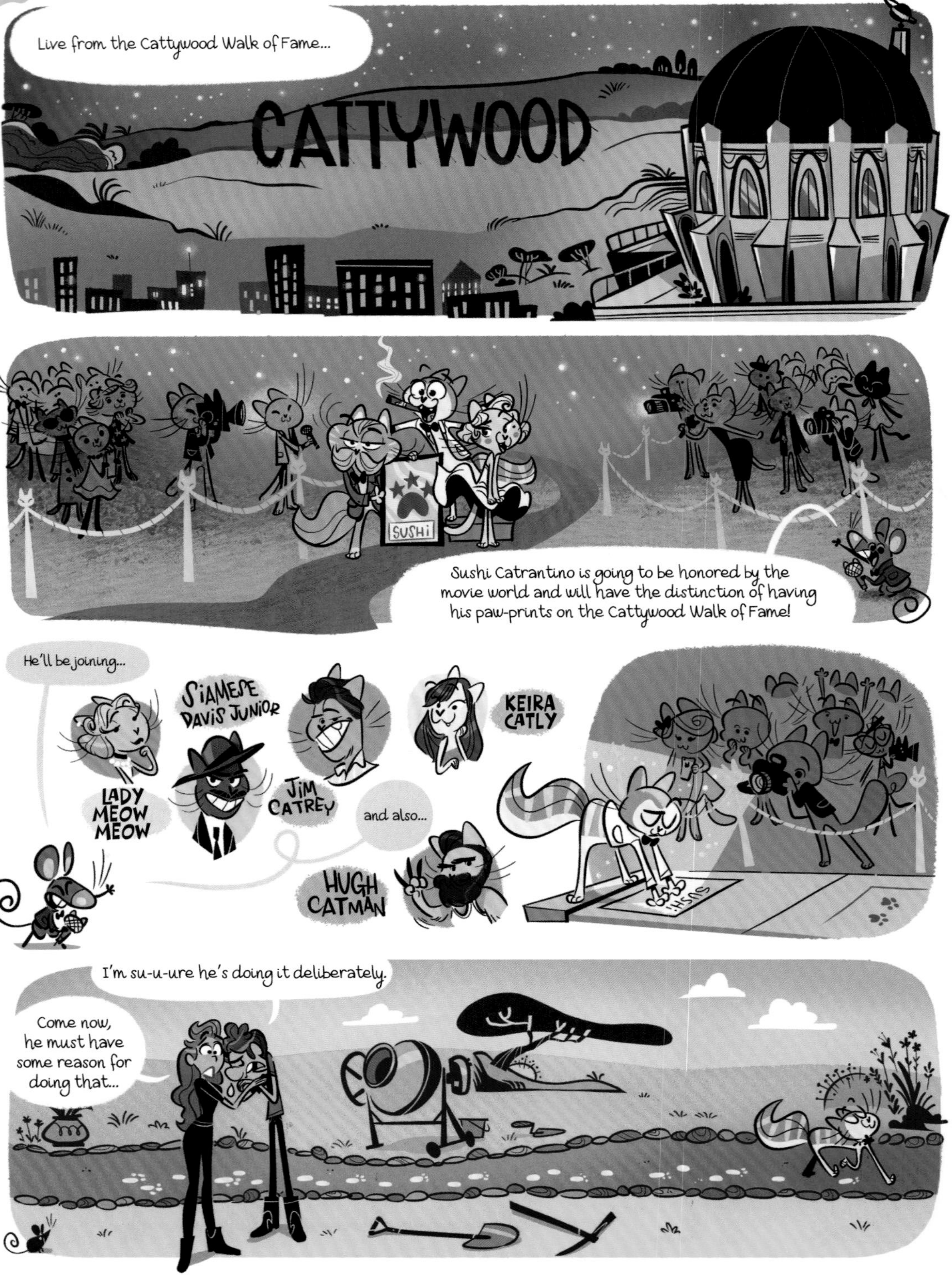
Live from the Cattywood Walk of Fame...
CATTYWOOD
SUSHI
Sushi Catrantino is going to be honored by the movie world and will have the distinction of having his paw-prints on the Cattywood Walk of Fame!
He'll be joining...
SIAMESE DAVIS JUNIOR
KEIRA CATLY
LADY MEOW MEOW
JIM CATREY
and also...
HUGH CATMAN
SUSHI
I'm su-u-ure he's doing it deliberately.
Come now, he must have some reason for doing that...

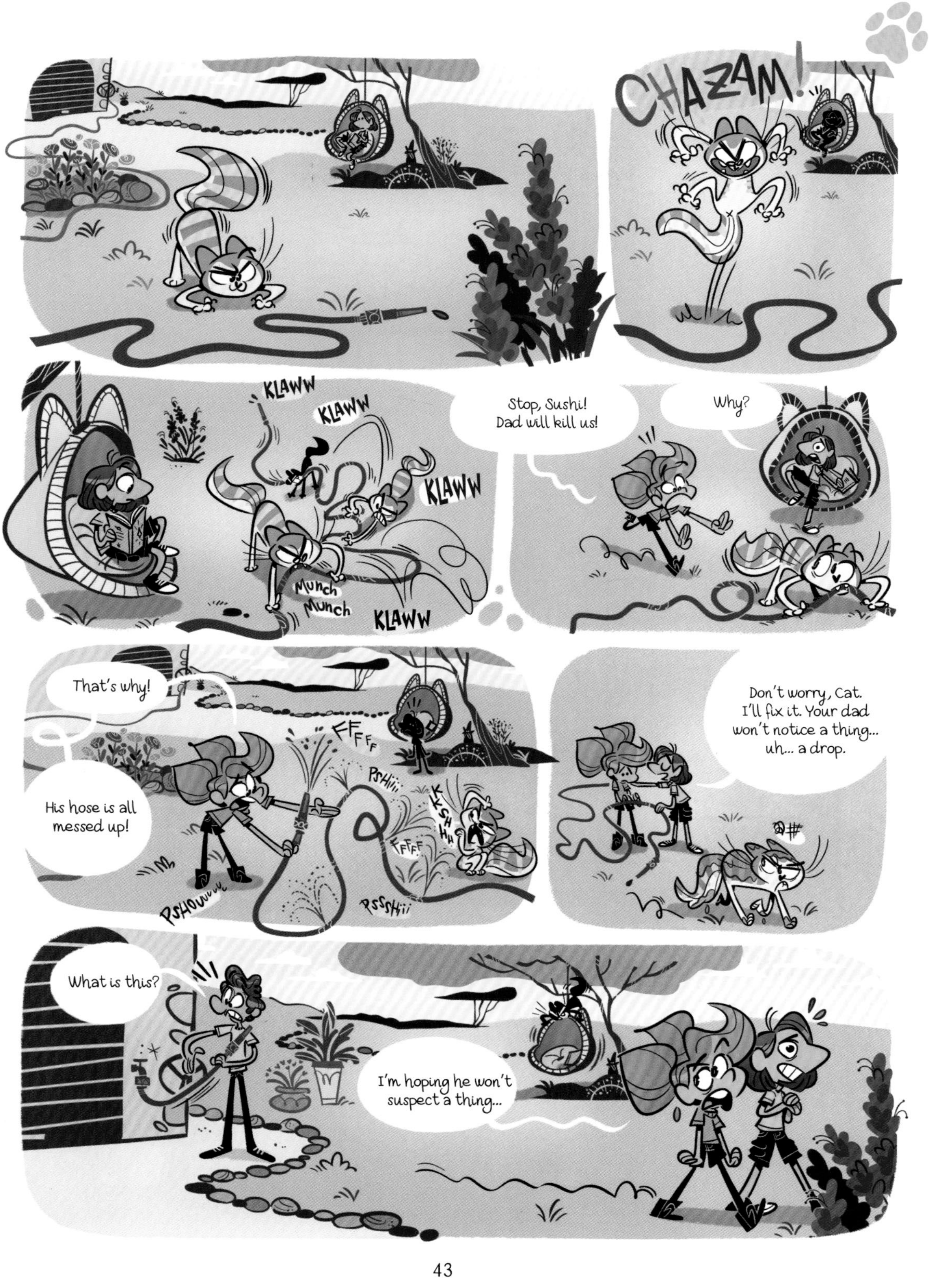
CHAZAM!
KLAWW
KLAWW
KLAWW
Munch
Munch
KLAWW
Stop, Sushi!
Dad will kill us!
Why?
That's why!
His hose is all messed up!
FFFFF
PSHiii
KKSHHH
FFFFF
PSHOUuuu
PSSSHiii
Don't worry, Cat. I'll fix it. Your dad won't notice a thing... uh... a drop.
What is this?
I'm hoping he won't suspect a thing...

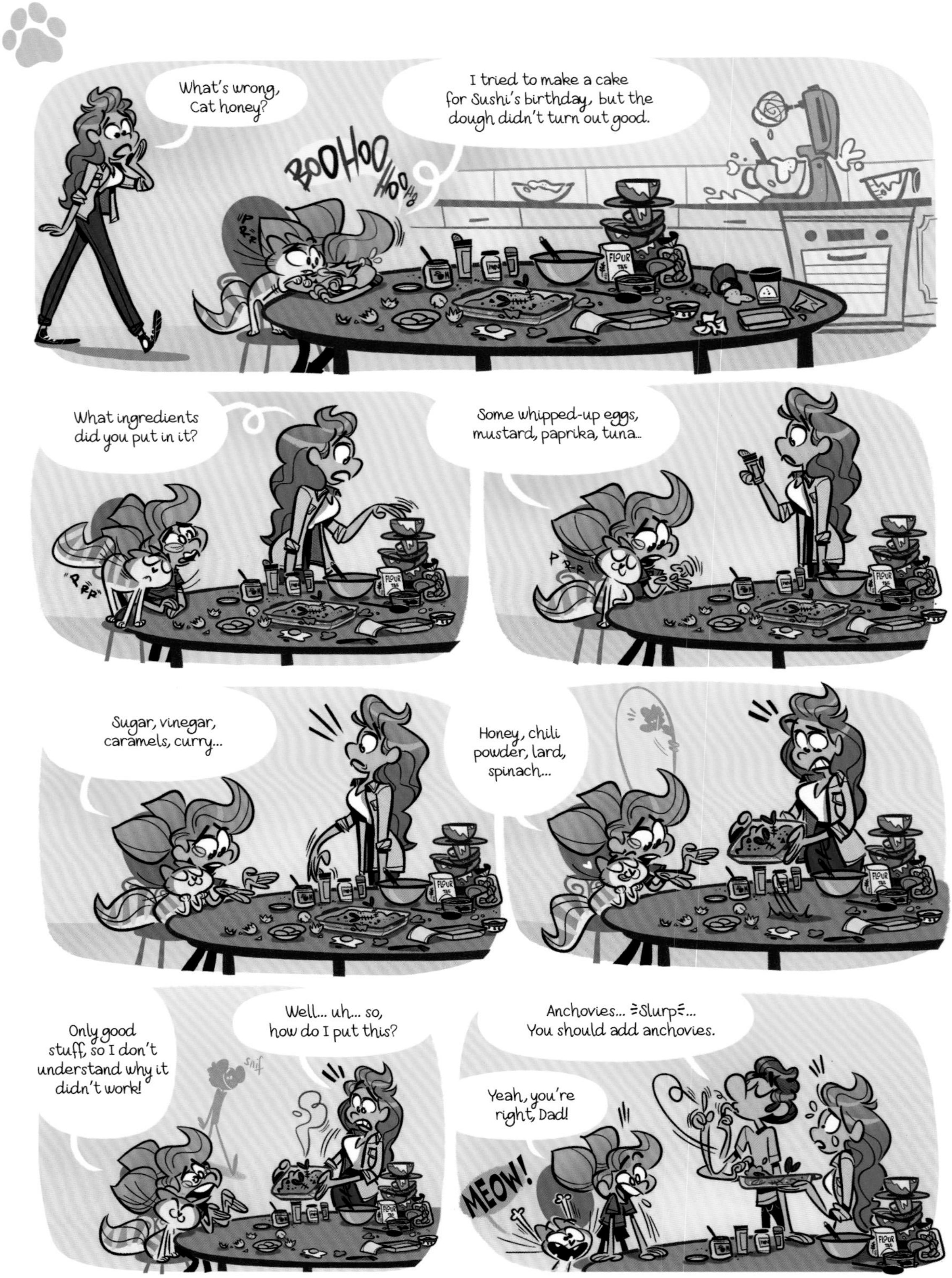

What's wrong, Cat honey?
I tried to make a cake for Sushi's birthday, but the dough didn't turn out good.
BOOHOO HOO HOO
What ingredients did you put in it?
Some whipped-up eggs, mustard, paprika, tuna...
Sugar, vinegar, caramels, curry...
Honey, chili powder, lard, spinach...
Only good stuff, so I don't understand why it didn't work!
Well... uh... so, how do I put this?
Anchovies... Slurp... You should add anchovies.
Yeah, you're right, Dad!
MEOW!

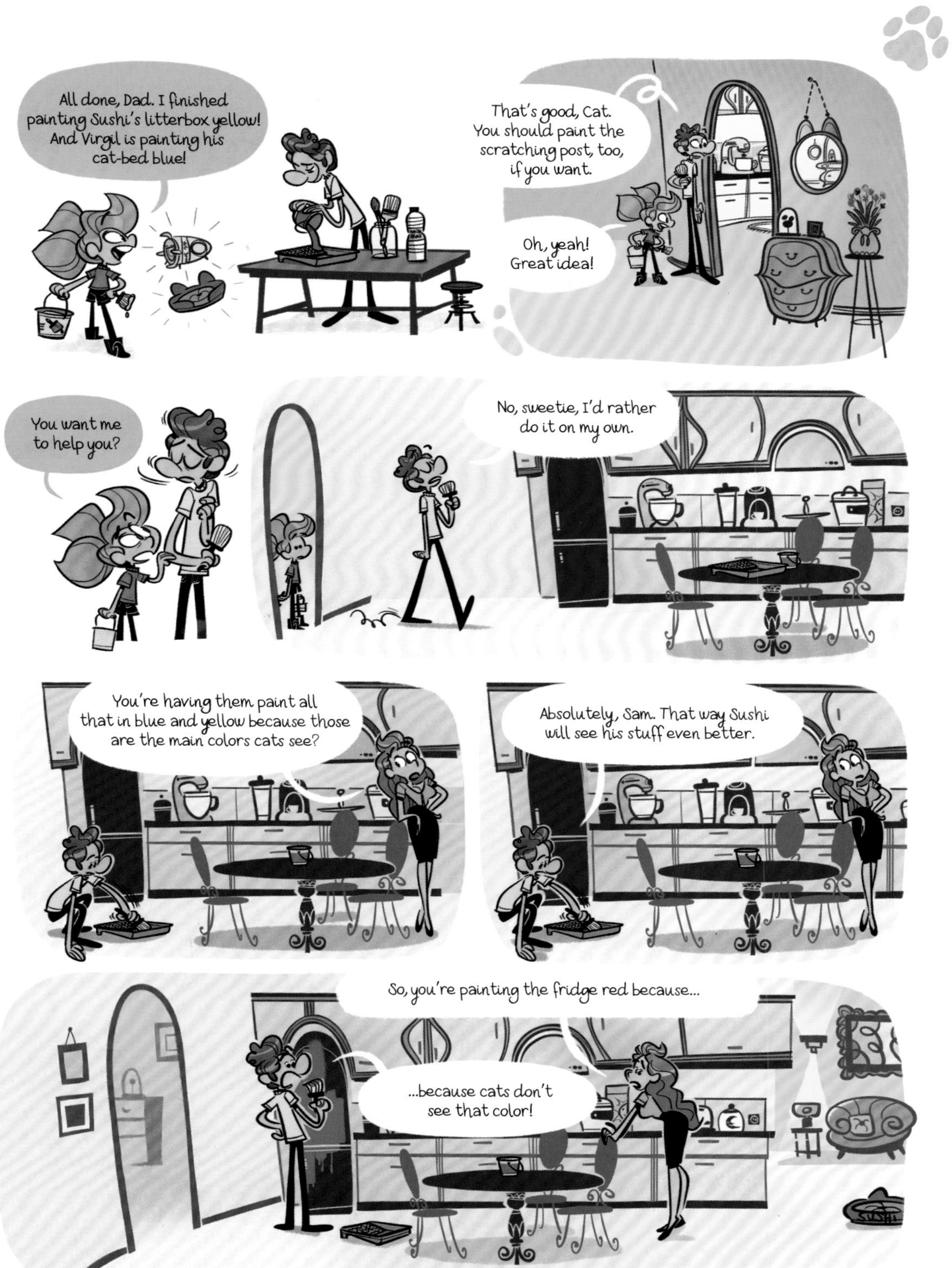
All done, Dad. I finished painting Sushi's litterbox yellow! And Virgil is painting his cat-bed blue!
That's good, Cat. You should paint the scratching post, too, if you want.
Oh, yeah! Great idea!
You want me to help you?
No, sweetie, I'd rather do it on my own.
You're having them paint all that in blue and yellow because those are the main colors cats see?
Absolutely, Sam. That way Sushi will see his stuff even better.
So, you're painting the fridge red because...
...because cats don't see that color!

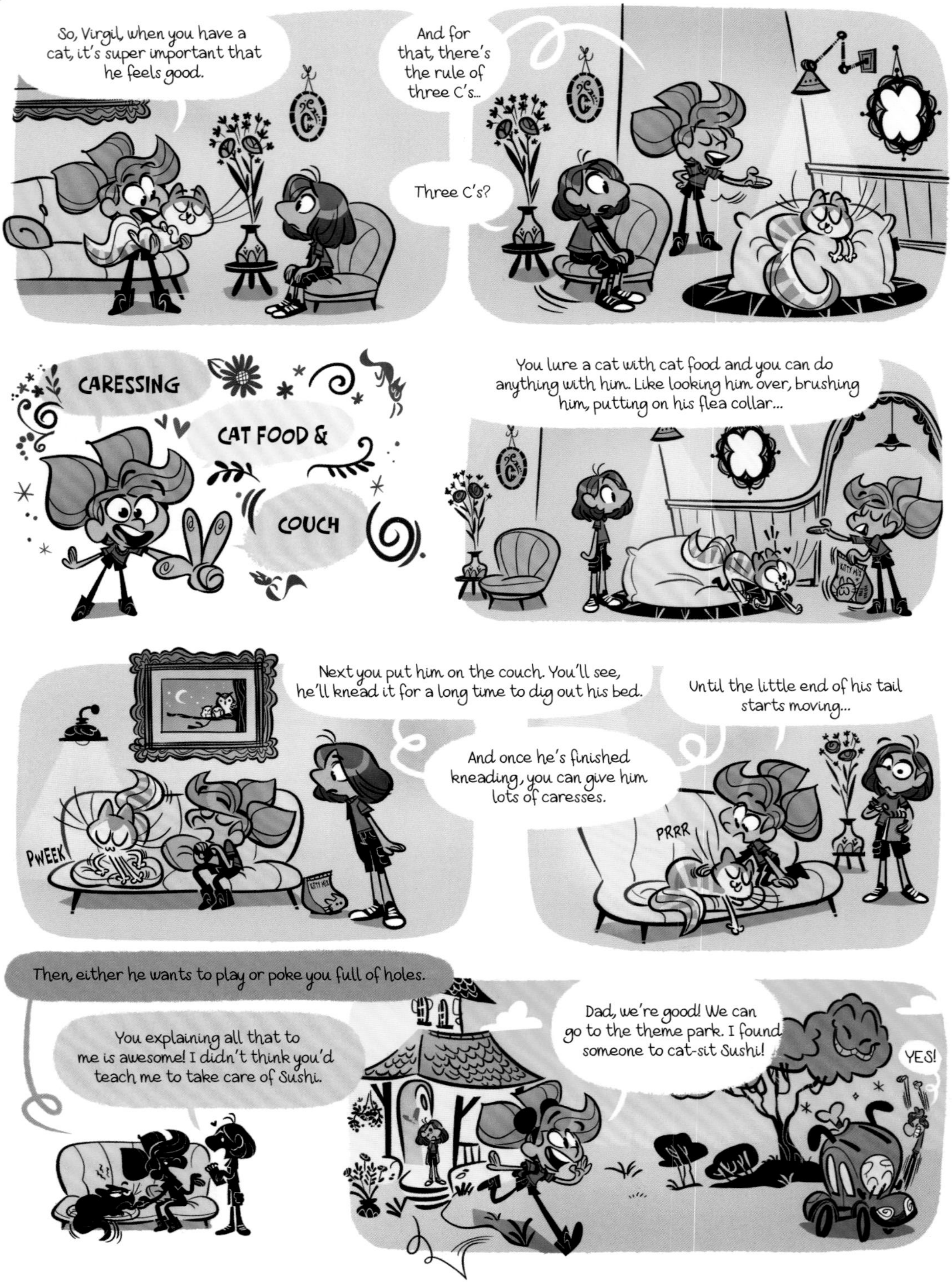
So, Virgil, when you have a cat, it's super important that he feels good.
And for that, there's the rule of three C's...
Three C's?
CARESSING
CAT FOOD &
COUCH
You lure a cat with cat food and you can do anything with him. Like looking him over, brushing him, putting on his flea collar...
Next you put him on the couch. You'll see, he'll knead it for a long time to dig out his bed.
PWEEK
And once he's finished kneading, you can give him lots of caresses.
Until the little end of his tail starts moving...
PRRR
Then, either he wants to play or poke you full of holes.
You explaining all that to me is awesome! I didn't think you'd teach me to take care of Sushi.
Dad, we're good! We can go to the theme park. I found someone to cat-sit Sushi!
YES!

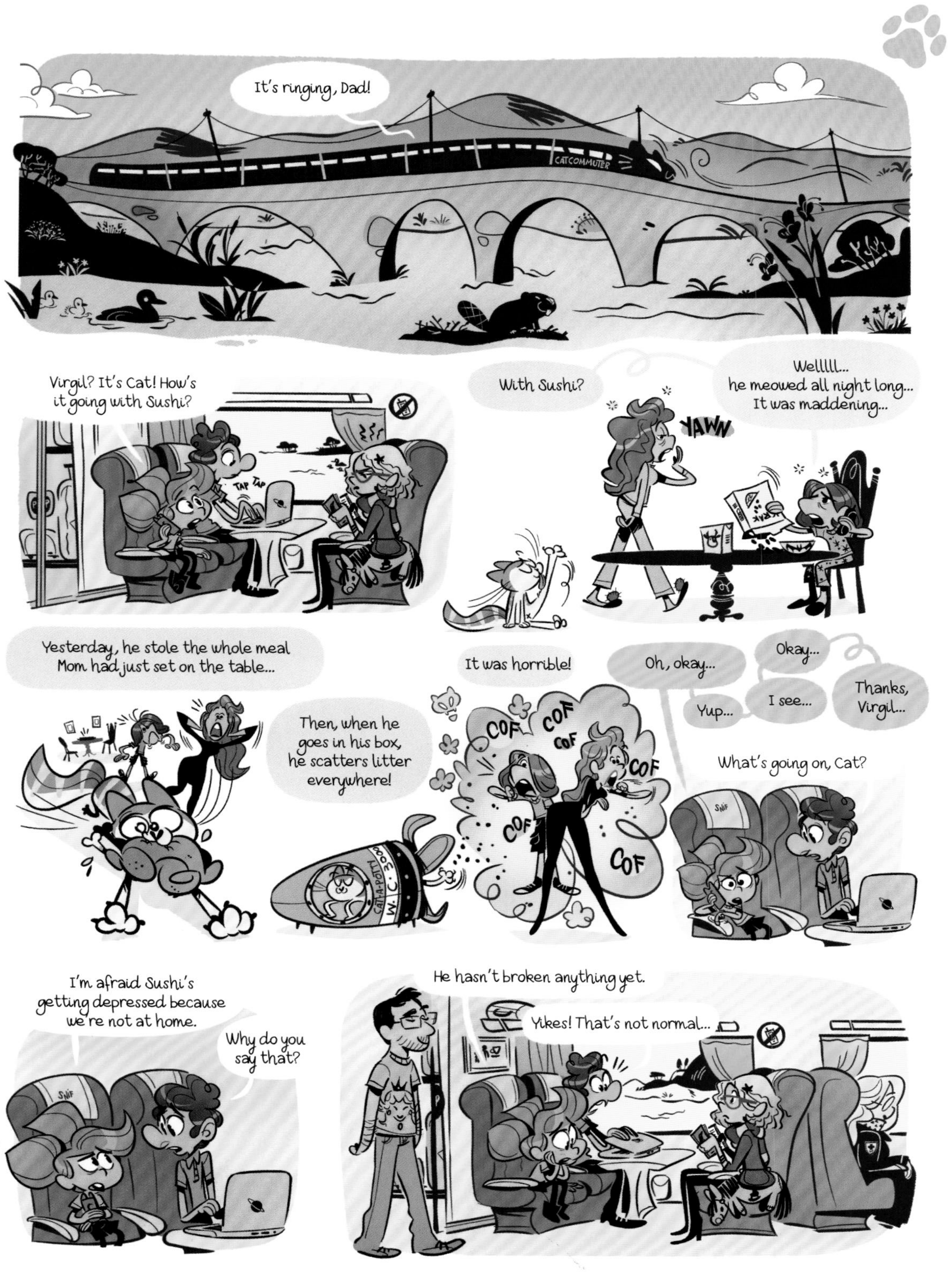

It's ringing, Dad!
CATCOMMUTER
Virgil? It's Cat! How's it going with Sushi?
TAP TAP
With Sushi?
YAWN
Welllll... he meowed all night long... It was maddening...
Yesterday, he stole the whole meal Mom had just set on the table...
Then, when he goes in his box, he scatters litter everywhere!
CAT-A-POTTY W.C. 3000
COF COF COF COF COF COF
It was horrible!
Oh, okay...
Yup...
Okay...
I see...
Thanks, Virgil...
What's going on, Cat?
SNIF
I'm afraid Sushi's getting depressed because we're not at home.
Why do you say that?
SNIF
He hasn't broken anything yet.
Yikes! That's not normal...

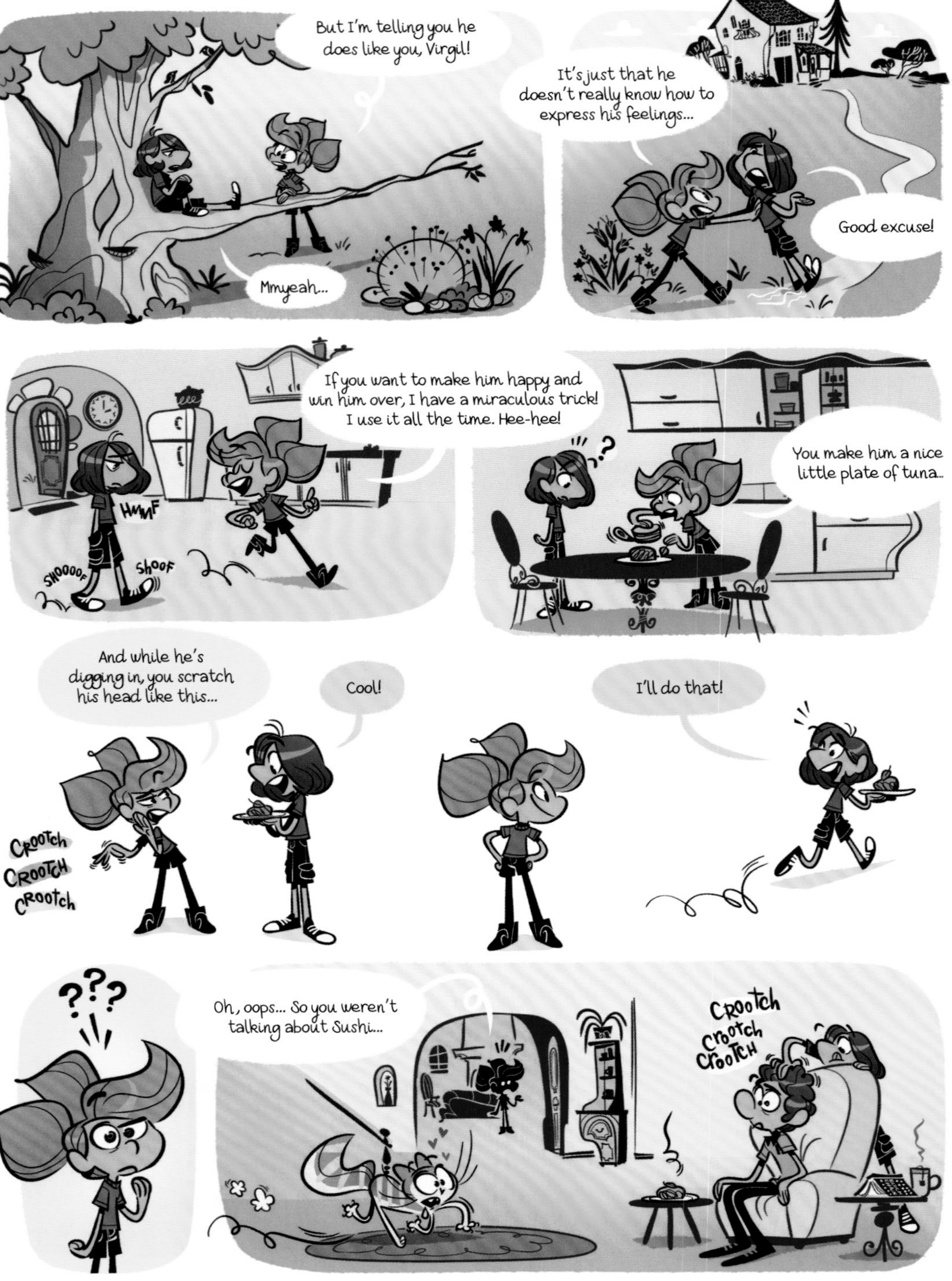
But I'm telling you he does like you, Virgil!
Mmyeah...
It's just that he doesn't really know how to express his feelings...
Good excuse!
HMMF
SHOOOOF
SHOOF
If you want to make him happy and win him over, I have a miraculous trick! I use it all the time. Hee-hee!
You make him a nice little plate of tuna...
And while he's digging in, you scratch his head like this...
CROOTCH
CROOTCH
CROOTCH
Cool!
I'll do that!
???
Oh, oops... So you weren't talking about Sushi...
CROOTCH
CROOTCH
CROOTCH

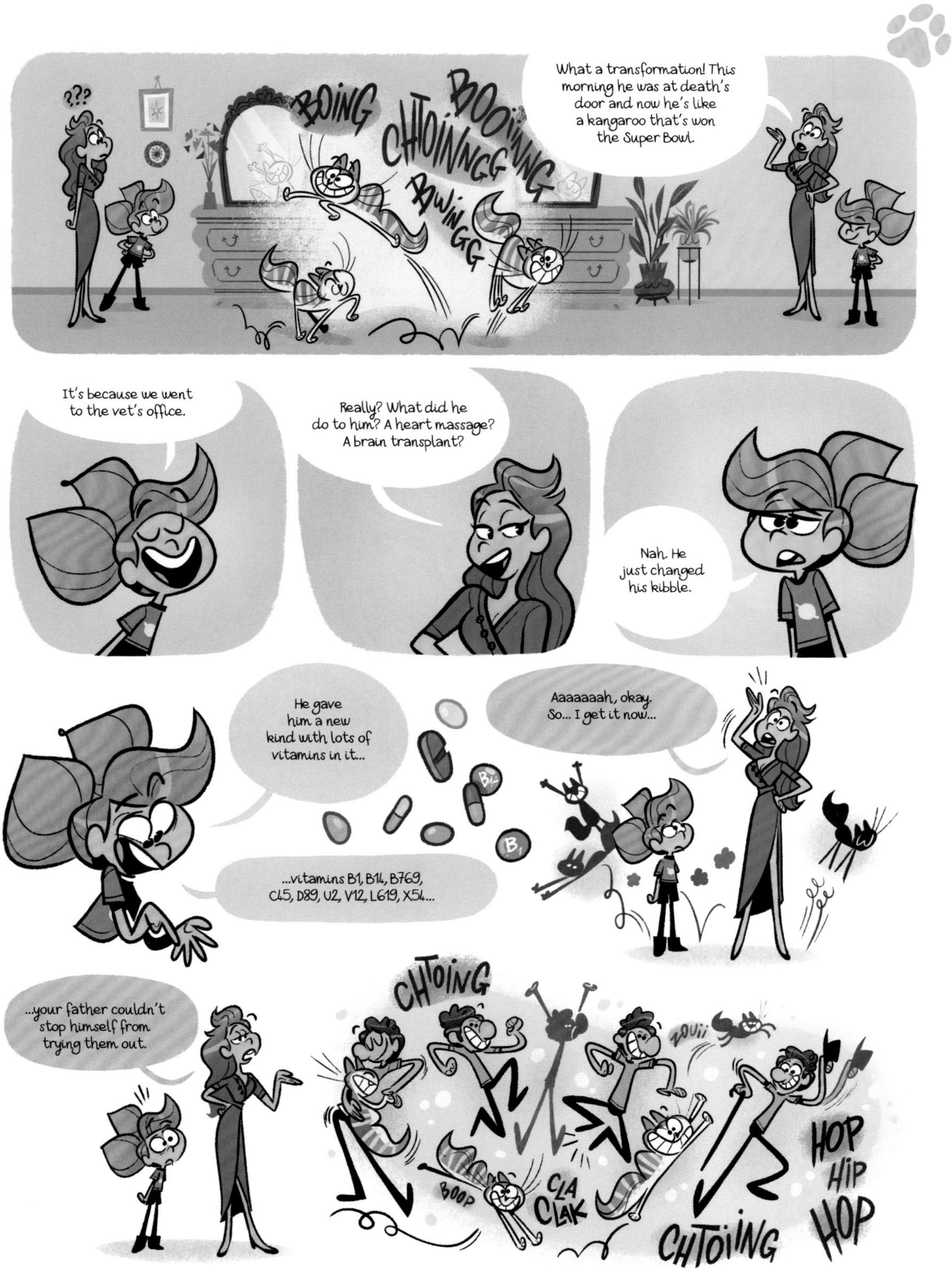
???
BOING
CHTOIINNGG
BOOÏNNNG
BWINGG
What a transformation! This morning he was at death's door and now he's like a kangaroo that's won the Super Bowl.
It's because we went to the vet's office.
Really? What did he do to him? A heart massage? A brain transplant?
Nah. He just changed his kibble.
He gave him a new kind with lots of vitamins in it...
...vitamins B1, B14, B769, C45, D89, U2, V12, L619, X54...
B14
B1
Aaaaaaah, okay. So... I get it now...
...your father couldn't stop himself from trying them out.
CHTOING
ZOUii
BOOP
CLA CLAK
CHTOIING
HOP HIP HOP

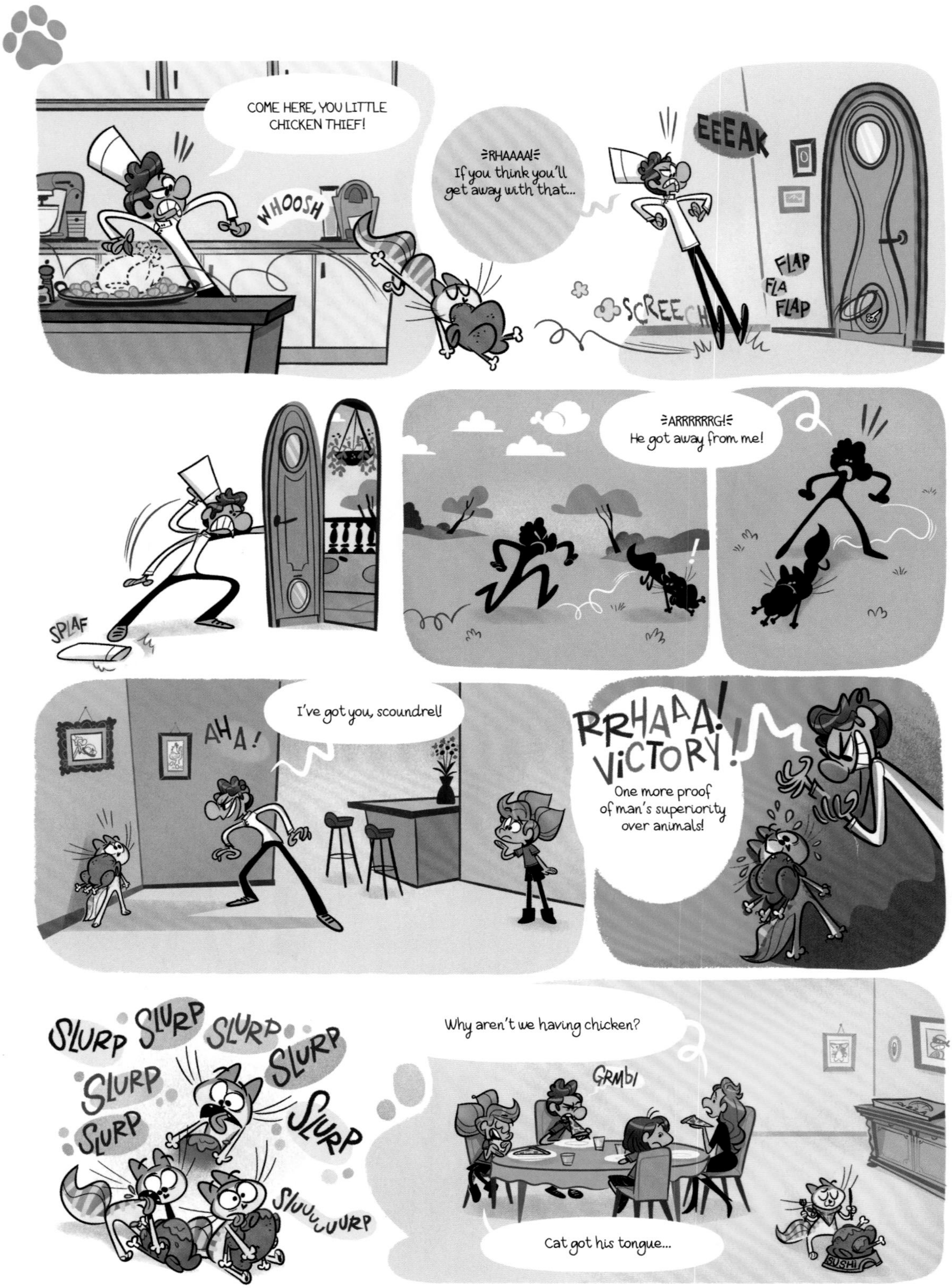

COME HERE, YOU LITTLE CHICKEN THIEF!
WHOOSH
RHAAAA! If you think you'll get away with that...
EEEAK
FLAP
FLA
FLAP
SCREECH
SPLAF
ARRRRRRG! He got away from me!
I've got you, scoundrel!
AHA!
RRHAAA! VICTORY!
One more proof of man's superiority over animals!
SLURP
SLURP
SLURP
SLURP
SLURP
SLURP
SLURP
SLUUUUUURP
Why aren't we having chicken?
GRMBL
Cat got his tongue...
SUSHI

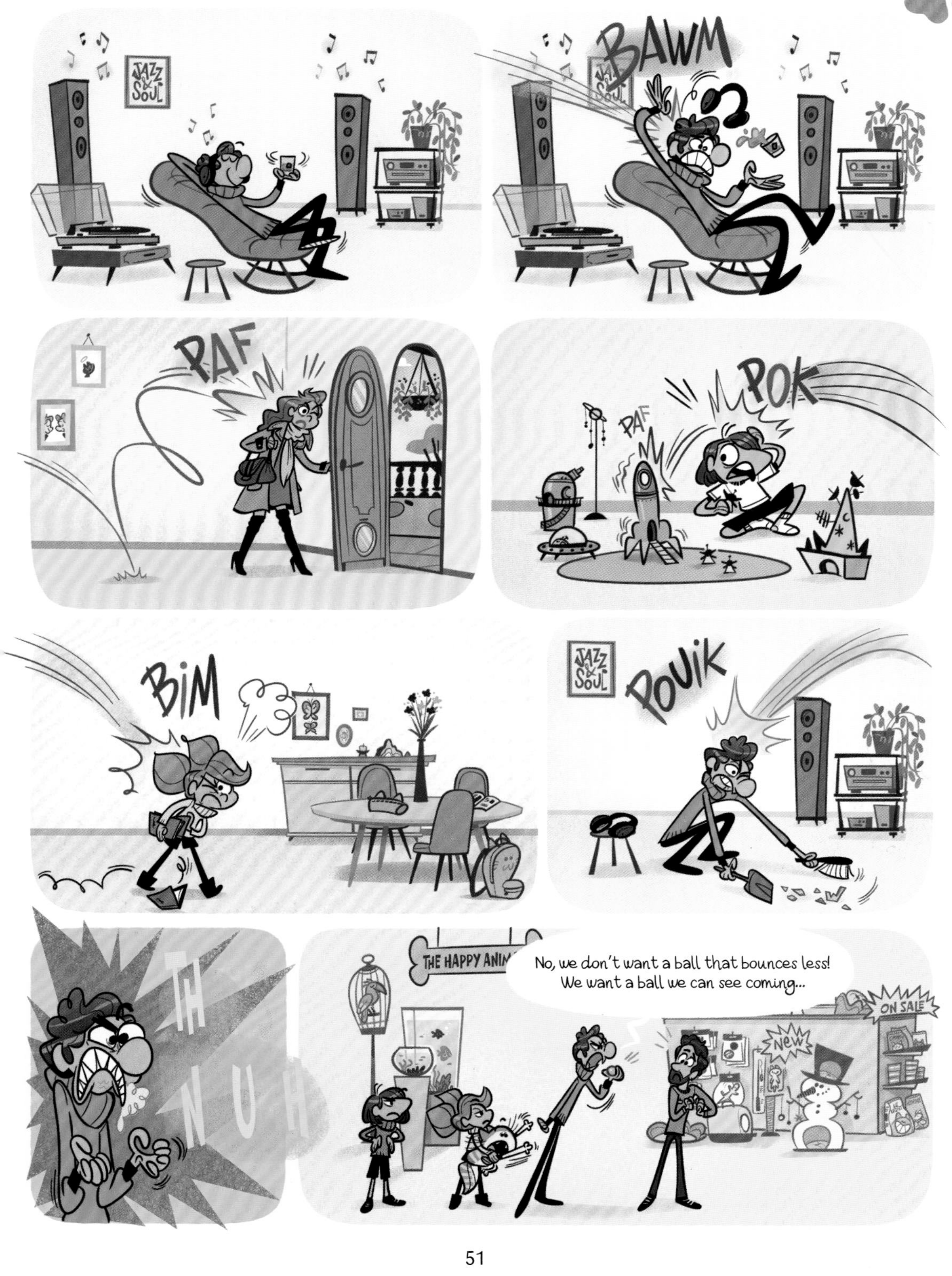
JAZZ & SOUL
BAWM
PAF
PAF
POK
BIM
JAZZ & SOUL
POUIK
TH
NUH
THE HAPPY ANIM
No, we don't want a ball that bounces less!
We want a ball we can see coming...
ON SALE
New

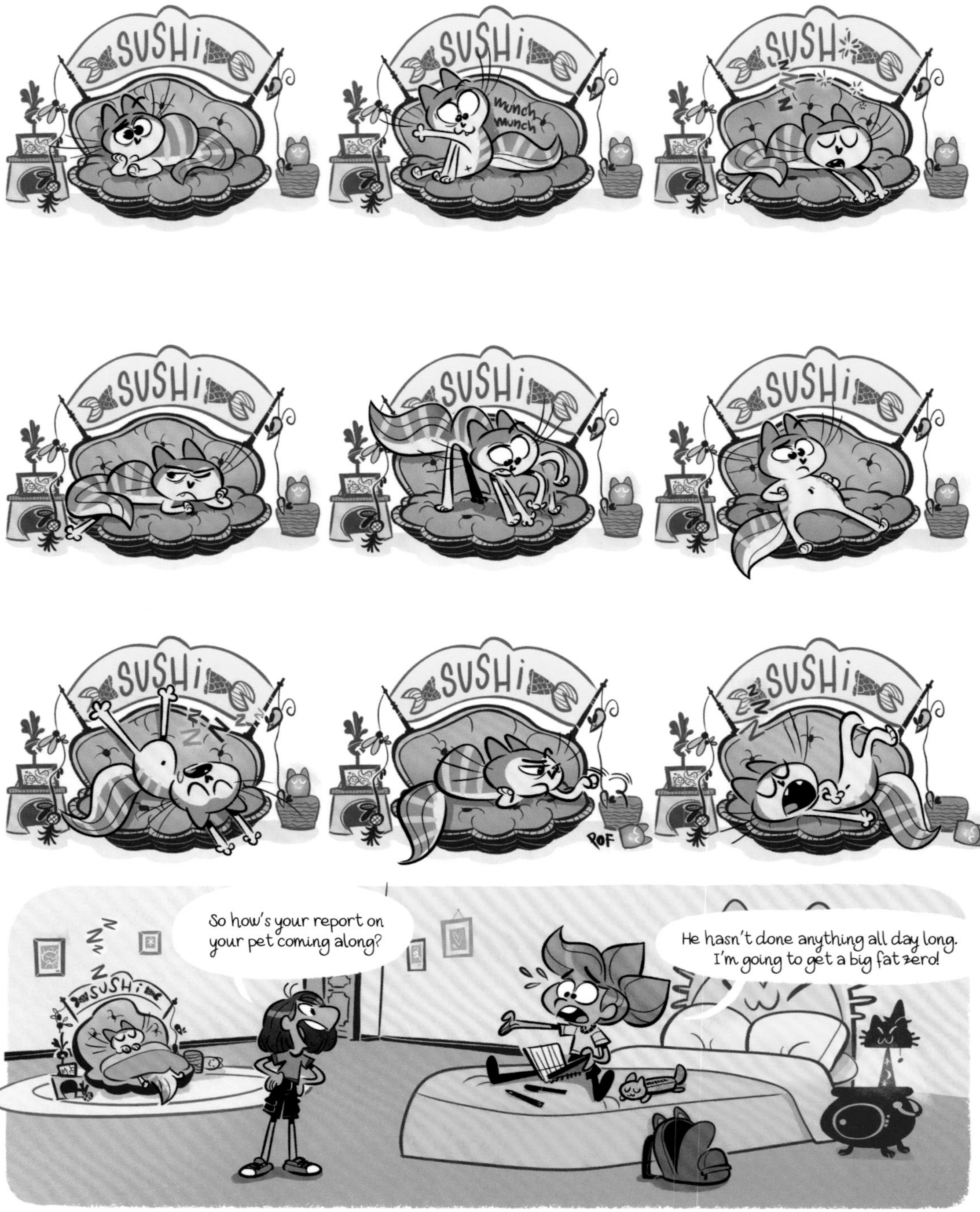
SUSHI
munch munch
POF
So how's your report on your pet coming along?
He hasn't done anything all day long. I'm going to get a big fat zero!

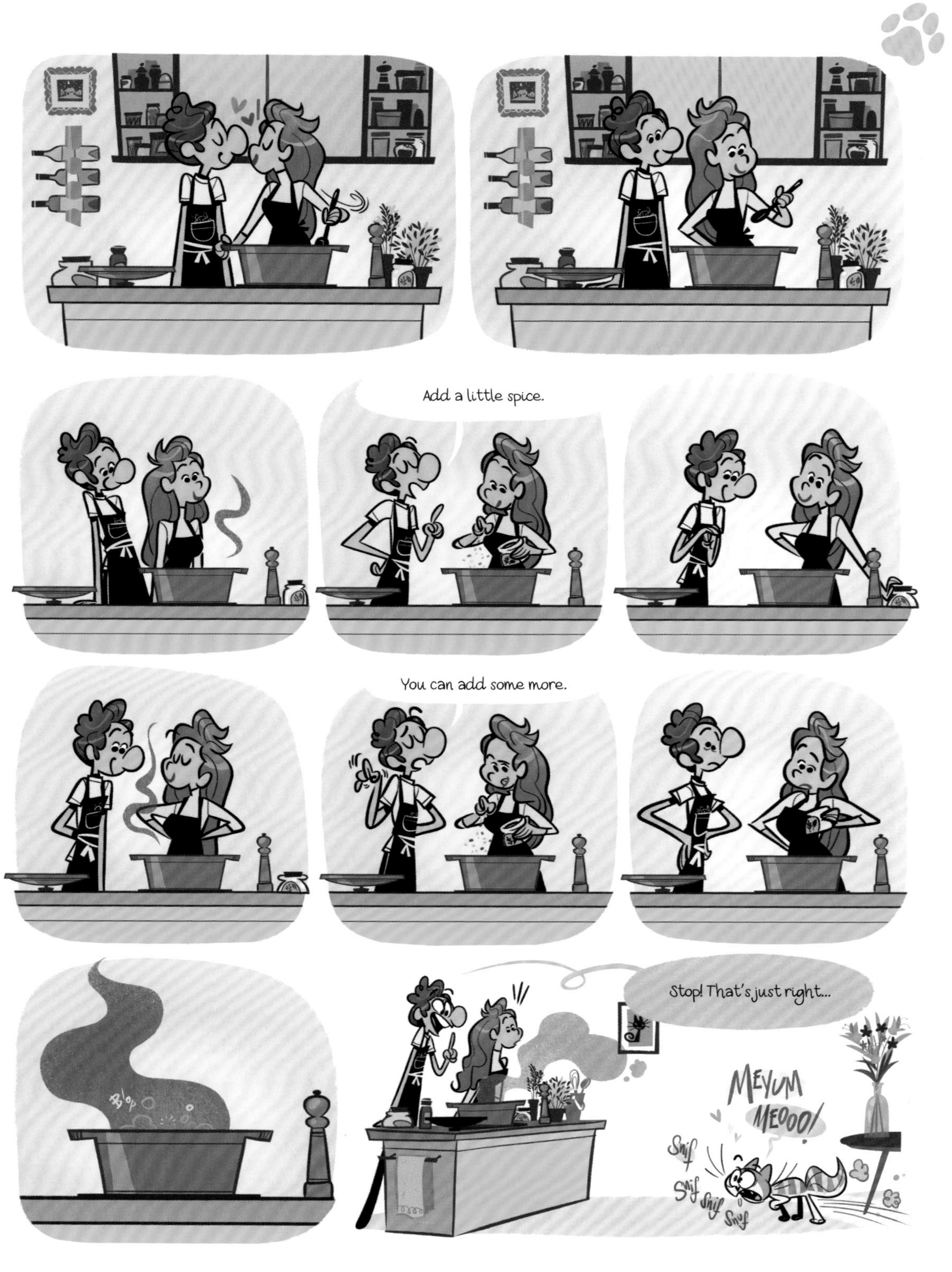

Add a little spice.
You can add some more.
Blop
Stop! That's just right...
MEYUM
MEOOO!
Snif
Snif
Snif
Snif

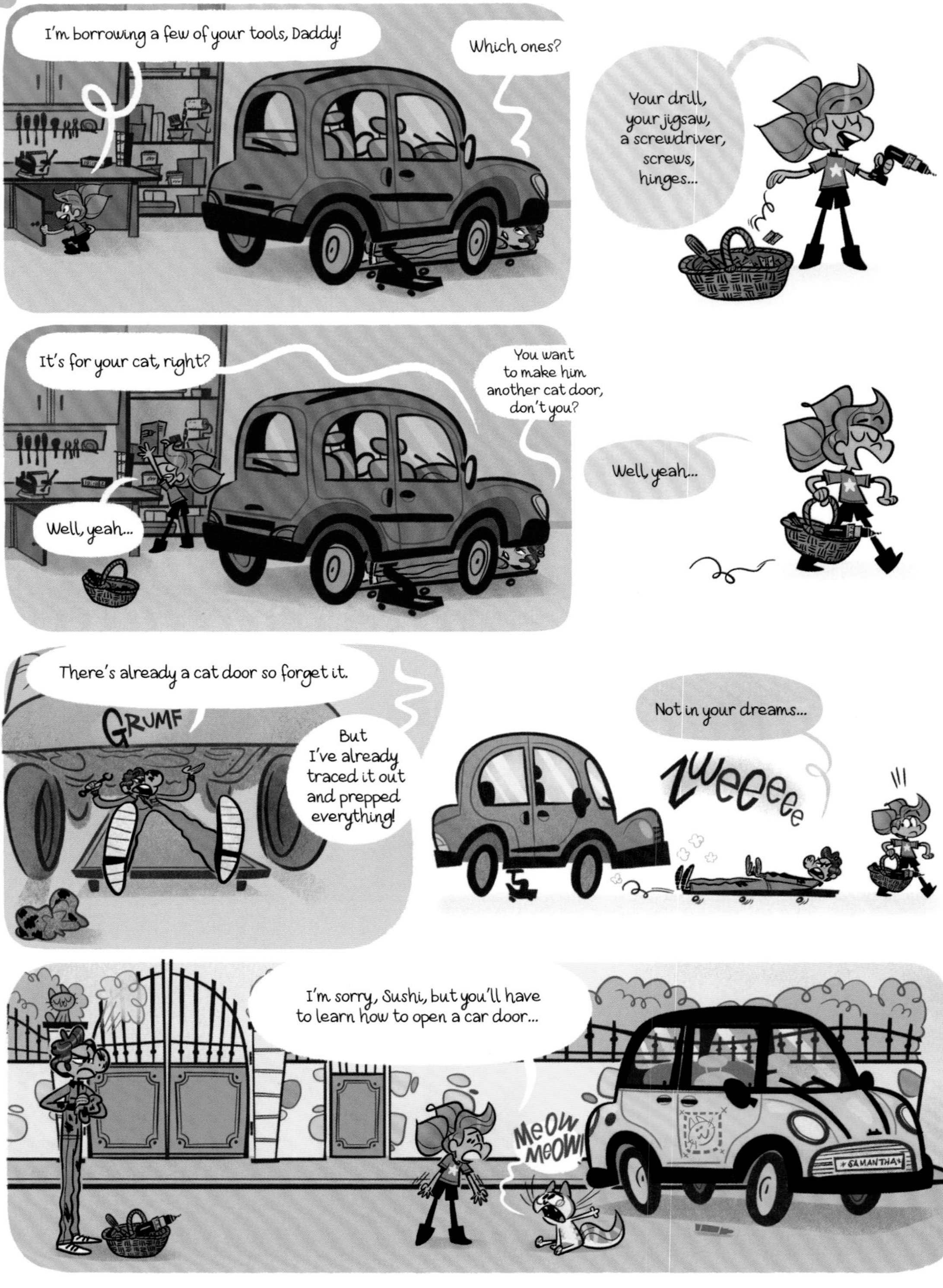
I'm borrowing a few of your tools, Daddy!
Which ones?
Your drill, your jigsaw, a screwdriver, screws, hinges...
It's for your cat, right?
Well, yeah...
You want to make him another cat door, don't you?
Well, yeah...
There's already a cat door so forget it.
GRUMF
But I've already traced it out and prepped everything!
Not in your dreams...
ZWEEEEEE
I'm sorry, Sushi, but you'll have to learn how to open a car door...
MEOW MEOW!
SAMANTHA

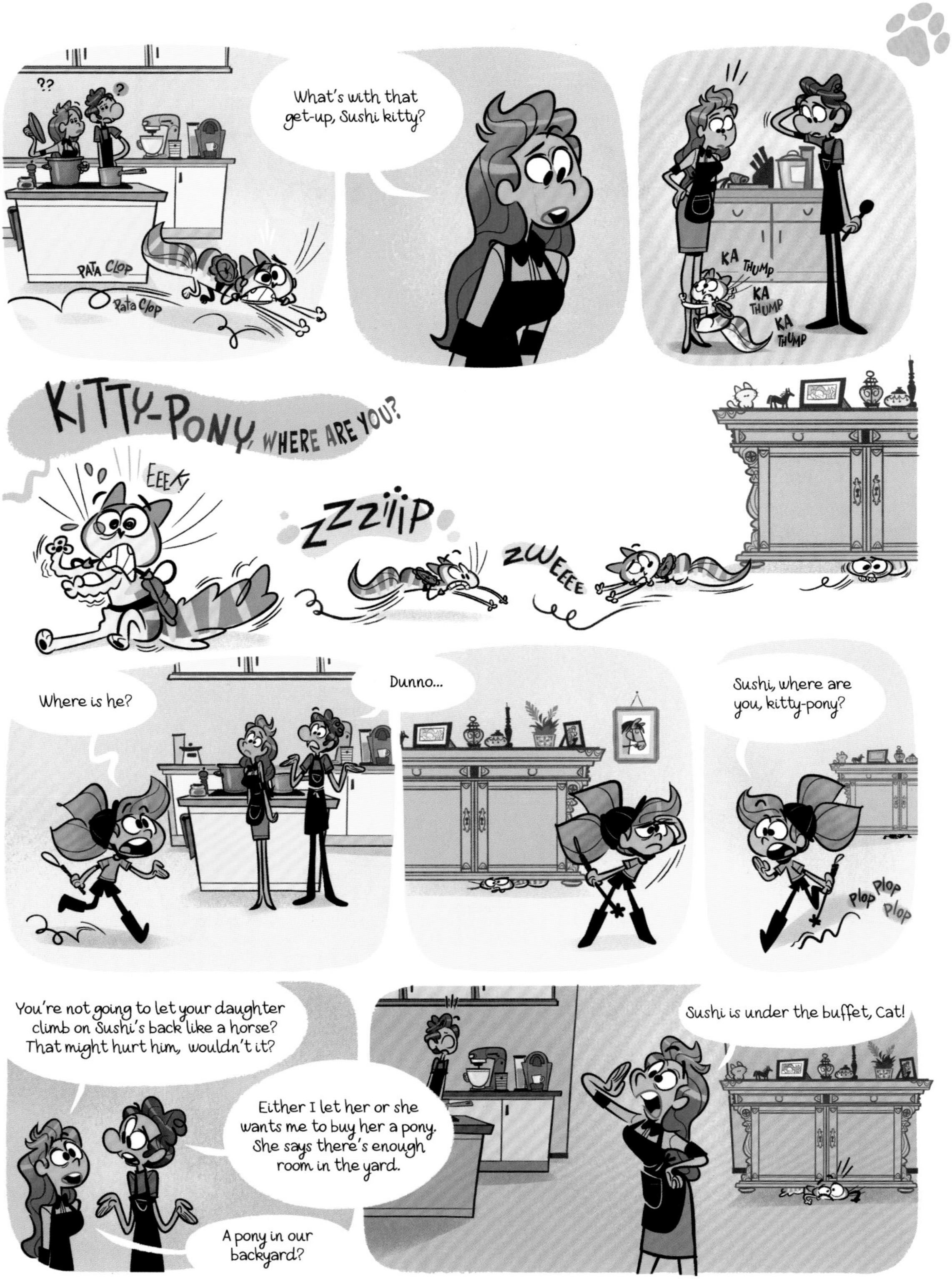
??
?
PATA CLOP
Pata Clop
What's with that get-up, Sushi kitty?
KA THUMP
KA THUMP
KA THUMP
KITTY-PONY, WHERE ARE YOU?
EEEK!
ZZZIIIP
ZWEEEE
Where is he?
Dunno...
Sushi, where are you, kitty-pony?
Plop Plop Plop
You're not going to let your daughter climb on Sushi's back like a horse? That might hurt him, wouldn't it?
Either I let her or she wants me to buy her a pony. She says there's enough room in the yard.
A pony in our backyard?
Sushi is under the buffet, Cat!

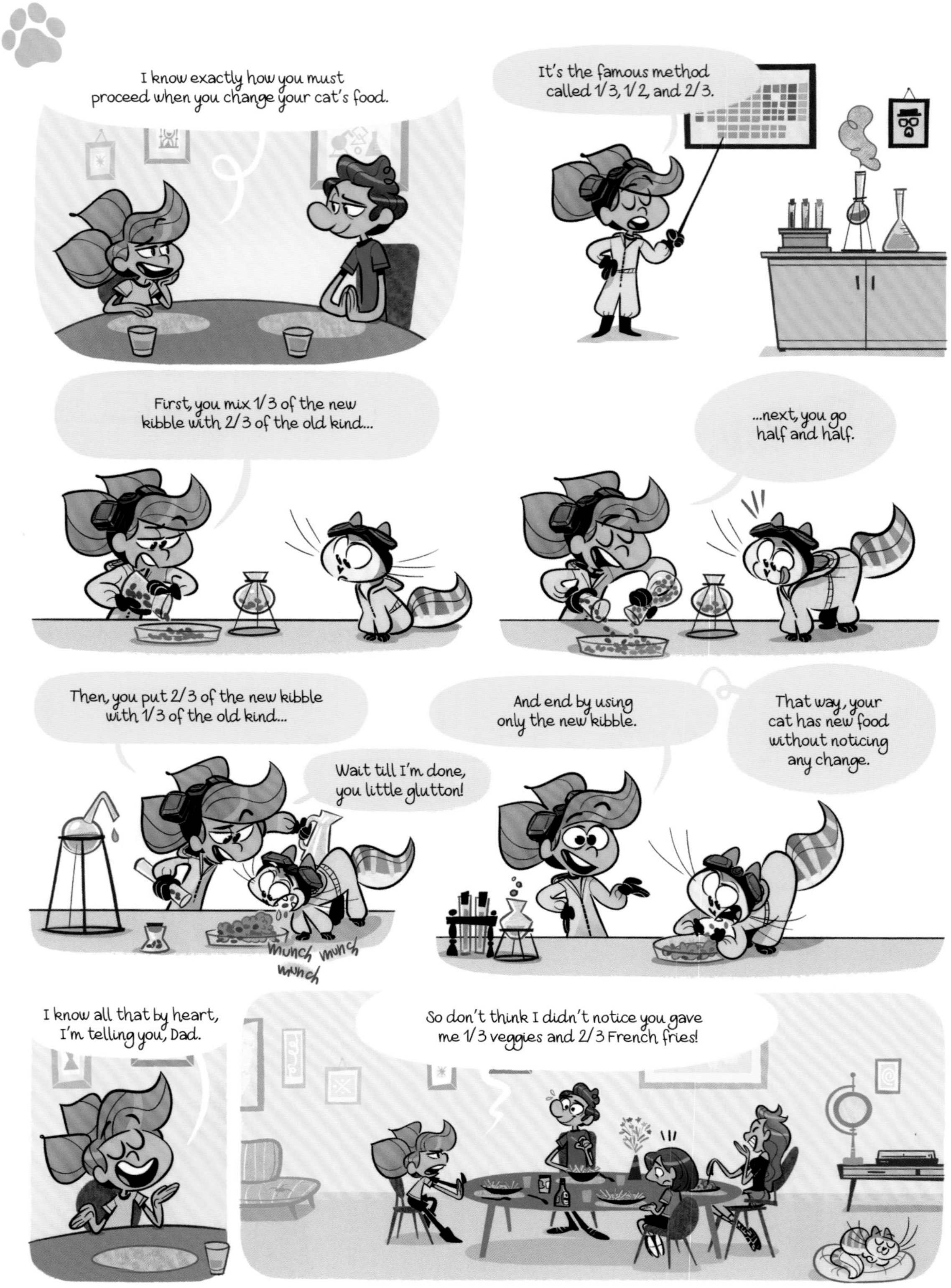
I know exactly how you must proceed when you change your cat's food.
It's the famous method called 1/3, 1/2, and 2/3.
First, you mix 1/3 of the new kibble with 2/3 of the old kind...
...next, you go half and half.
Then, you put 2/3 of the new kibble with 1/3 of the old kind...
Wait till I'm done, you little glutton!
munch munch munch
And end by using only the new kibble.
That way, your cat has new food without noticing any change.
I know all that by heart, I'm telling you, Dad.
So don't think I didn't notice you gave me 1/3 veggies and 2/3 French fries!

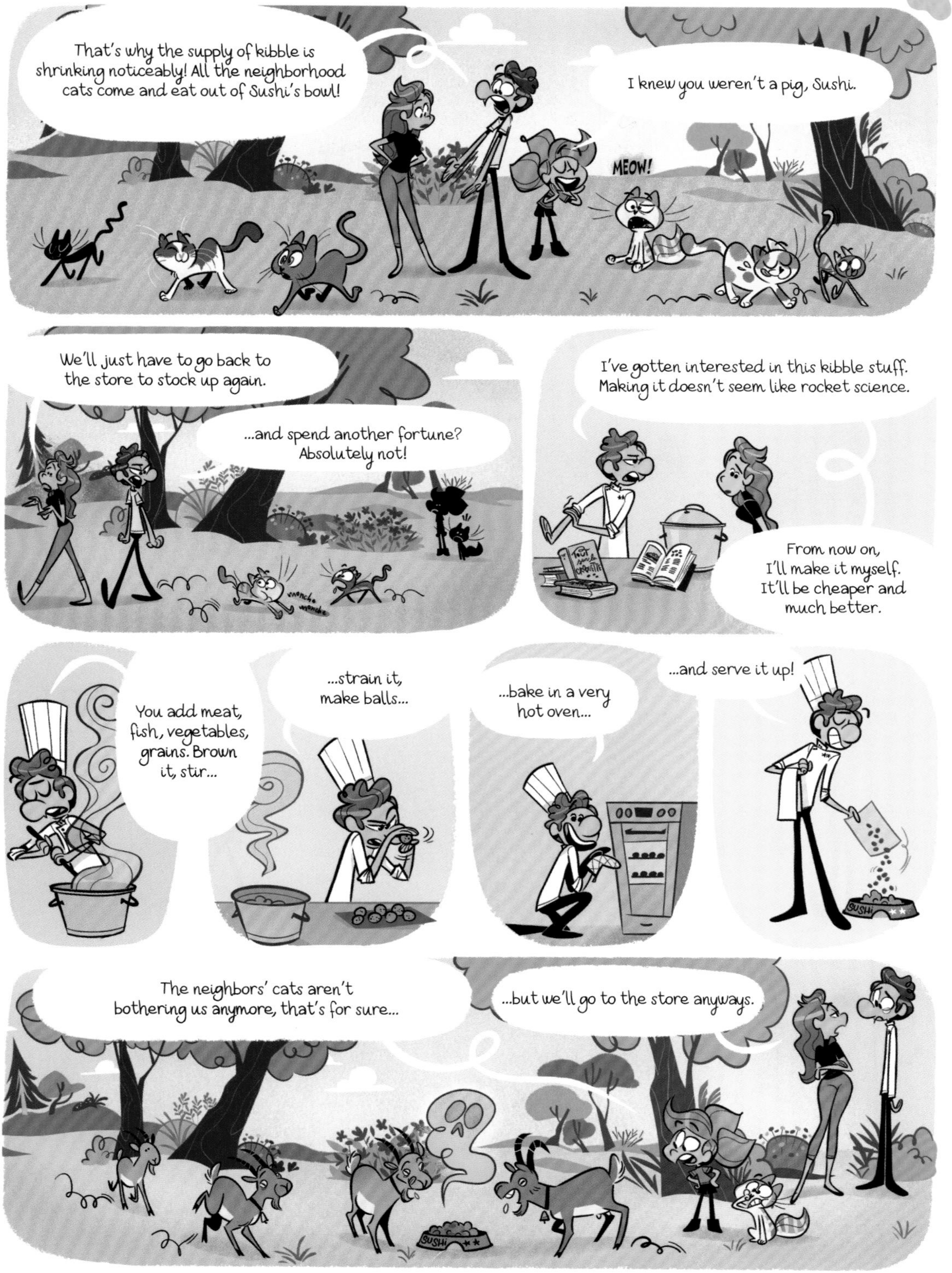
That's why the supply of kibble is shrinking noticeably! All the neighborhood cats come and eat out of Sushi's bowl!
I knew you weren't a pig, Sushi.
MEOW!
We'll just have to go back to the store to stock up again.
...and spend another fortune? Absolutely not!
I've gotten interested in this kibble stuff. Making it doesn't seem like rocket science.
From now on, I'll make it myself. It'll be cheaper and much better.
You add meat, fish, vegetables, grains. Brown it, stir...
...strain it, make balls...
...bake in a very hot oven...
...and serve it up!
SUSHI
The neighbors' cats aren't bothering us anymore, that's for sure...
...but we'll go to the store anyways.
SUSHI

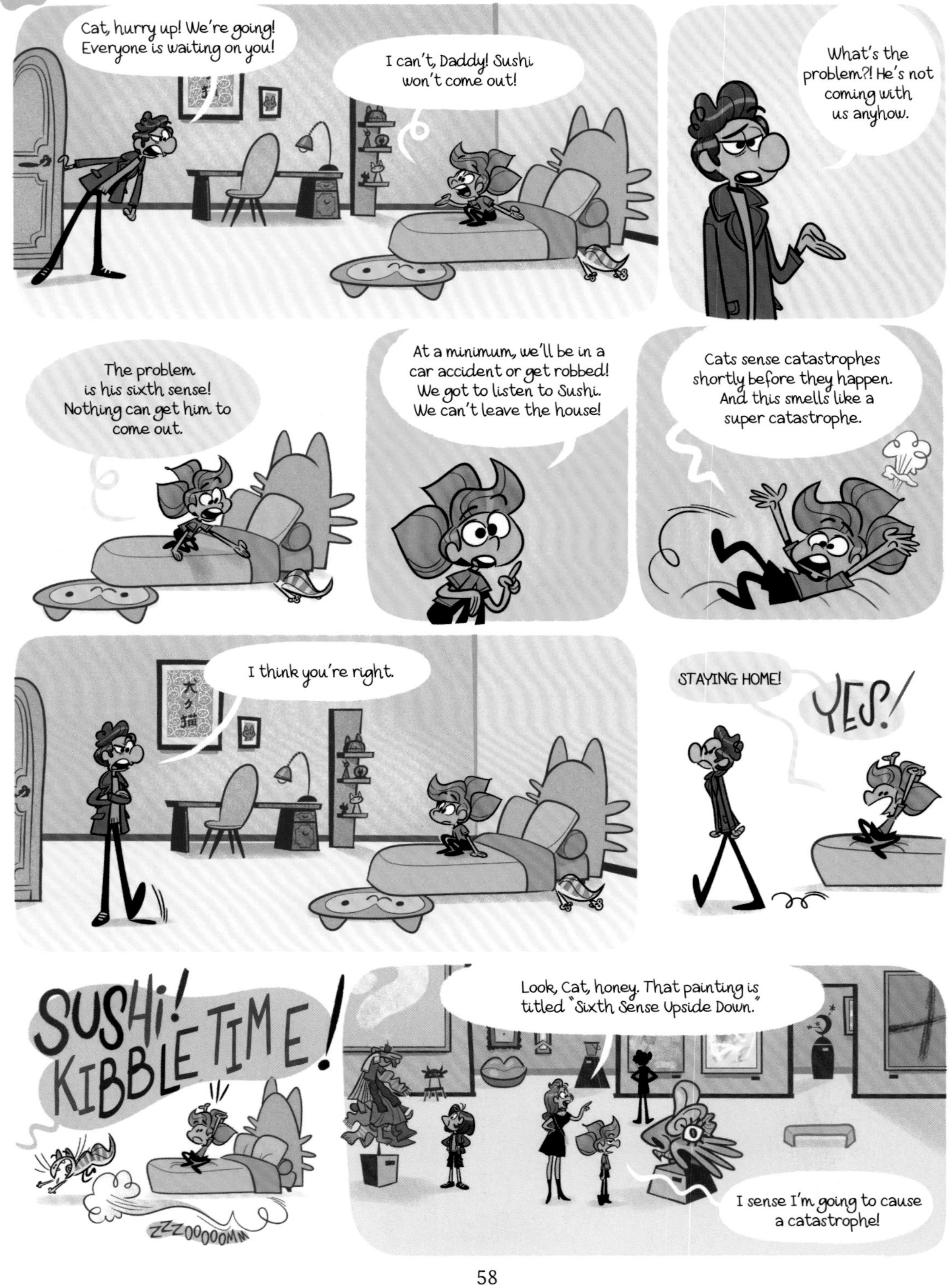
Cat, hurry up! We're going! Everyone is waiting on you!
I can't, Daddy! Sushi won't come out!
What's the problem?! He's not coming with us anyhow.
The problem is his sixth sense! Nothing can get him to come out.
At a minimum, we'll be in a car accident or get robbed! We got to listen to Sushi. We can't leave the house!
Cats sense catastrophes shortly before they happen. And this smells like a super catastrophe.
I think you're right.
STAYING HOME!
YES!
SUSHI! KIBBLE TIME!
ZZZOOOOOMM
Look, Cat, honey. That painting is titled "Sixth Sense Upside Down."
I sense I'm going to cause a catastrophe!

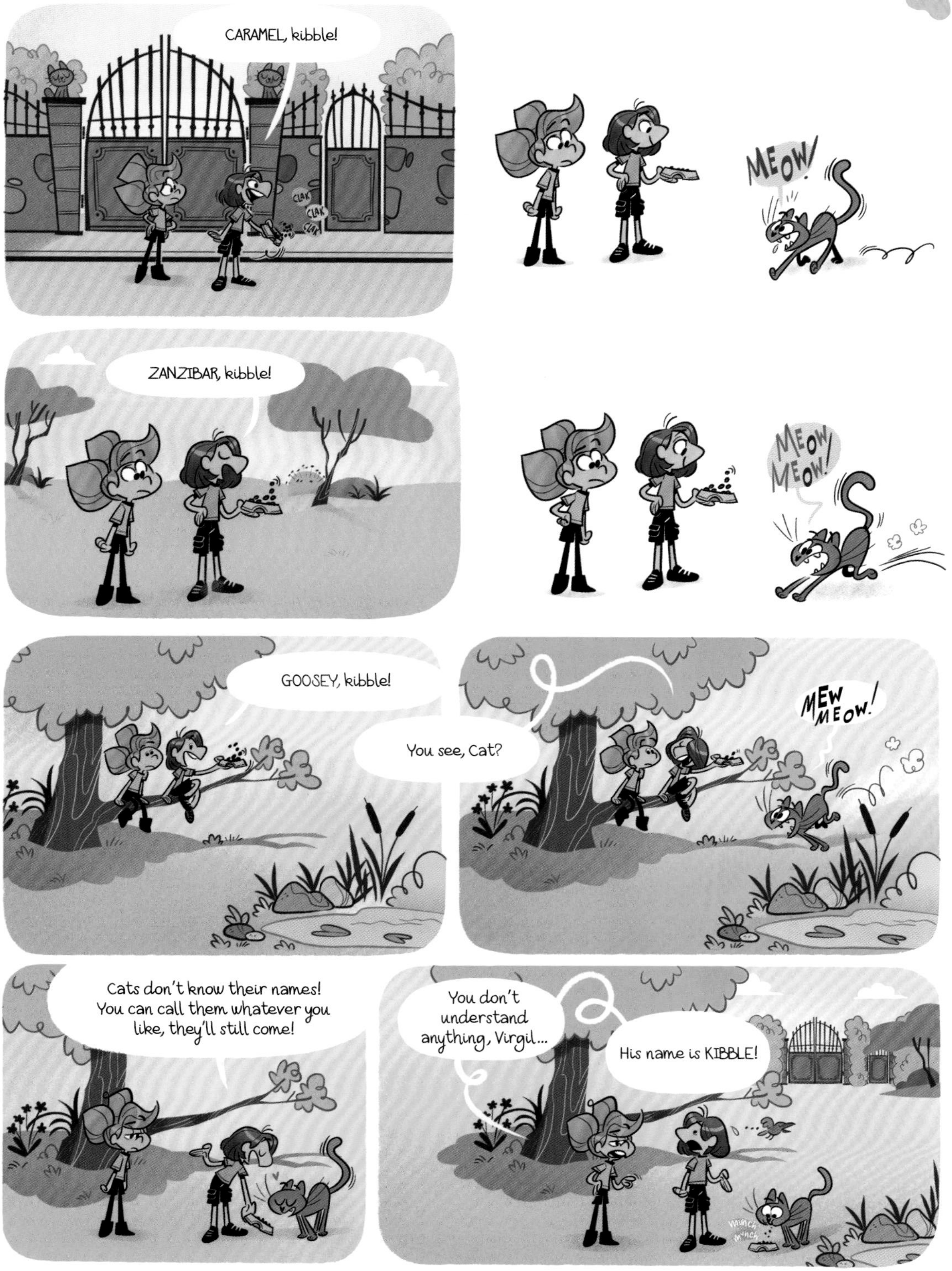
CARAMEL, kibble!
CLAK
CLAK
CLAK
MEOW!
ZANZIBAR, kibble!
MEOW MEOW!
GOOSEY, kibble!
You see, Cat?
MEW MEOW!
Cats don't know their names! You can call them whatever you like, they'll still come!
You don't understand anything, Virgil...
His name is KIBBLE!
munch munch

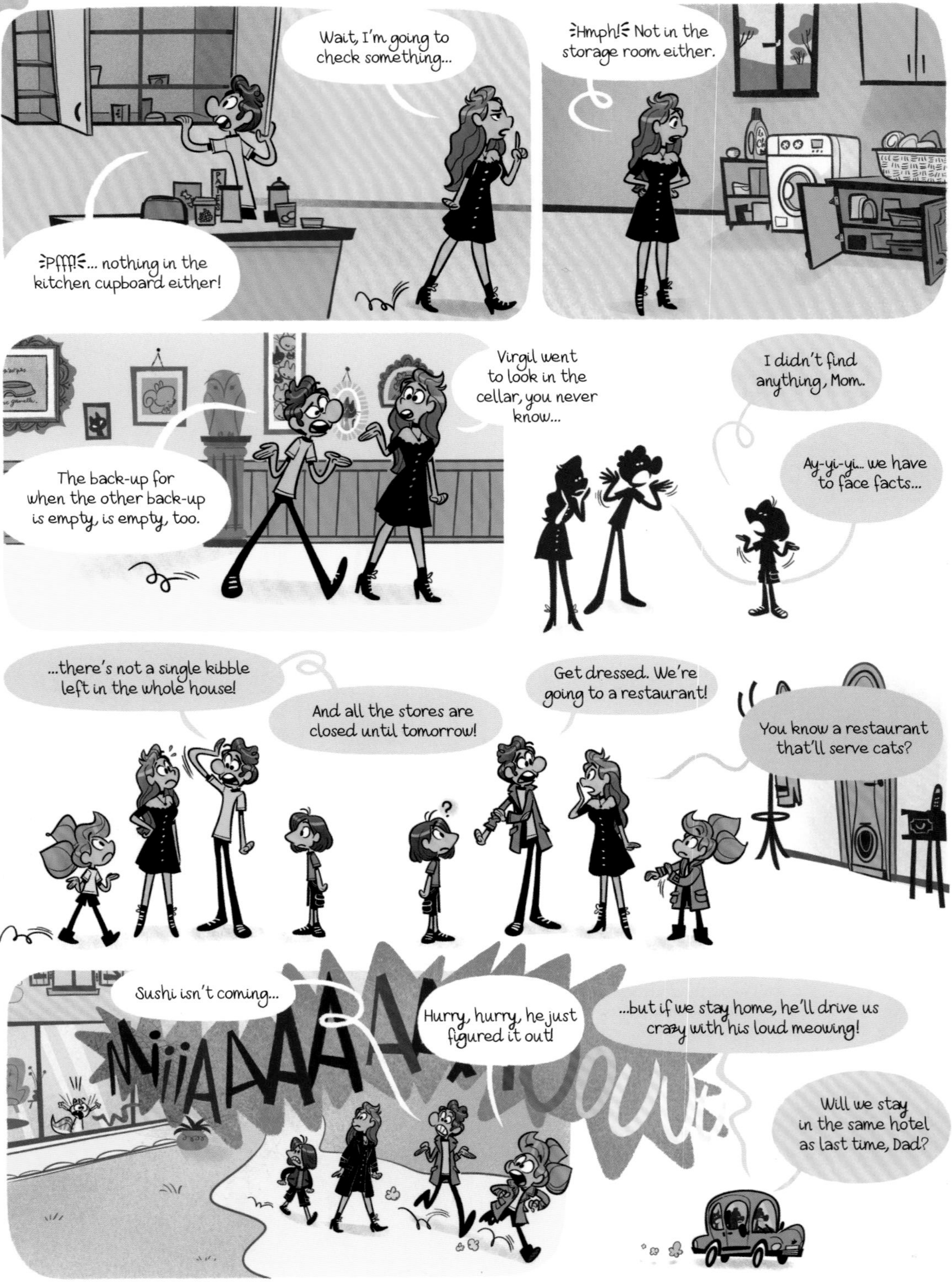
Wait, I'm going to check something...
⸗Pfff!⸗... nothing in the kitchen cupboard either!
⸗Hmph!⸗ Not in the storage room either.
Virgil went to look in the cellar, you never know...
The back-up for when the other back-up is empty, is empty, too.
I didn't find anything, Mom.
Ay-yi-yi... we have to face facts...
...there's not a single kibble left in the whole house!
And all the stores are closed until tomorrow!
Get dressed. We're going to a restaurant!
You know a restaurant that'll serve cats?
Sushi isn't coming...
Hurry, hurry, he just figured it out!
...but if we stay home, he'll drive us crazy with his loud meowing!
Will we stay in the same hotel as last time, Dad?

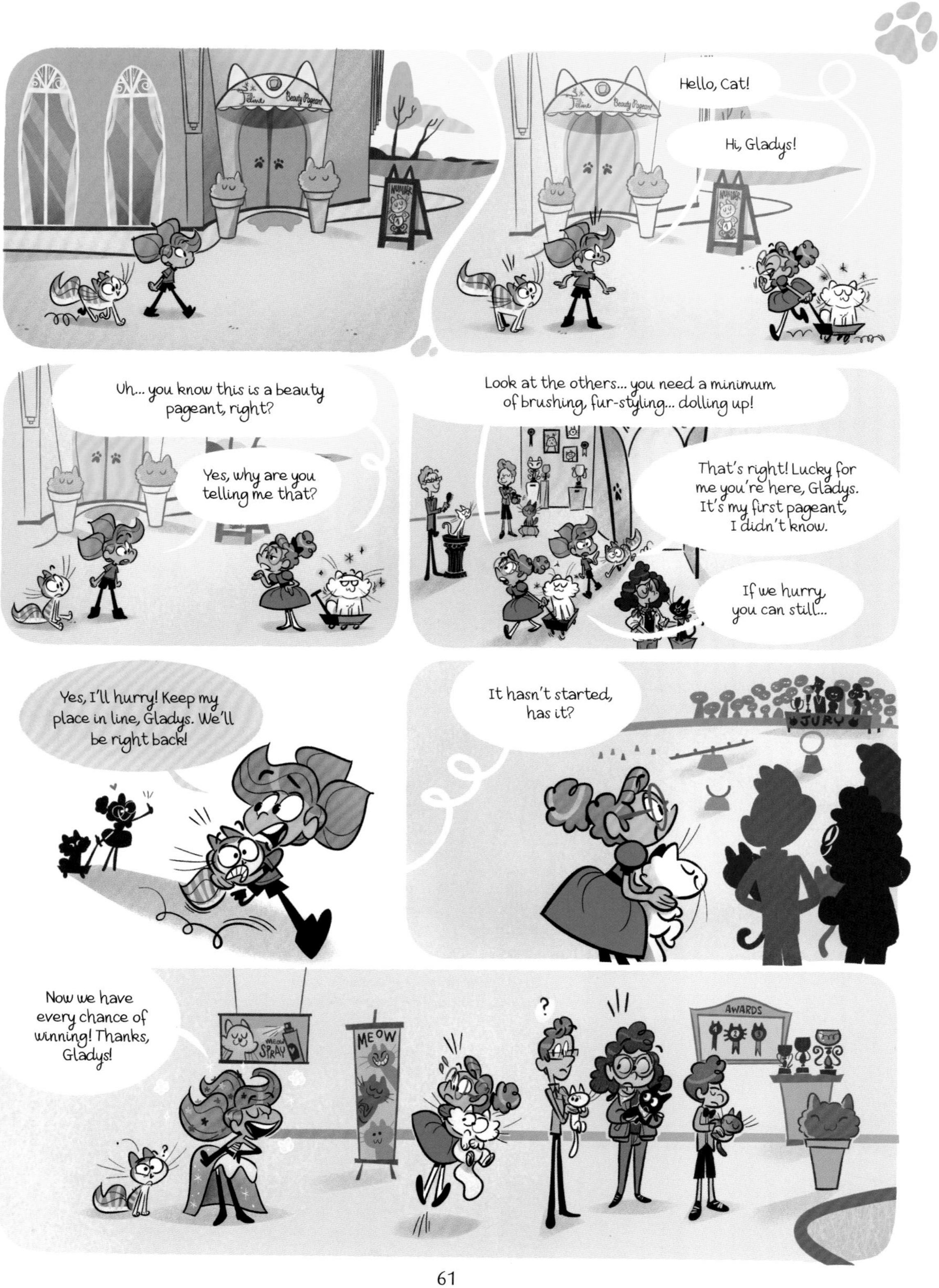
Féline Beauty Pageant
NUMBER
Hello, Cat!
Hi, Gladys!
Uh... you know this is a beauty pageant, right?
Yes, why are you telling me that?
Look at the others... you need a minimum of brushing, fur-styling... dolling up!
That's right! Lucky for me you're here, Gladys. It's my first pageant, I didn't know.
If we hurry, you can still...
Yes, I'll hurry! Keep my place in line, Gladys. We'll be right back!
It hasn't started, has it?
JURY
Now we have every chance of winning! Thanks, Gladys!
MEOW SPRAY
MEOW
AWARDS

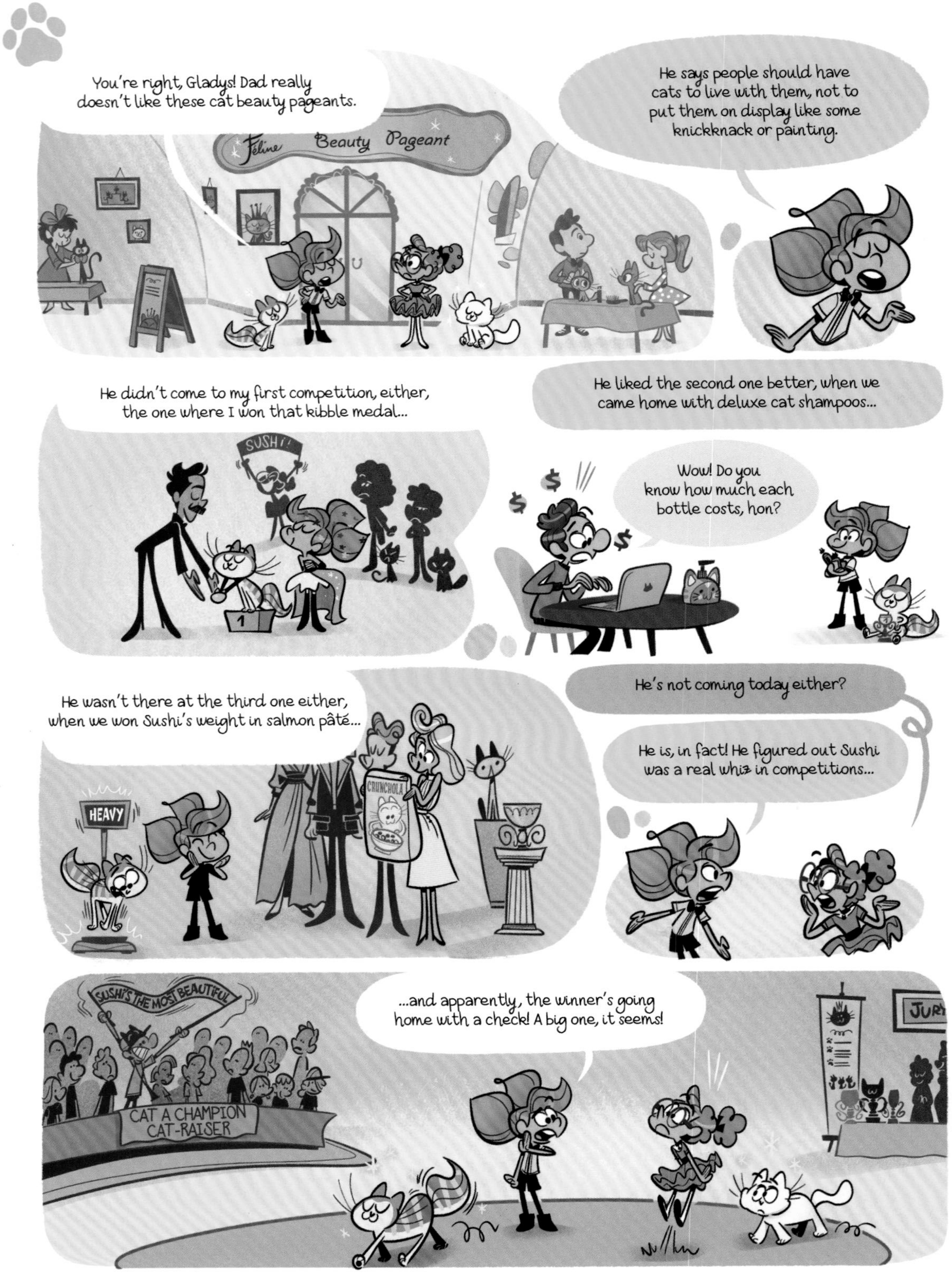
You're right, Gladys! Dad really doesn't like these cat beauty pageants.
Féline Beauty Pageant
He says people should have cats to live with them, not to put them on display like some knickknack or painting.
He didn't come to my first competition, either, the one where I won that kibble medal...
SUSHI!
1
He liked the second one better, when we came home with deluxe cat shampoos...
Wow! Do you know how much each bottle costs, hon?
He wasn't there at the third one either, when we won Sushi's weight in salmon pâté...
HEAVY
CRUNCHOLA
He's not coming today either?
He is, in fact! He figured out Sushi was a real whiz in competitions...
SUSHI'S THE MOST BEAUTIFUL
CAT A CHAMPION CAT-RAISER
...and apparently, the winner's going home with a check! A big one, it seems!
JURY

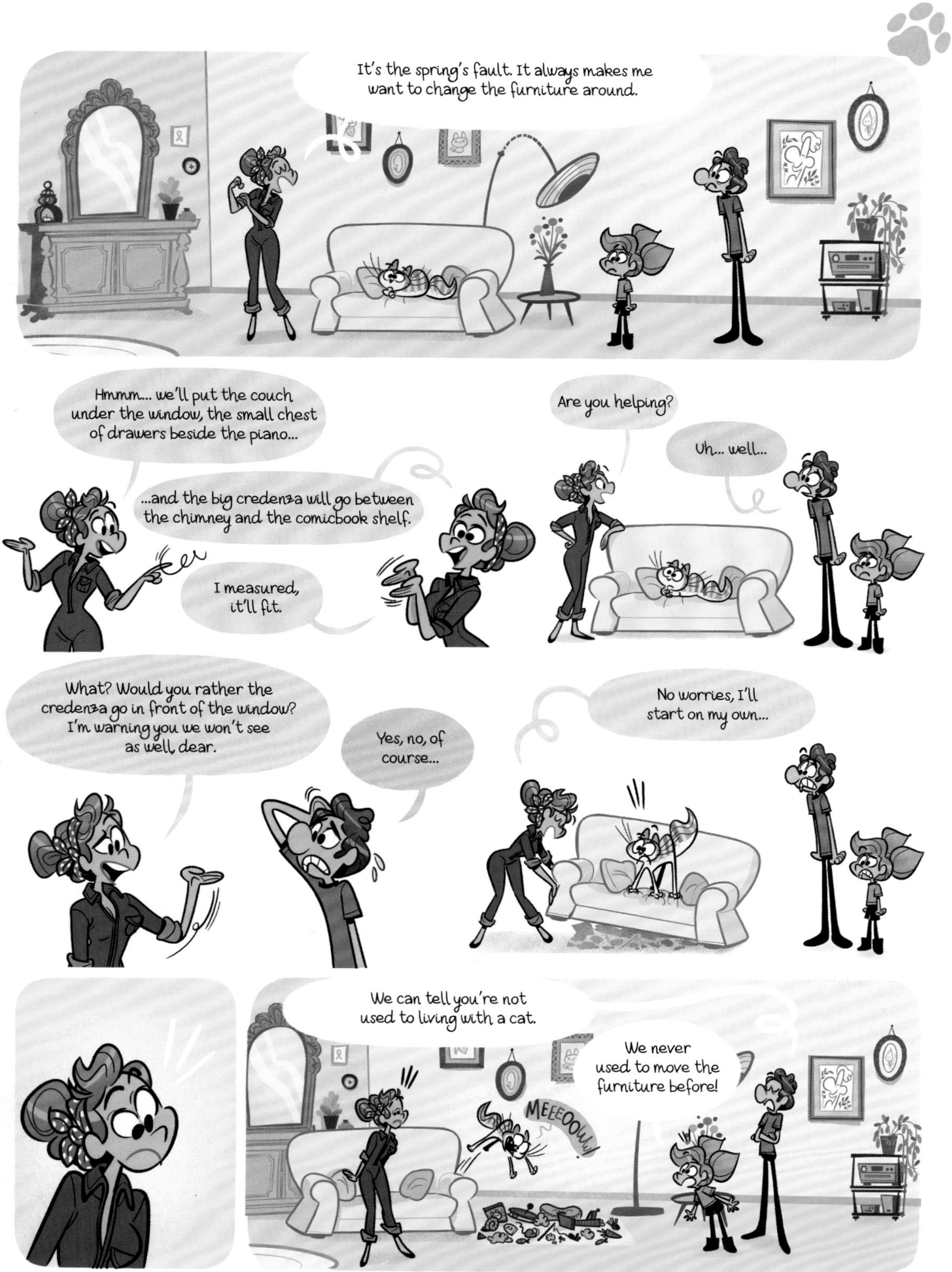

It's the spring's fault. It always makes me want to change the furniture around.
Hmmm... we'll put the couch under the window, the small chest of drawers beside the piano...
...and the big credenza will go between the chimney and the comicbook shelf.
I measured, it'll fit.
Are you helping?
Uh... well...
What? Would you rather the credenza go in front of the window? I'm warning you we won't see as well, dear.
Yes, no, of course...
No worries, I'll start on my own...
We can tell you're not used to living with a cat.
MEEEOOW!
We never used to move the furniture before!

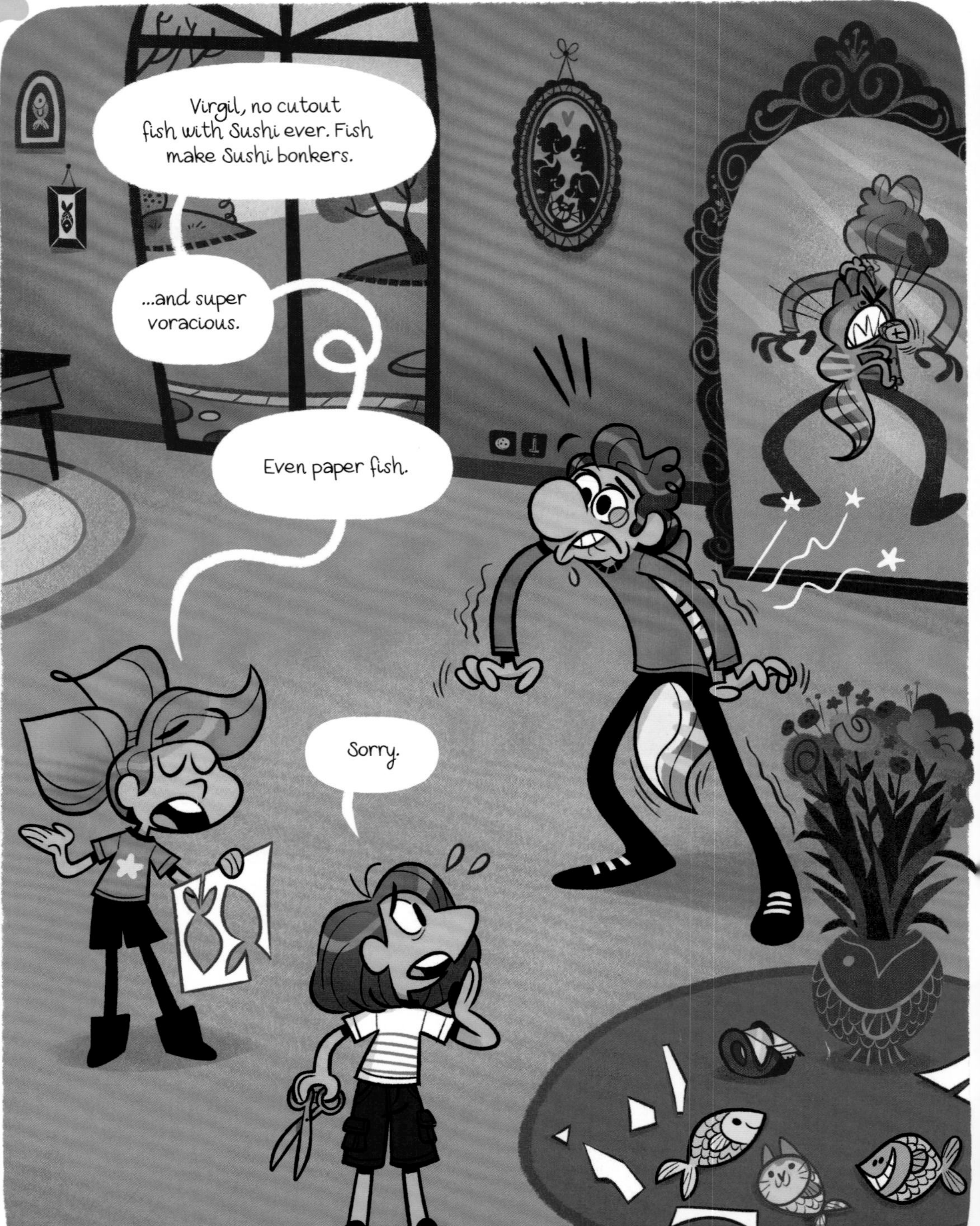
Virgil, no cutout fish with Sushi ever. Fish make Sushi bonkers.
...and super voracious.
Even paper fish.
Sorry.

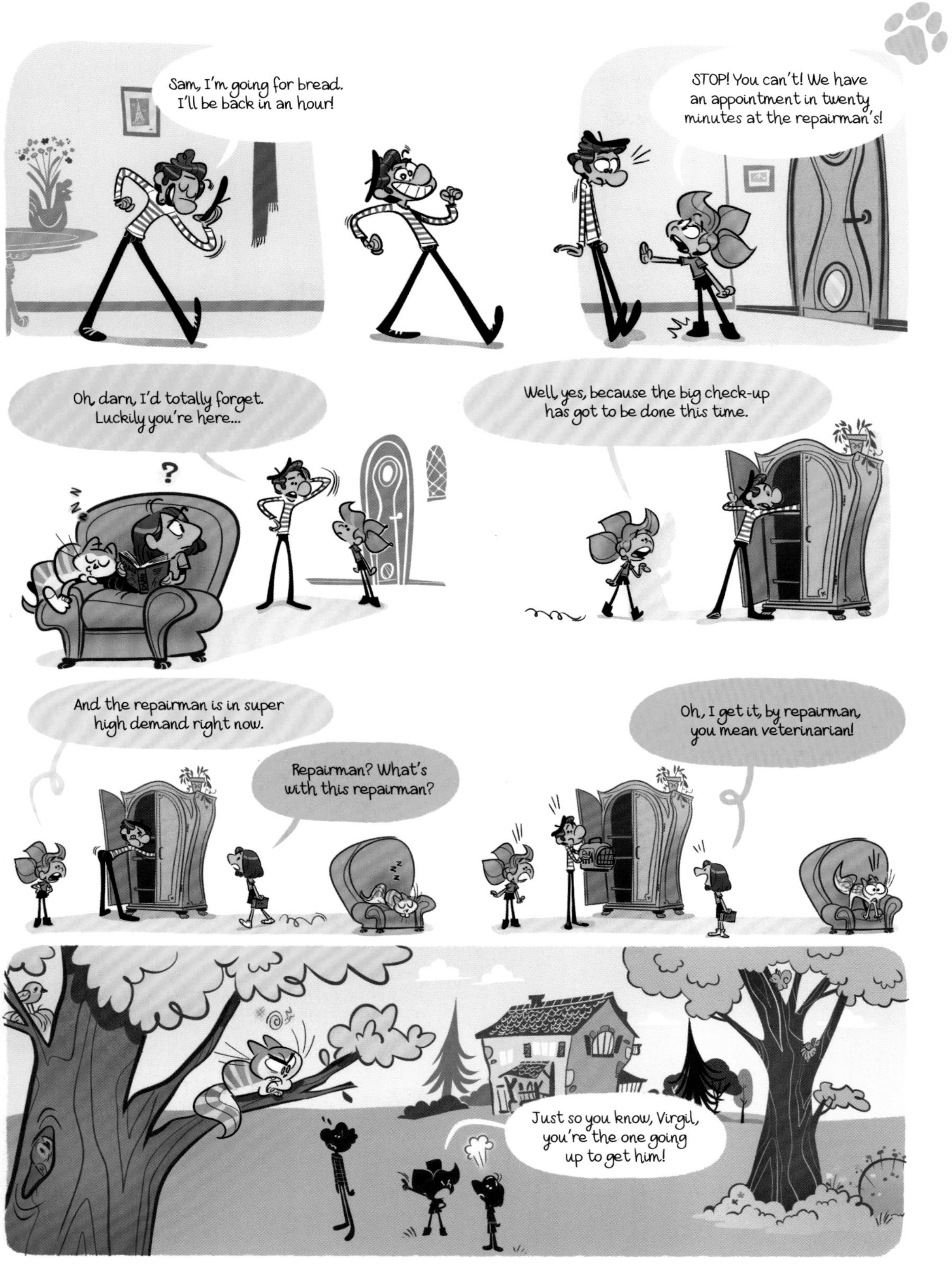
Sam, I'm going for bread. I'll be back in an hour!
STOP! You can't! We have an appointment in twenty minutes at the repairman's!
Oh, darn, I'd totally forget. Luckily you're here...
?
Well, yes, because the big check-up has got to be done this time.
And the repairman is in super high demand right now.
Repairman? What's with this repairman?
Oh, I get it, by repairman, you mean veterinarian!
Just so you know, Virgil, you're the one going up to get him!

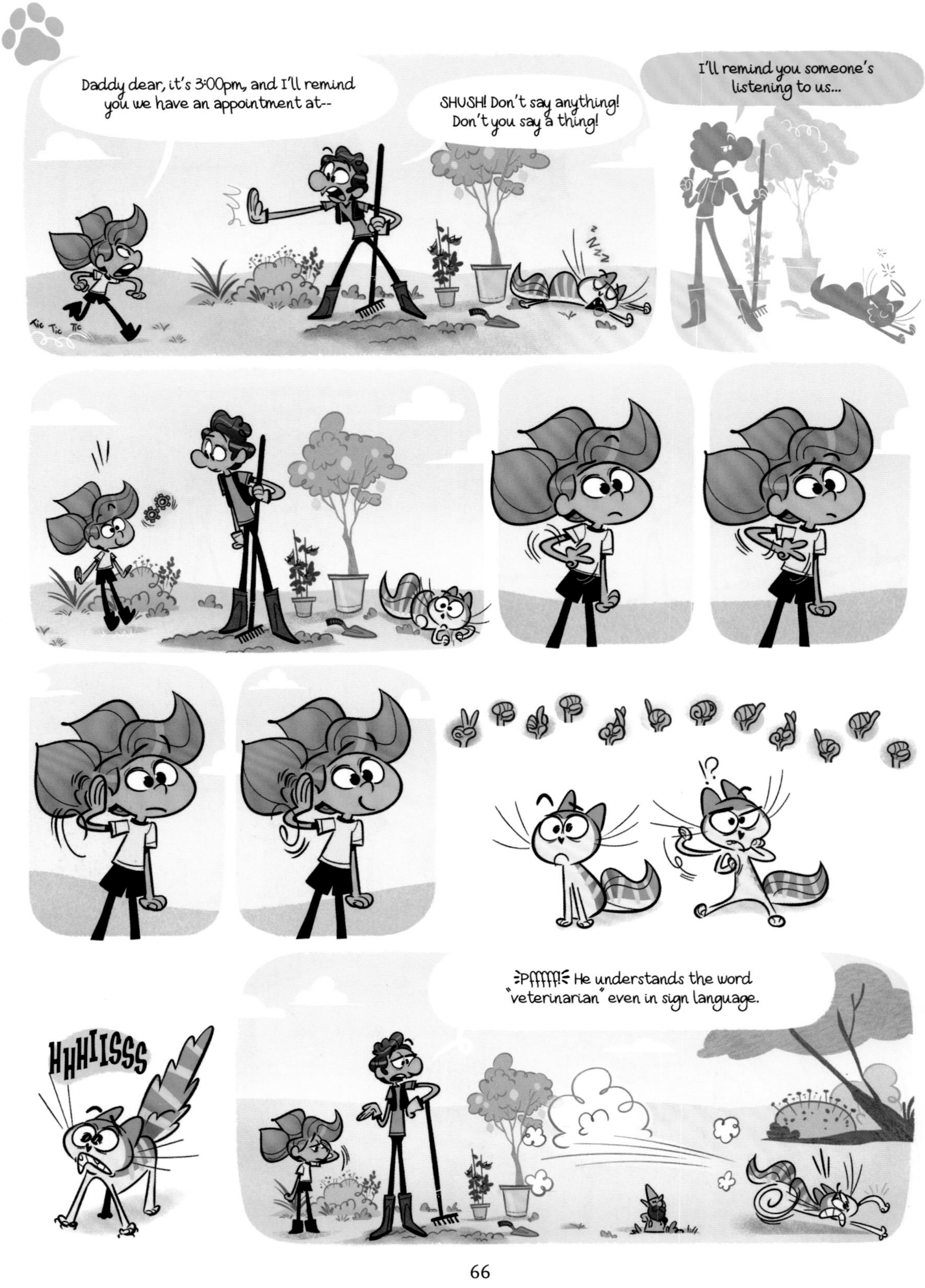
Daddy dear, it's 3:00pm, and I'll remind you we have an appointment at--
Tic Tic Tic
SHUSH! Don't say anything! Don't you say a thing!
ZZZ
I'll remind you someone's listening to us...
!?
HHHIISSS
ƎPfffff!Ǝ He understands the word "veterinarian" even in sign language.

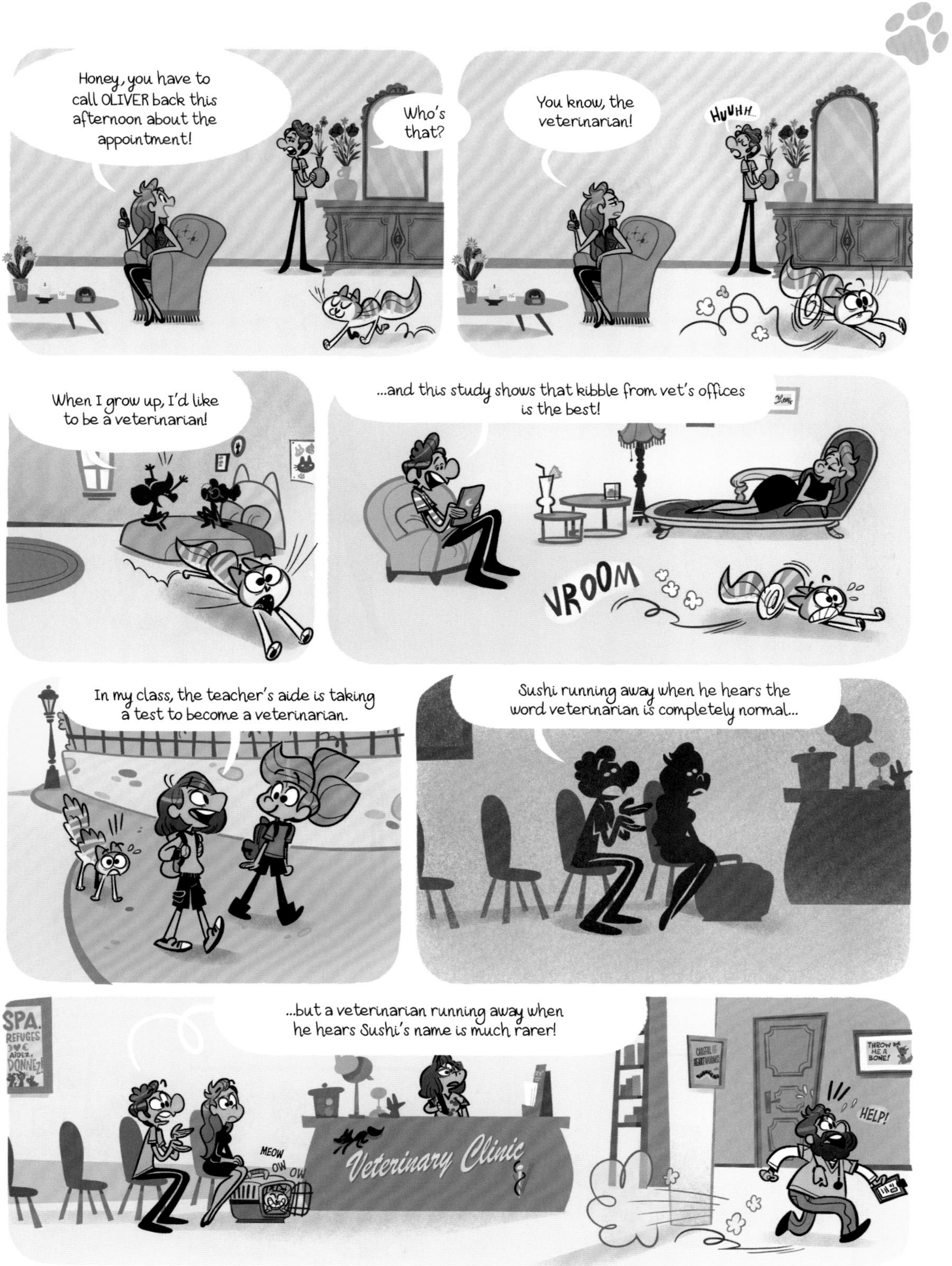
Honey, you have to call OLIVER back this afternoon about the appointment!
Who's that?
You know, the veterinarian!
HUUHH...
When I grow up, I'd like to be a veterinarian!
...and this study shows that kibble from vet's offices is the best!
VROOM
In my class, the teacher's aide is taking a test to become a veterinarian.
Sushi running away when he hears the word veterinarian is completely normal...
...but a veterinarian running away when he hears Sushi's name is much rarer!
SPA.
REFUGES
AIDEZ,
DONNEZ!
MEOW
OW
OW
Veterinary Clinic
THROW ME A BONE!
HELP!

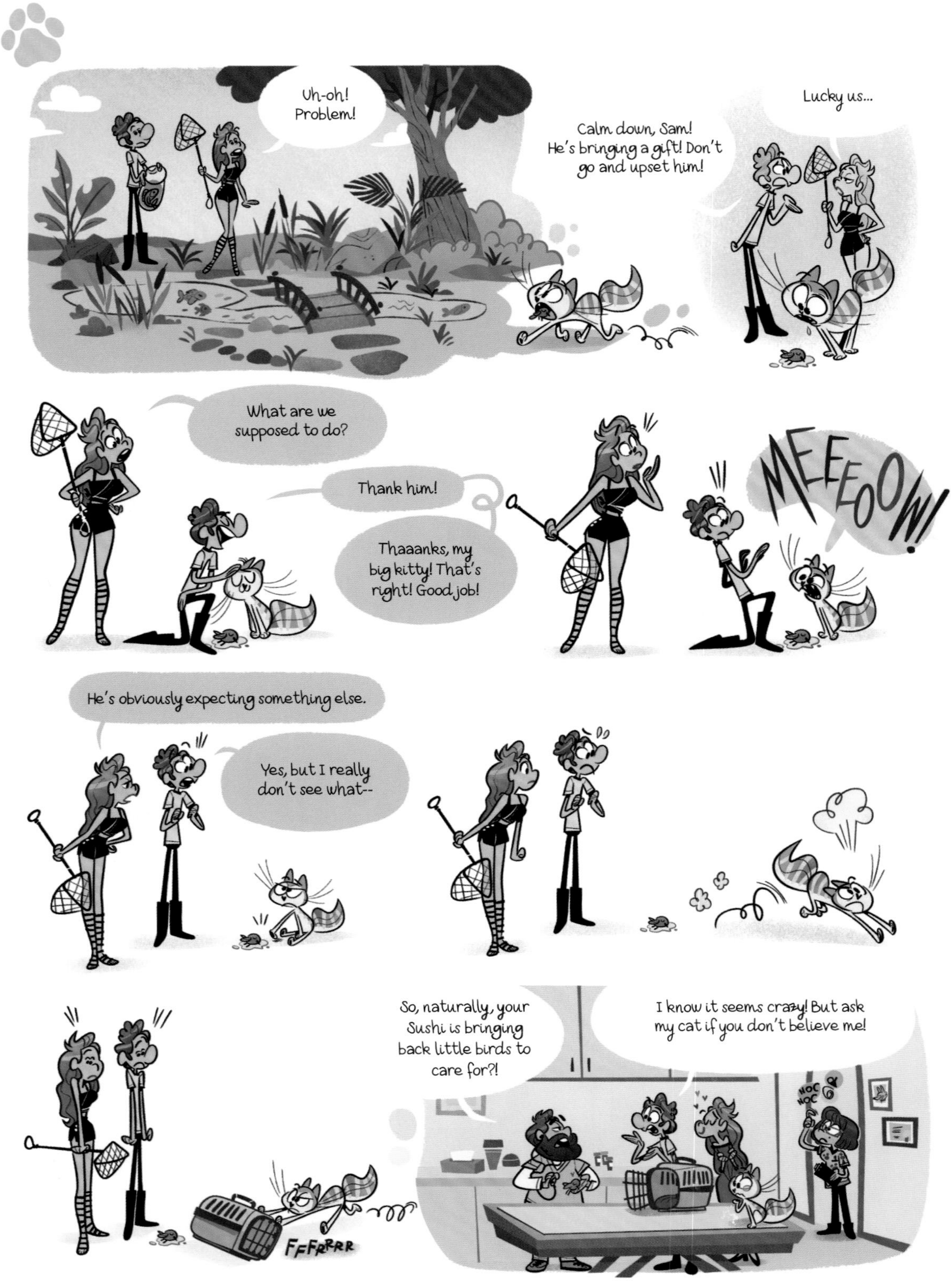
Uh-oh!
Problem!
Calm down, Sam! He's bringing a gift! Don't go and upset him!
Lucky us...
What are we supposed to do?
Thank him!
Thaaanks, my big kitty! That's right! Good job!
MEEEOOW!
He's obviously expecting something else.
Yes, but I really don't see what--
FFFRRRR
So, naturally, your Sushi is bringing back little birds to care for?!
I know it seems crazy! But ask my cat if you don't believe me!
NOC NOC

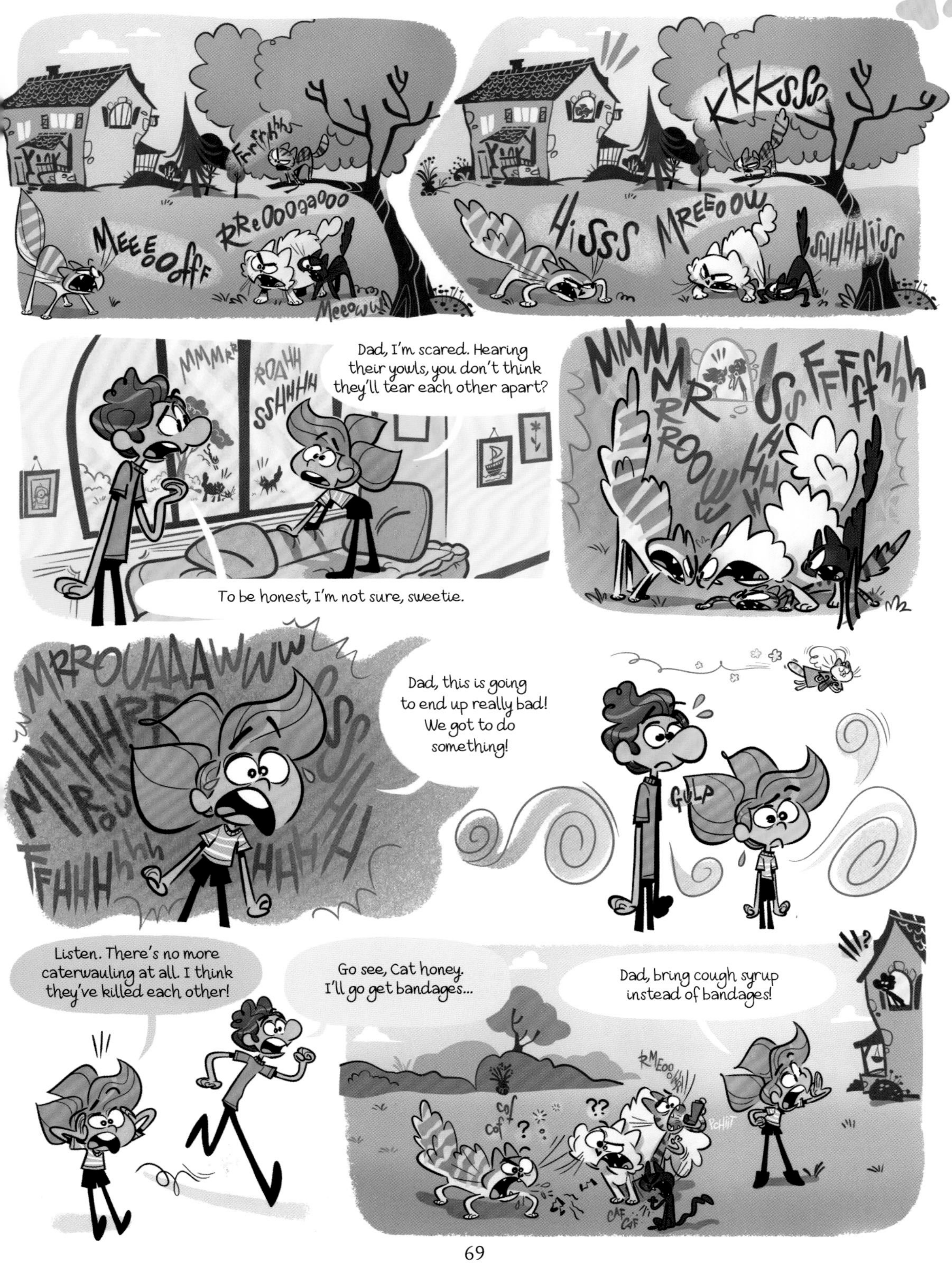

Dad, I'm scared. Hearing their youls, you don't think they'll tear each other apart?
To be honest, I'm not sure, sweetie.
Dad, this is going to end up really bad! We got to do something!
GULP
Listen. There's no more caterwauling at all. I think they've killed each other!
Go see, Cat honey. I'll go get bandages...
Dad, bring cough syrup instead of bandages!

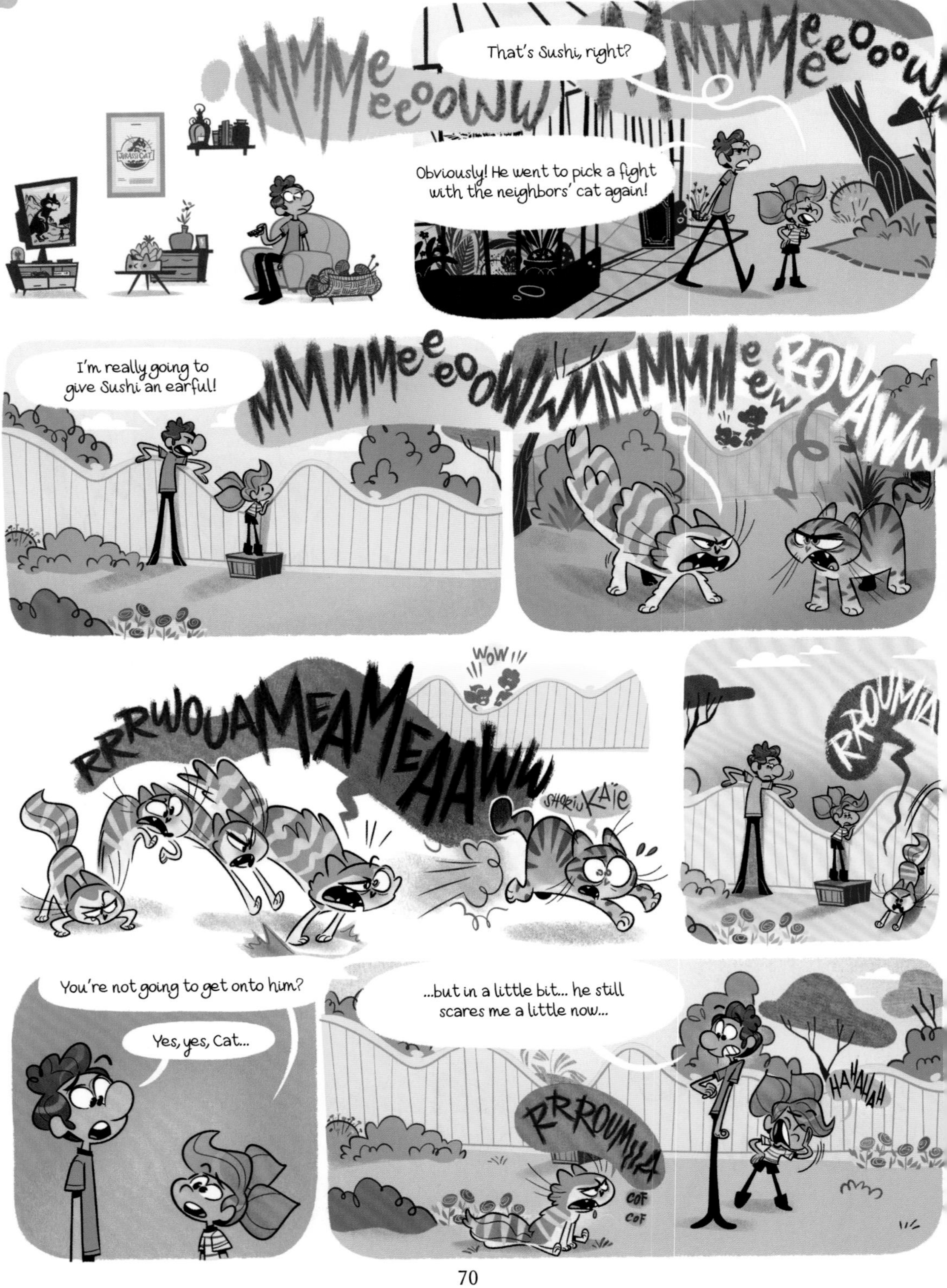
That's Sushi, right?
Obviously! He went to pick a fight with the neighbors' cat again!
I'm really going to give Sushi an earful!
WOW
You're not going to get onto him?
Yes, yes, Cat...
...but in a little bit... he still scares me a little now...
COF COF
HAHAHAH

I've always dreamed of being a catupuncturist! And today's the day!

Catupuncture consists of introducing thin needles like these into well-chosen places in the body in order to restore health.

It can sting a little.

In Chinese medicine, a balanced person is a person in good health.

And these needles allow you to reestablish a person's energy balance.

In fact, the human body contains 12 meridians upon which there are 361 acupuncture points.

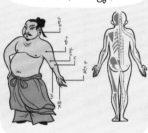
The meridians are passageways in the body through which life energy flows.

The acupuncture points are the places on the skin's surface where you poke the needles.

JBONVINGG

PÒUING

Stimulation of those points can cure or relax.

So, hon, is that relaxing?

GNIIIHH

71

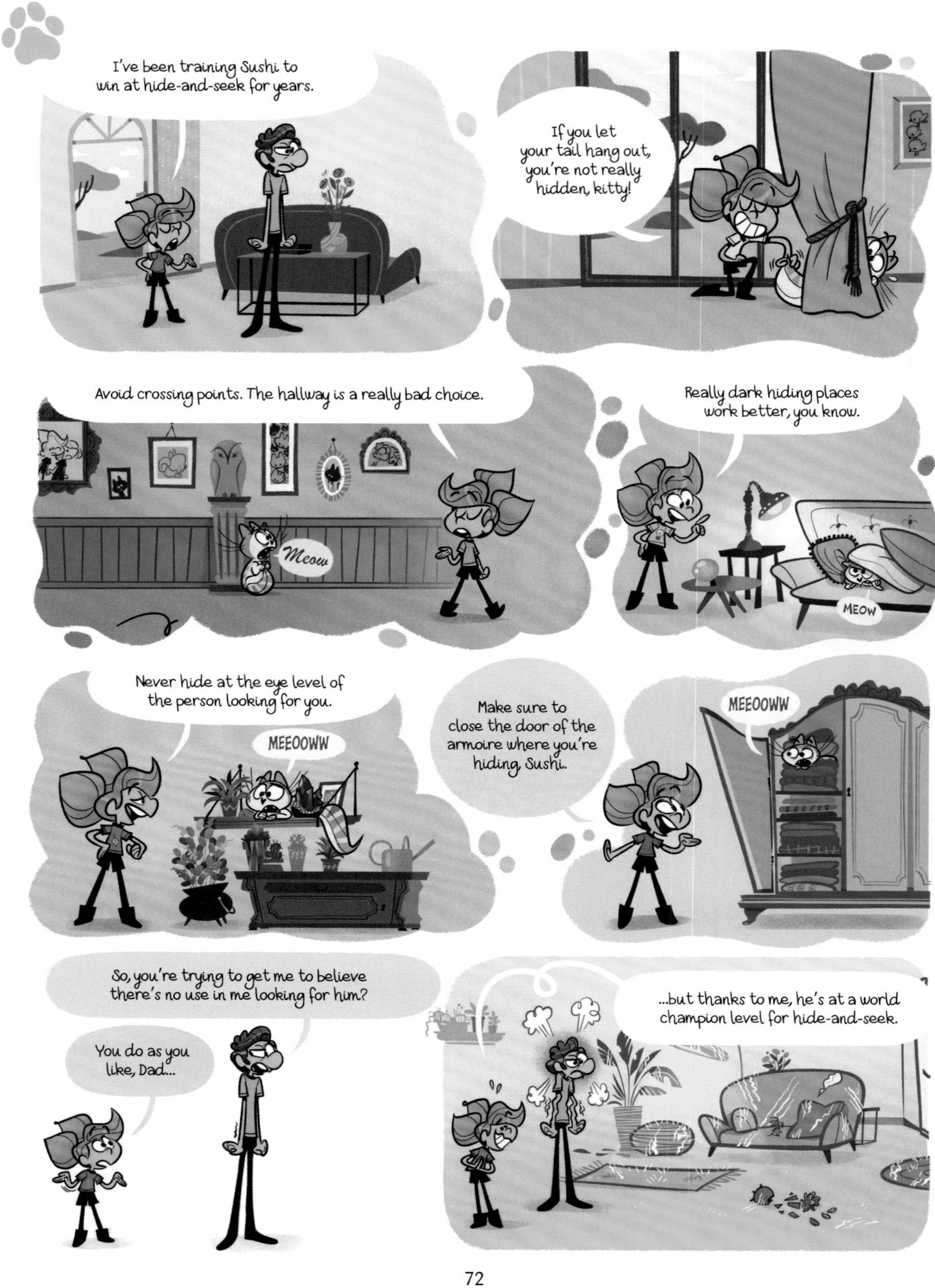

I've been training Sushi to win at hide-and-seek for years.
If you let your tail hang out, you're not really hidden, kitty!
Avoid crossing points. The hallway is a really bad choice.
Meow
Really dark hiding places work better, you know.
MEOW
Never hide at the eye level of the person looking for you.
MEEOOWW
Make sure to close the door of the armoire where you're hiding, Sushi.
MEEOOWW
So, you're trying to get me to believe there's no use in me looking for him?
You do as you like, Dad...
...but thanks to me, he's at a world champion level for hide-and-seek.

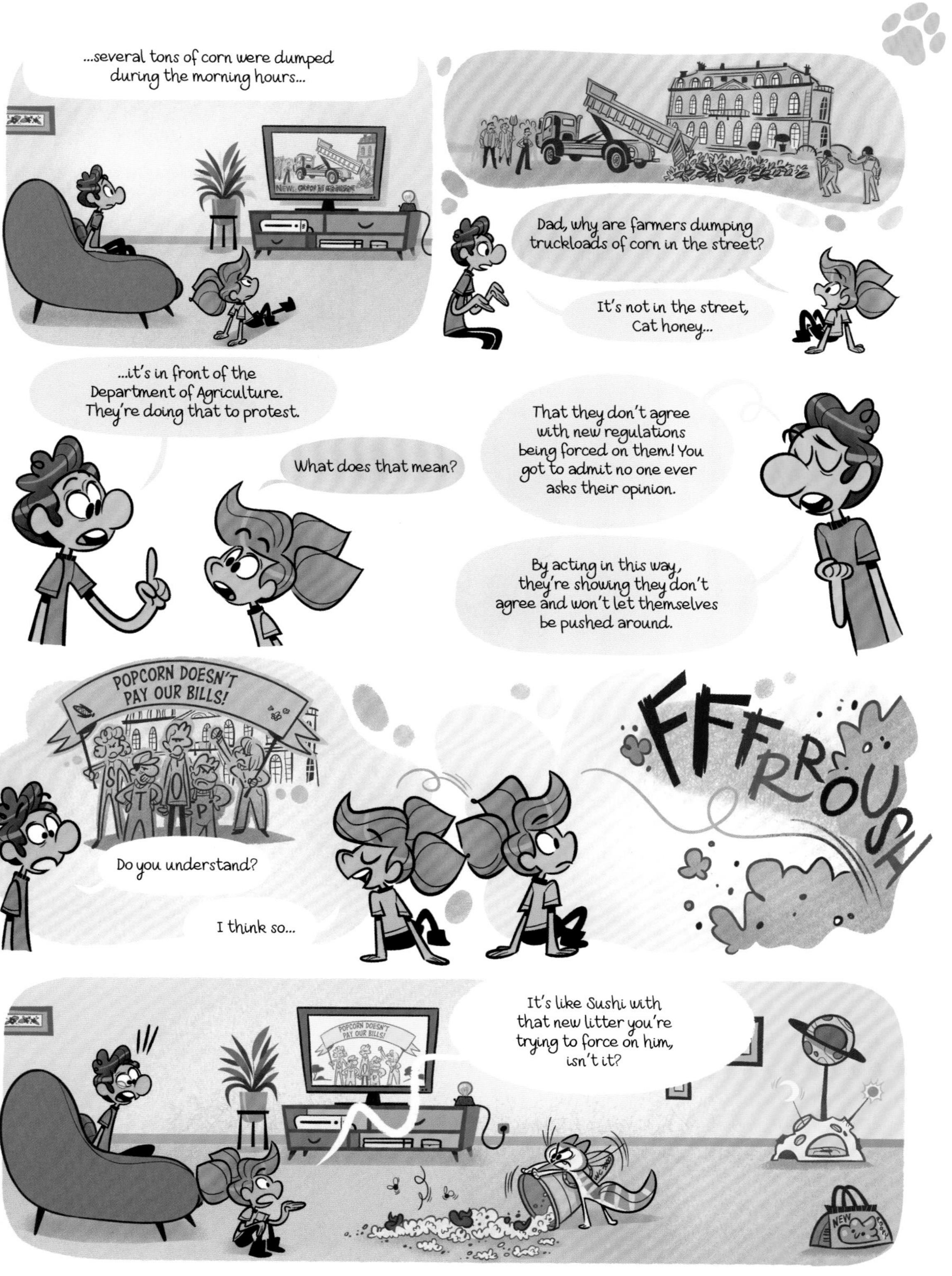
...several tons of corn were dumped during the morning hours...
Dad, why are farmers dumping truckloads of corn in the street?
It's not in the street, Cat honey...
...it's in front of the Department of Agriculture. They're doing that to protest.
What does that mean?
That they don't agree with new regulations being forced on them! You got to admit no one ever asks their opinion.
By acting in this way, they're showing they don't agree and won't let themselves be pushed around.
POPCORN DOESN'T PAY OUR BILLS!
S T O P
Do you understand?
I think so...
FFFRROUSH
POPCORN DOESN'T PAY OUR BILLS!
It's like Sushi with that new litter you're trying to force on him, isn't it?
NEW

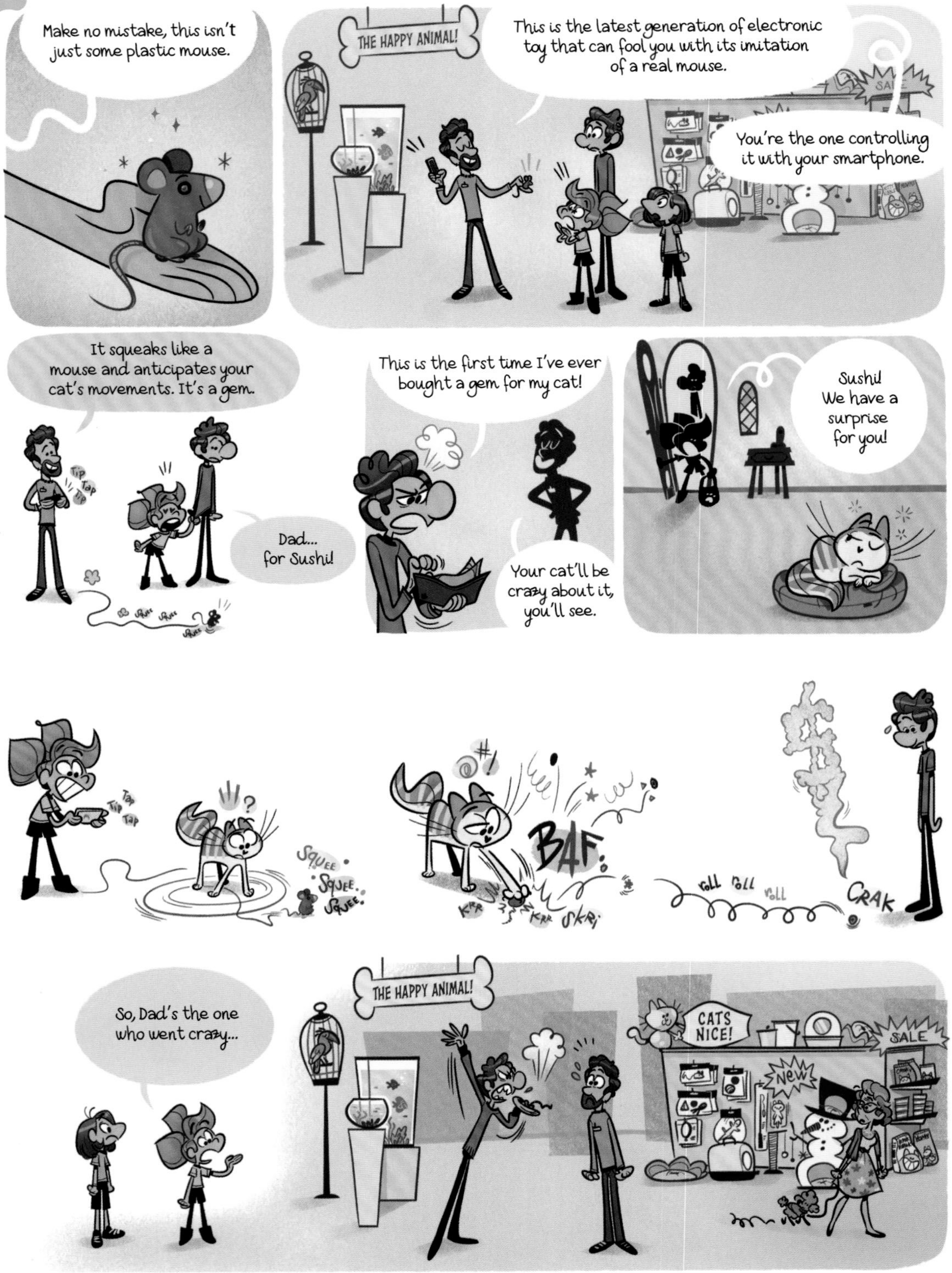

Make no mistake, this isn't just some plastic mouse.
THE HAPPY ANIMAL!
This is the latest generation of electronic toy that can fool you with its imitation of a real mouse.
You're the one controlling it with your smartphone.
It squeaks like a mouse and anticipates your cat's movements. It's a gem.
TIP TAP TIP
Dad... for Sushi!
This is the first time I've ever bought a gem for my cat!
Your cat'll be crazy about it, you'll see.
Sushi! We have a surprise for you!
TIP TAP TAP
SQUEE SQUEE SQUEE
BAF
SKRI
ROLL ROLL ROLL
CRAK
So, Dad's the one who went crazy...
THE HAPPY ANIMAL!
CATS NICE!
NEW
SALE

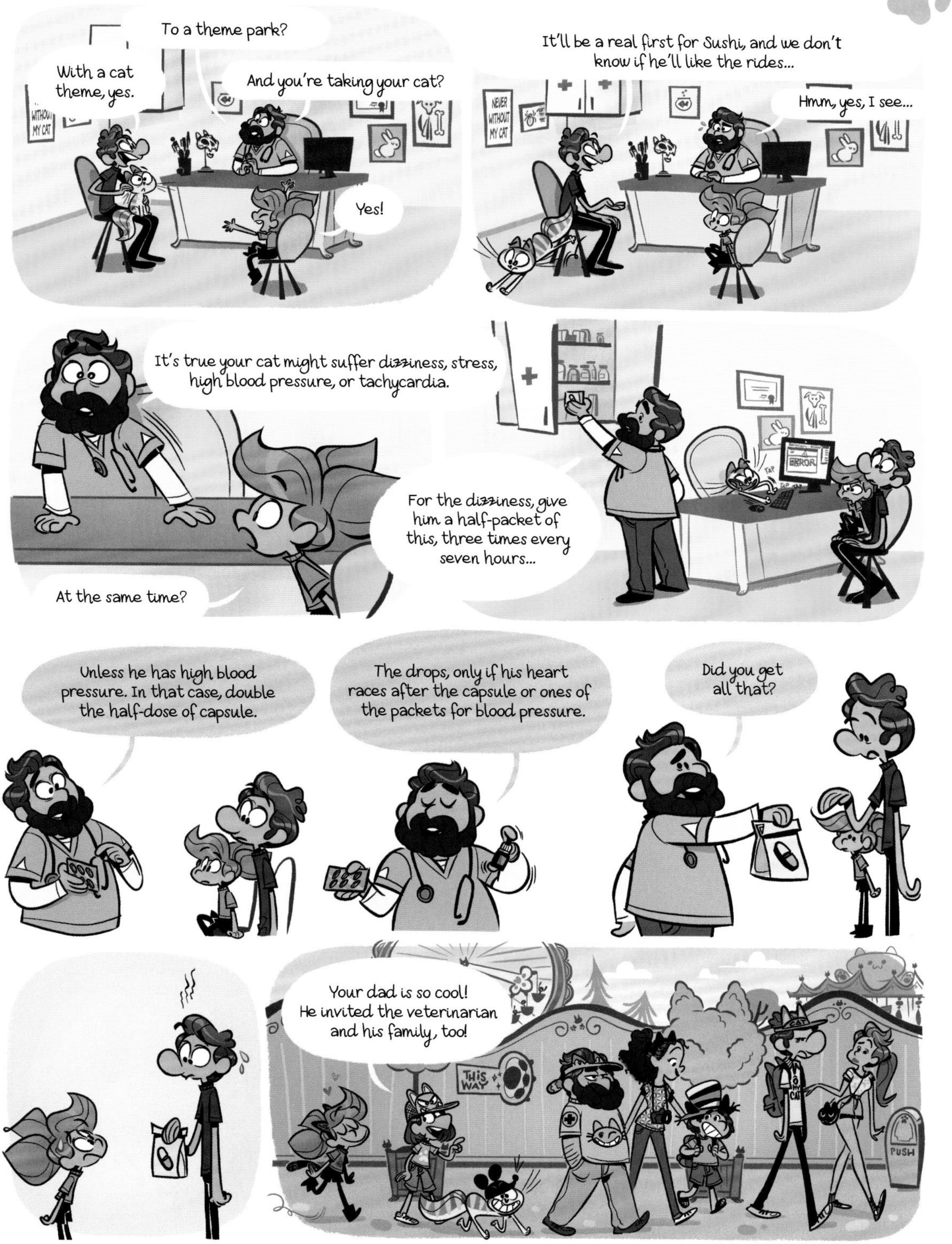
To a theme park?
With a cat theme, yes.
And you're taking your cat?
Yes!
NEVER WITHOUT MY CAT
It'll be a real first for Sushi, and we don't know if he'll like the rides...
Hmm, yes, I see...
It's true your cat might suffer dizziness, stress, high blood pressure, or tachycardia.
At the same time?
For the dizziness, give him a half-packet of this, three times every seven hours...
ERROR
TAP TAP TAP
Unless he has high blood pressure. In that case, double the half-dose of capsule.
The drops, only if his heart races after the capsule or ones of the packets for blood pressure.
Did you get all that?
Your dad is so cool! He invited the veterinarian and his family, too!
THIS WAY
CAT
PUSH

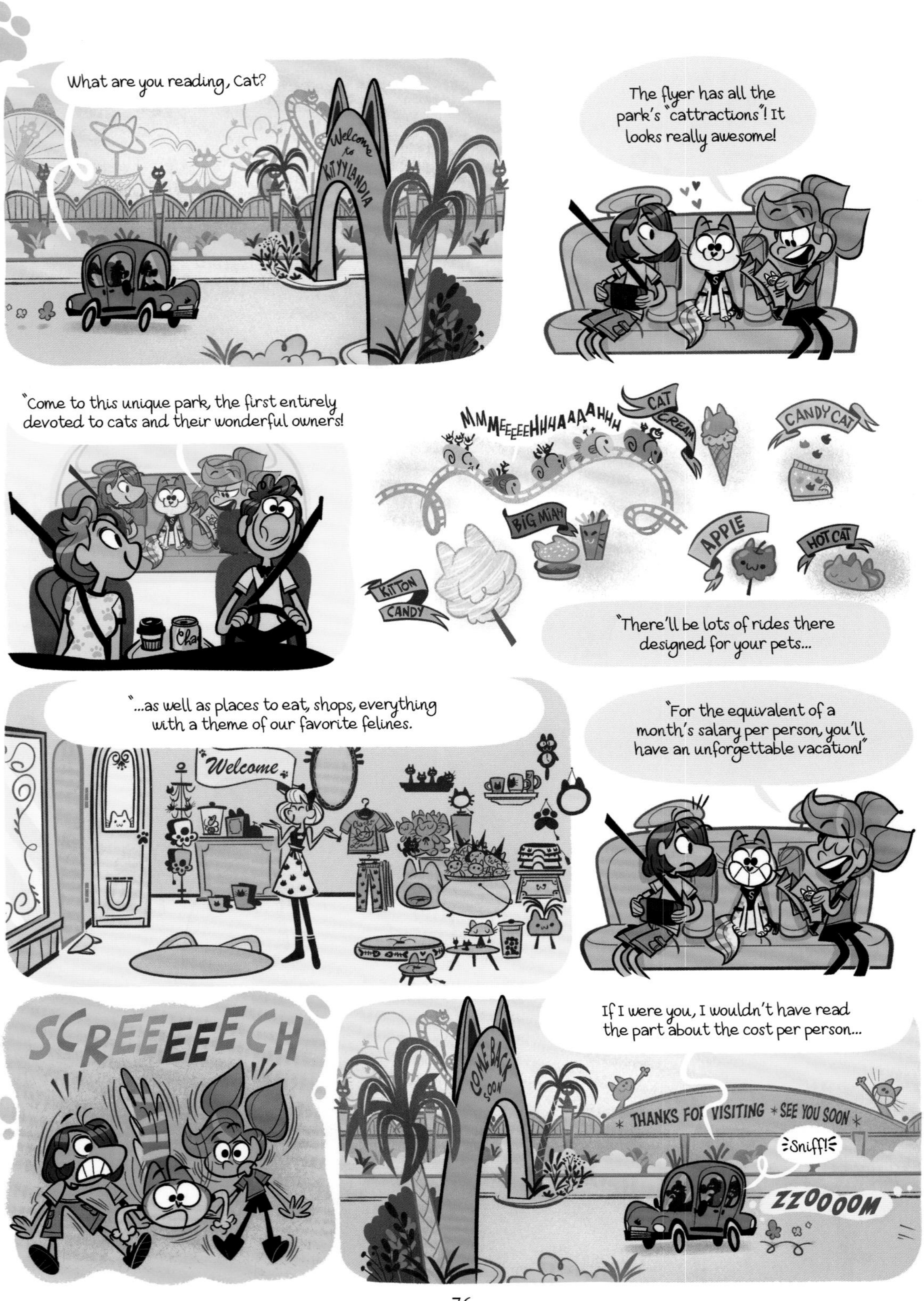
What are you reading, Cat?
Welcome to KITYYLANDIA
The flyer has all the park's "cattractions"! It looks really awesome!
"Come to this unique park, the first entirely devoted to cats and their wonderful owners!
MMMEEEEEHHHAAAAHHH
CAT CREAM
CANDY CAT
BIG MIAU
APPLE
HOT CAT
KITTON CANDY
"There'll be lots of rides there designed for your pets...
"...as well as places to eat, shops, everything with a theme of our favorite felines.
Welcome
"For the equivalent of a month's salary per person, you'll have an unforgettable vacation!"
SCREEEEEECH
COME BACK SOON
If I were you, I wouldn't have read the part about the cost per person...
THANKS FOR VISITING * SEE YOU SOON
Sniff!
ZZOOOOM

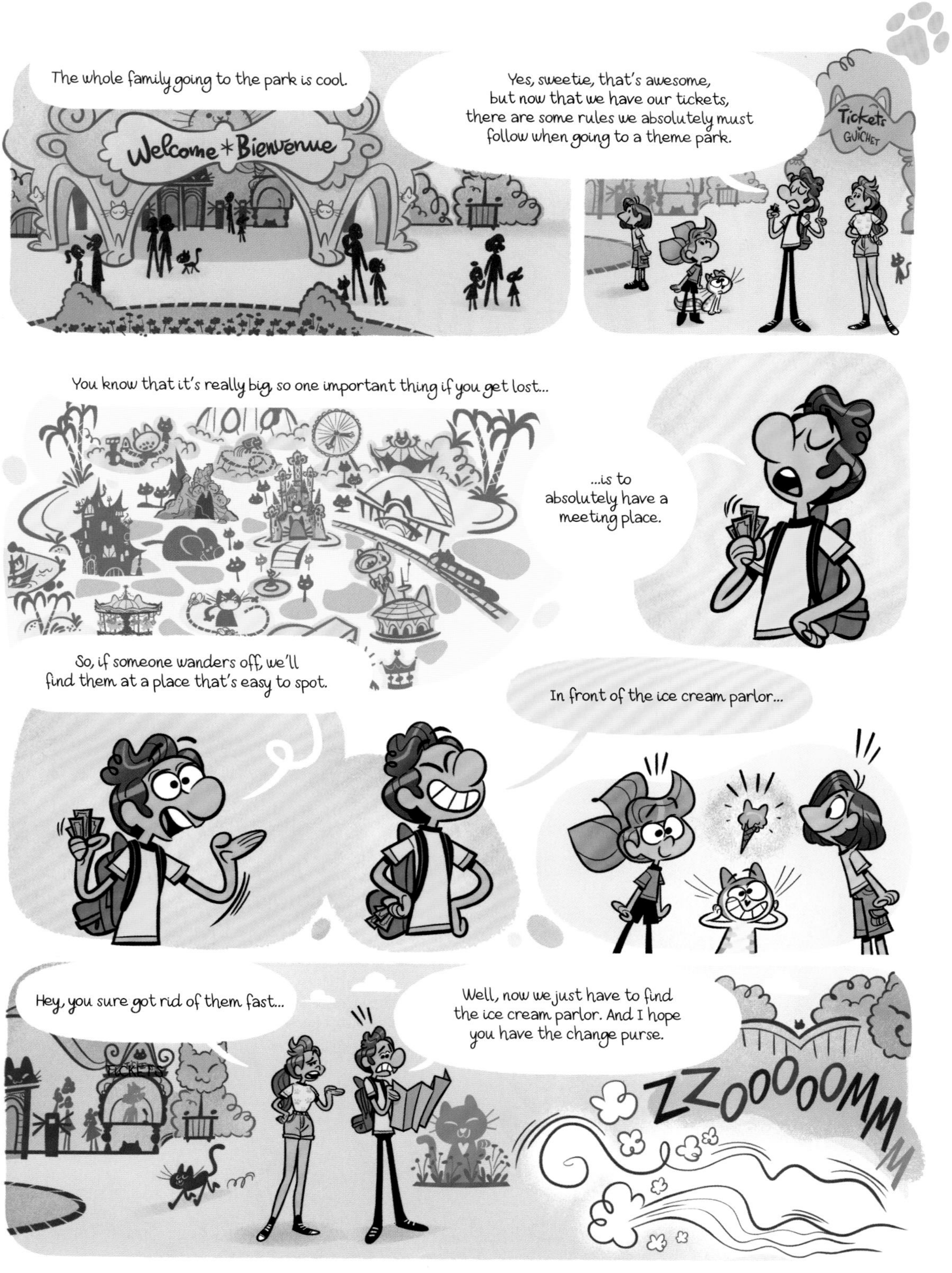

The whole family going to the park is cool.
Welcome * Bienvenue
Yes, sweetie, that's awesome, but now that we have our tickets, there are some rules we absolutely must follow when going to a theme park.
Tickets GUICHET
You know that it's really big, so one important thing if you get lost...
...is to absolutely have a meeting place.
So, if someone wanders off, we'll find them at a place that's easy to spot.
In front of the ice cream parlor...
Hey, you sure got rid of them fast...
Well, now we just have to find the ice cream parlor. And I hope you have the change purse.
ZZOOOOOMMM

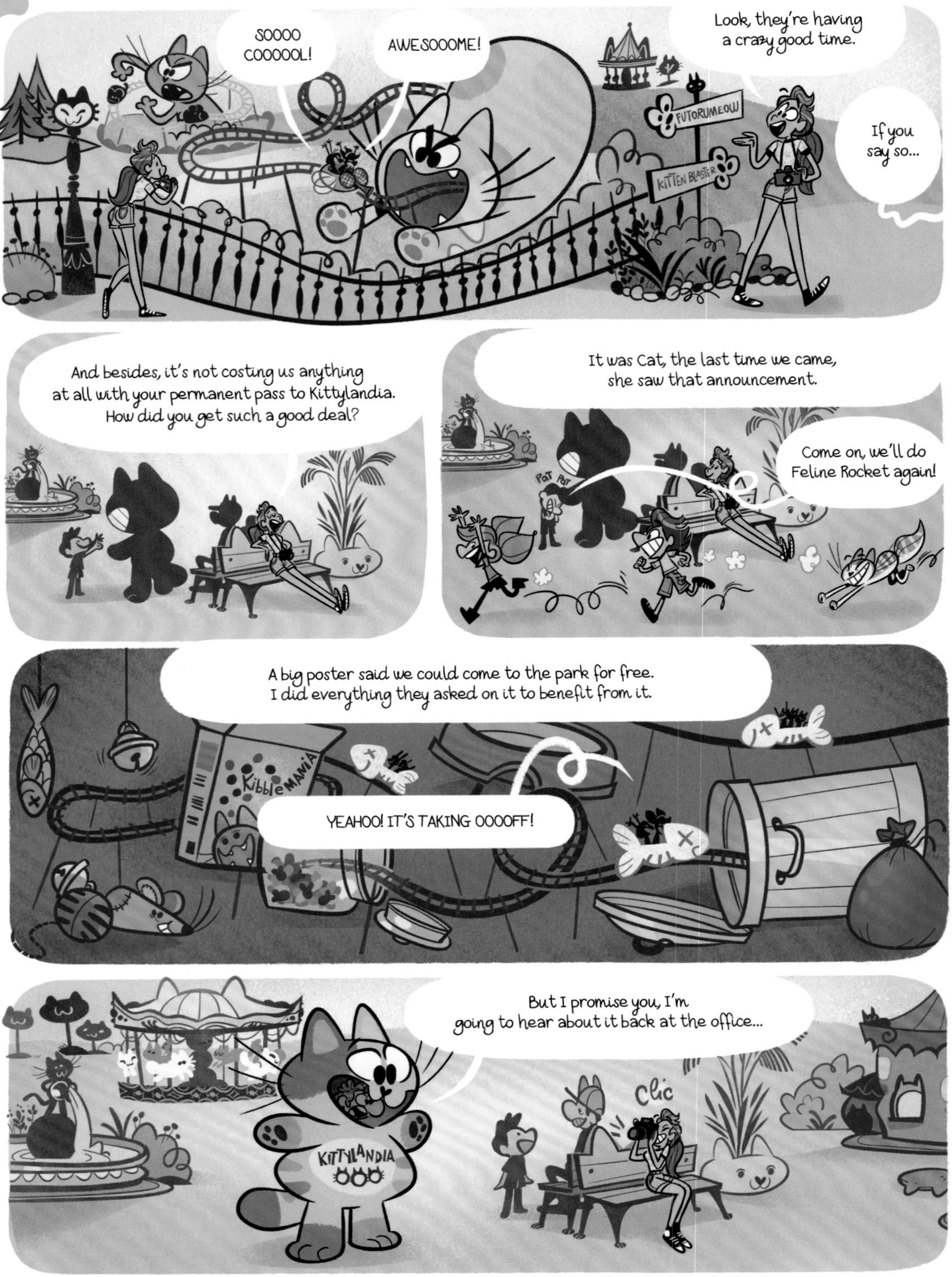
SOOOO COOOOOOL!
AWESOOOME!
Look, they're having a crazy good time.
FUTORUMEOW
KITTEN BLASTER
If you say so...
And besides, it's not costing us anything at all with your permanent pass to Kittylandia. How did you get such a good deal?
It was Cat, the last time we came, she saw that announcement.
PAT PAT
Come on, we'll do Feline Rocket again!
A big poster said we could come to the park for free. I did everything they asked on it to benefit from it.
KibbleMANIA
YEAHOO! IT'S TAKING OOOOFF!
But I promise you, I'm going to hear about it back at the office...
Clic
KITTYLANDIA

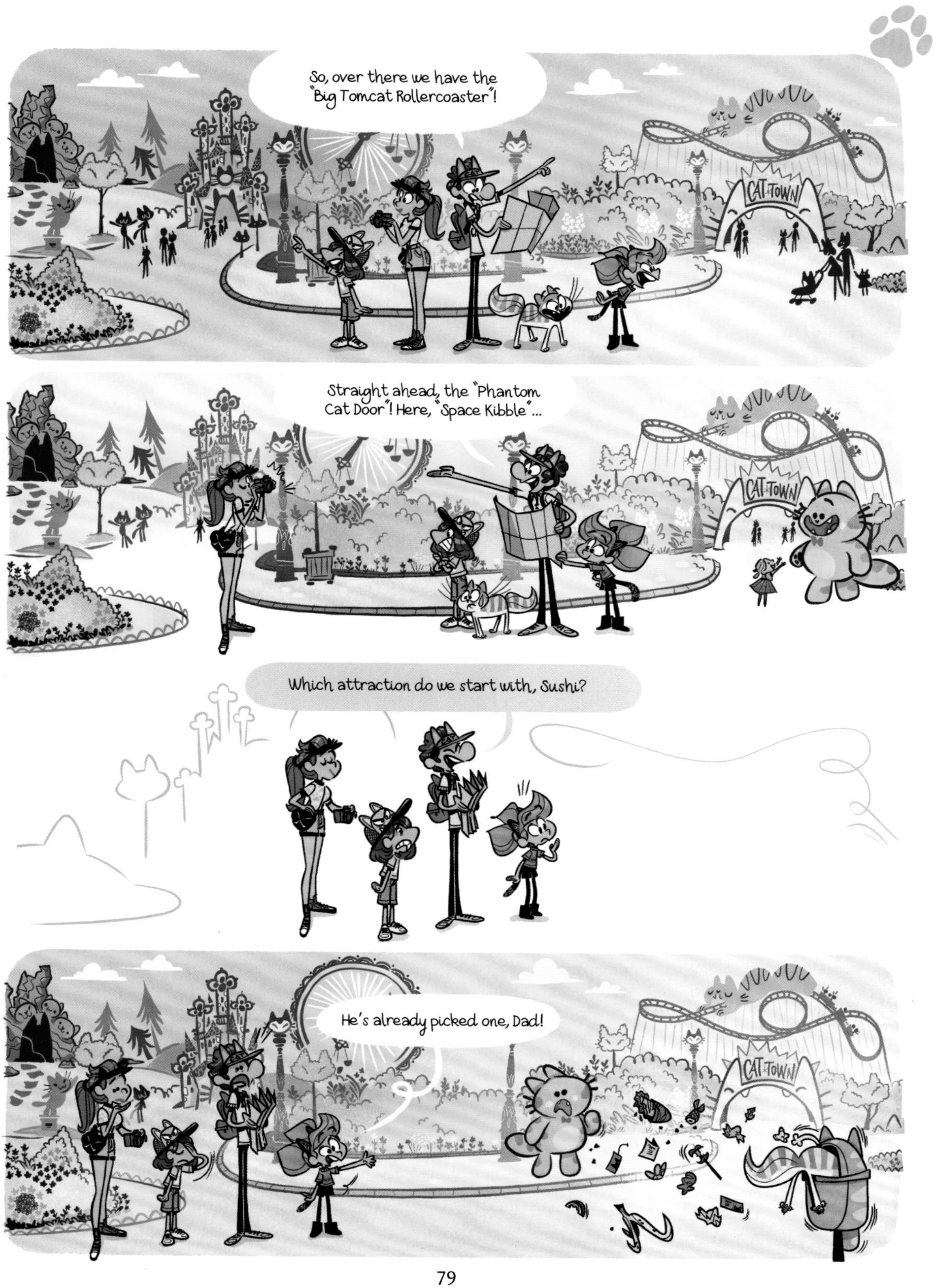
So, over there we have the "Big Tomcat Rollercoaster"!
CAT TOWN
Straight ahead, the "Phantom Cat Door"! Here, "Space Kibble"...
CAT TOWN
Which attraction do we start with, Sushi?
He's already picked one, Dad!
CAT TOWN

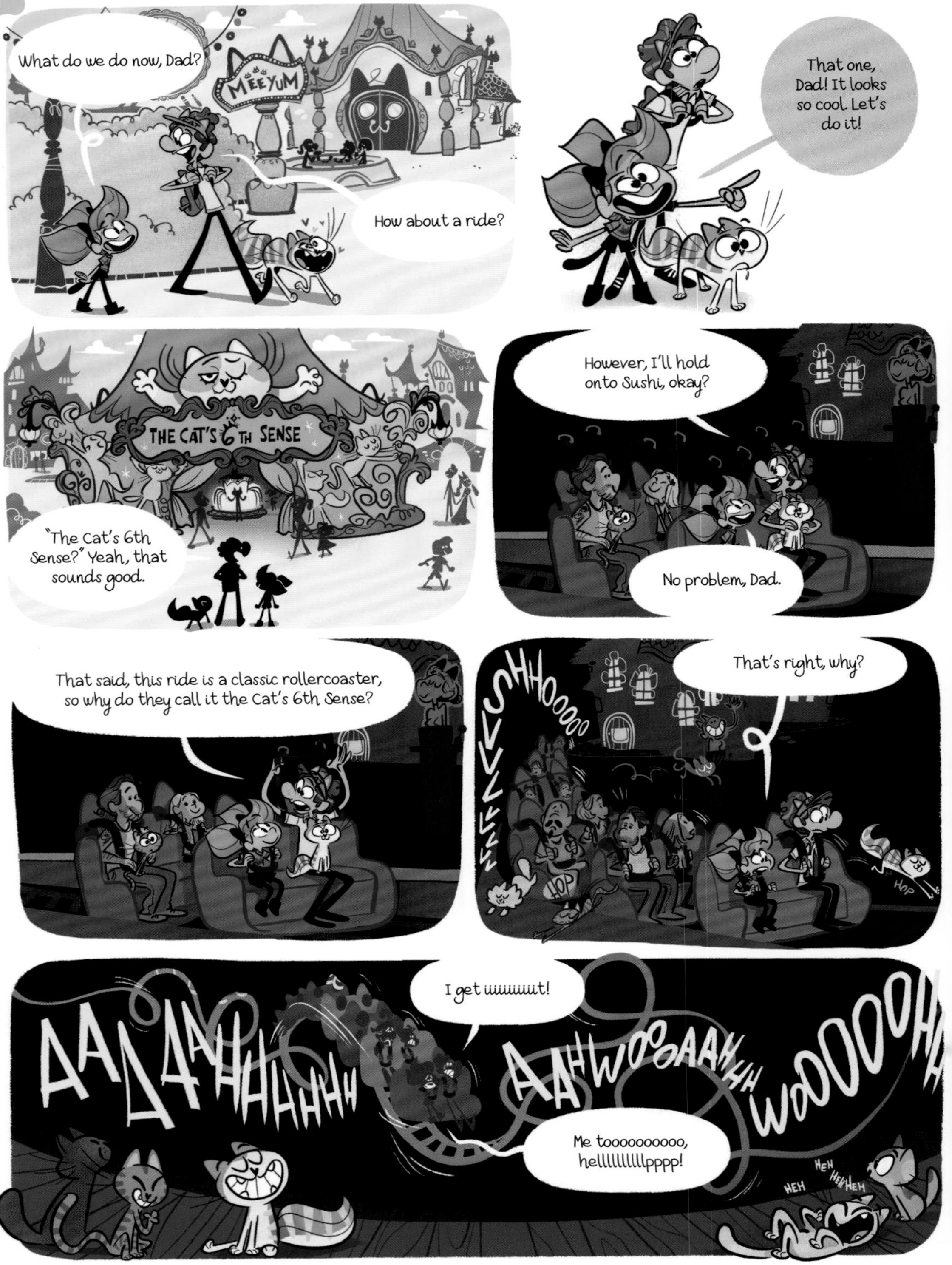

What do we do now, Dad?
MEEYUM
How about a ride?
That one, Dad! It looks so cool. Let's do it!
THE CAT'S 6TH SENSE
"The Cat's 6th Sense?" Yeah, that sounds good.
However, I'll hold onto Sushi, okay?
No problem, Dad.
That said, this ride is a classic rollercoaster, so why do they call it the Cat's 6th Sense?
That's right, why?
SHHOOOOO
HOP
HOP
AAAAHHHHHHH
I get iiiiiiiiiiit!
AAHWOOAAHHH
WOOOOOHH
Me toooooooooo, helllllllllpppp!
HEH HEH HEH HEH

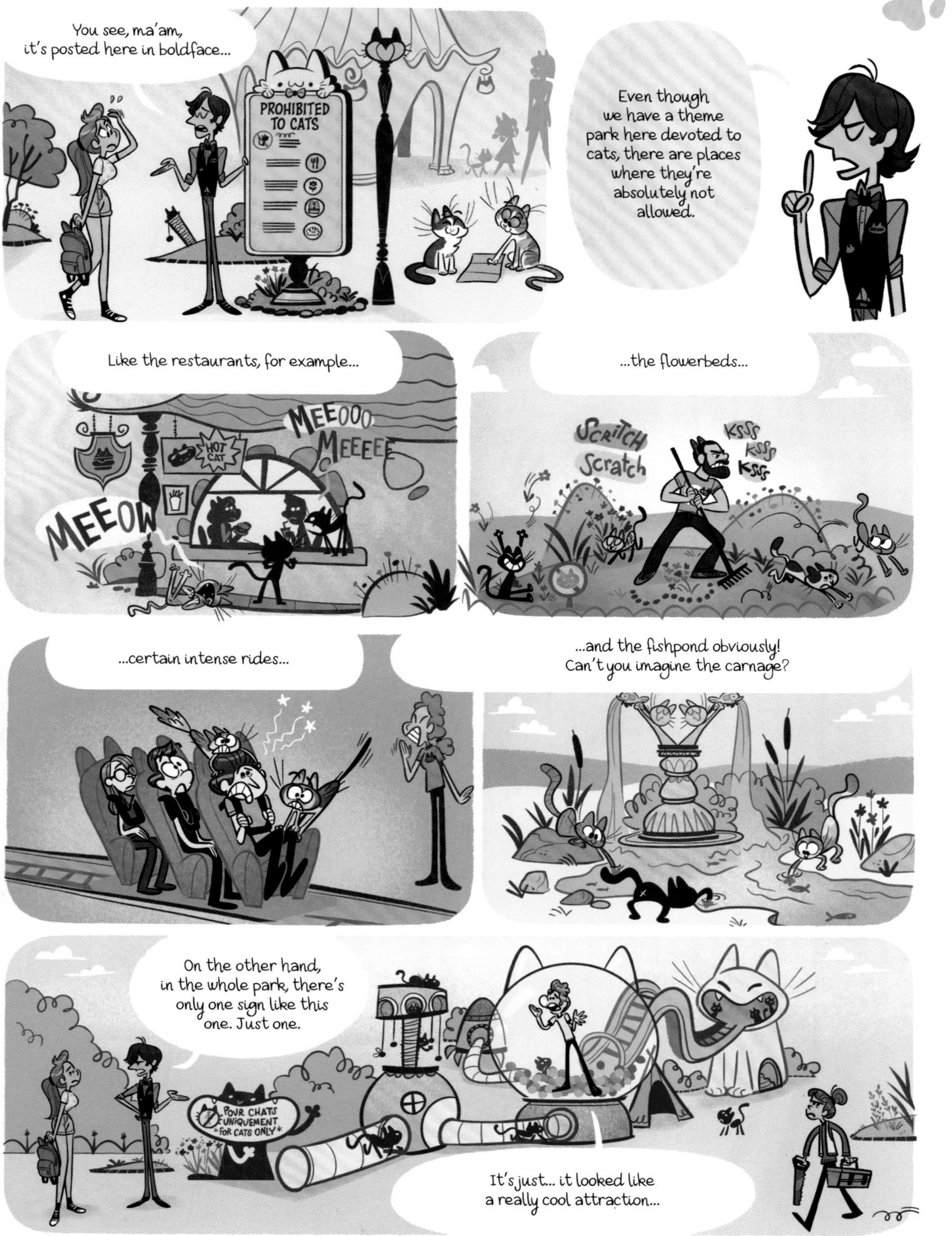
You see, ma'am, it's posted here in boldface...
PROHIBITED TO CATS
Even though we have a theme park here devoted to cats, there are places where they're absolutely not allowed.
Like the restaurants, for example...
MEEOOO
MEEEEE
HOT CAT
MEEOW
...the flowerbeds...
SCRITCH
Scratch
KSSS
KSSS
KSSS
...certain intense rides...
...and the fishpond obviously! Can't you imagine the carnage?
On the other hand, in the whole park, there's only one sign like this one. Just one.
POUR CHATS UNIQUEMENT
* FOR CATS ONLY *
It's just... it looked like a really cool attraction...

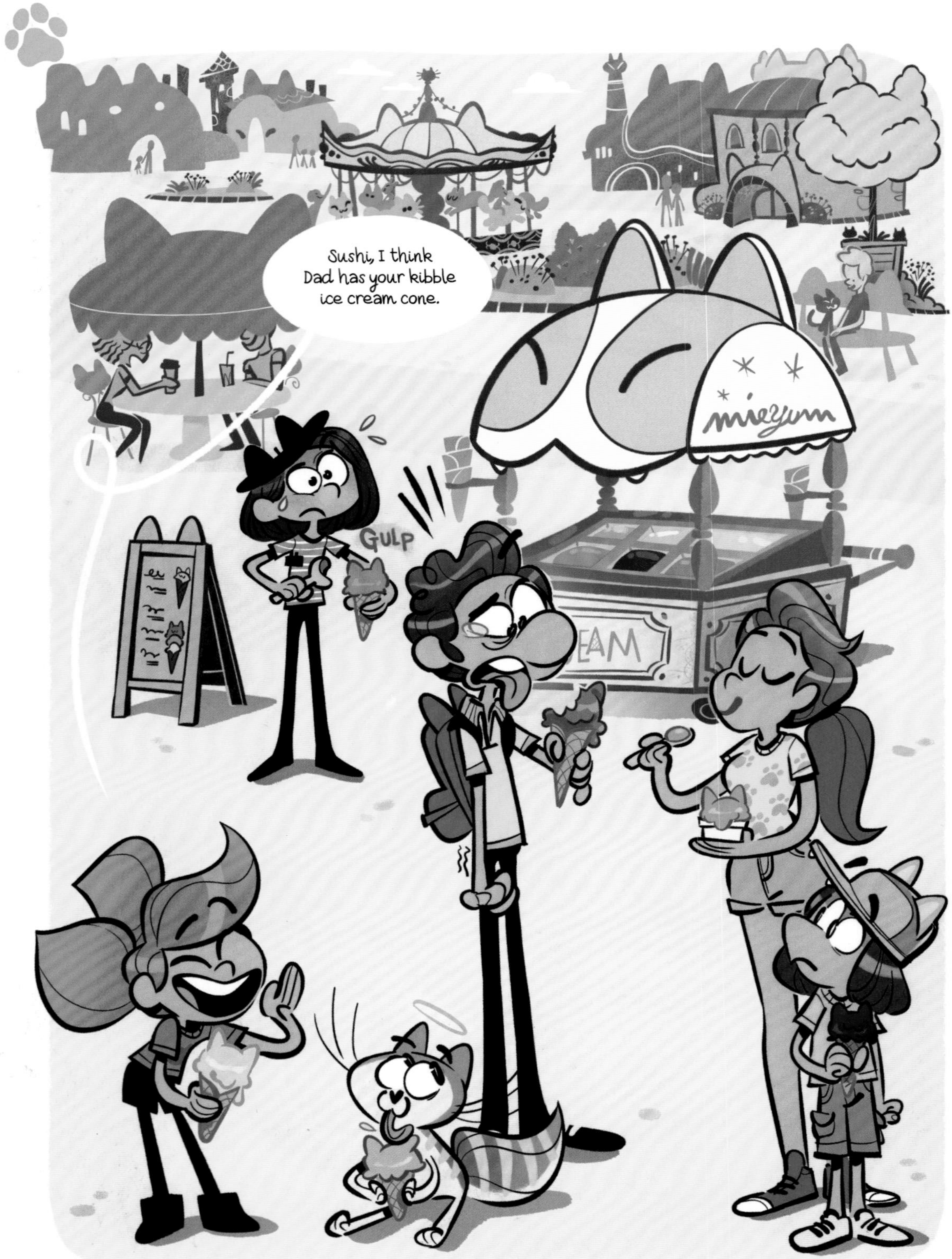
Sushi, I think Dad has your kibble ice cream cone.
GULP
mieyum
EAM

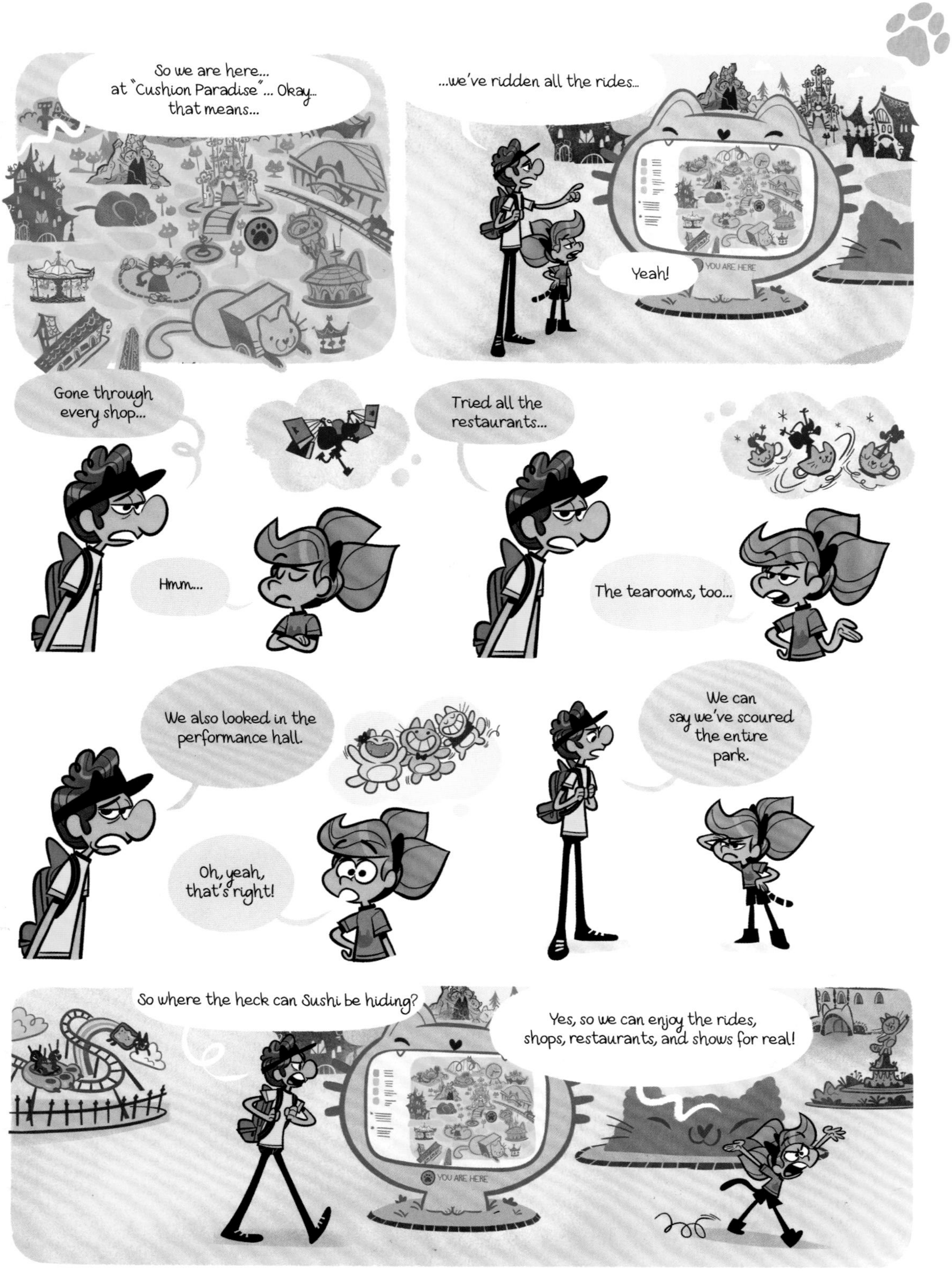

So we are here... at "Cushion Paradise"... Okay... that means...
...we've ridden all the rides...
YOU ARE HERE
Yeah!
Gone through every shop...
Hmm...
Tried all the restaurants...
The tearooms, too...
We also looked in the performance hall.
Oh, yeah, that's right!
We can say we've scoured the entire park.
So where the heck can Sushi be hiding?
YOU ARE HERE
Yes, so we can enjoy the rides, shops, restaurants, and shows for real!

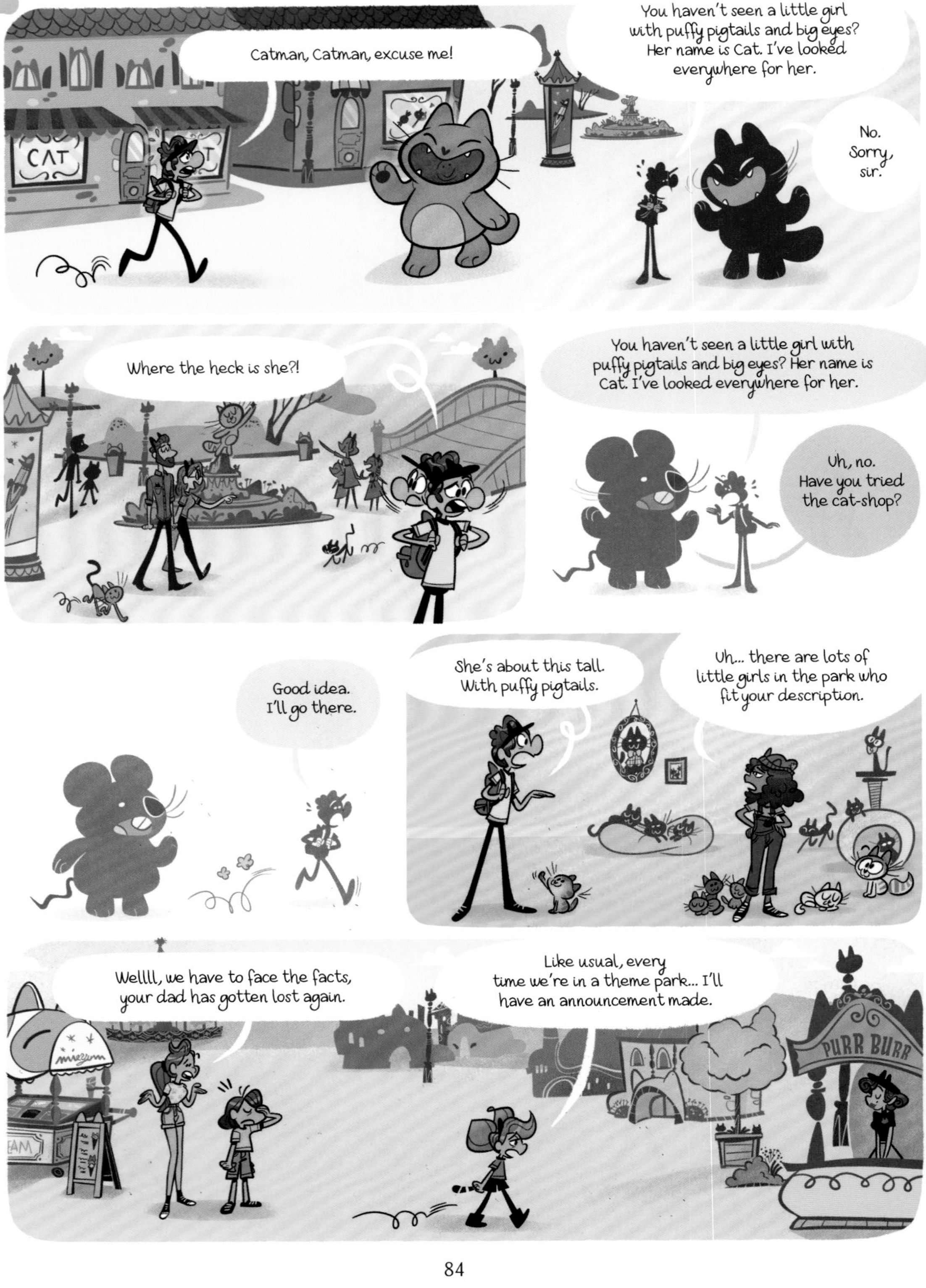
CAT
Catman, Catman, excuse me!
You haven't seen a little girl with puffy pigtails and big eyes? Her name is Cat. I've looked everywhere for her.
No. Sorry, sir.
Where the heck is she?!
You haven't seen a little girl with puffy pigtails and big eyes? Her name is Cat. I've looked everywhere for her.
Uh, no. Have you tried the cat-shop?
Good idea. I'll go there.
She's about this tall. With puffy pigtails.
Uh... there are lots of little girls in the park who fit your description.
Wellll, we have to face the facts, your dad has gotten lost again.
Like usual, every time we're in a theme park... I'll have an announcement made.
PURR BURR

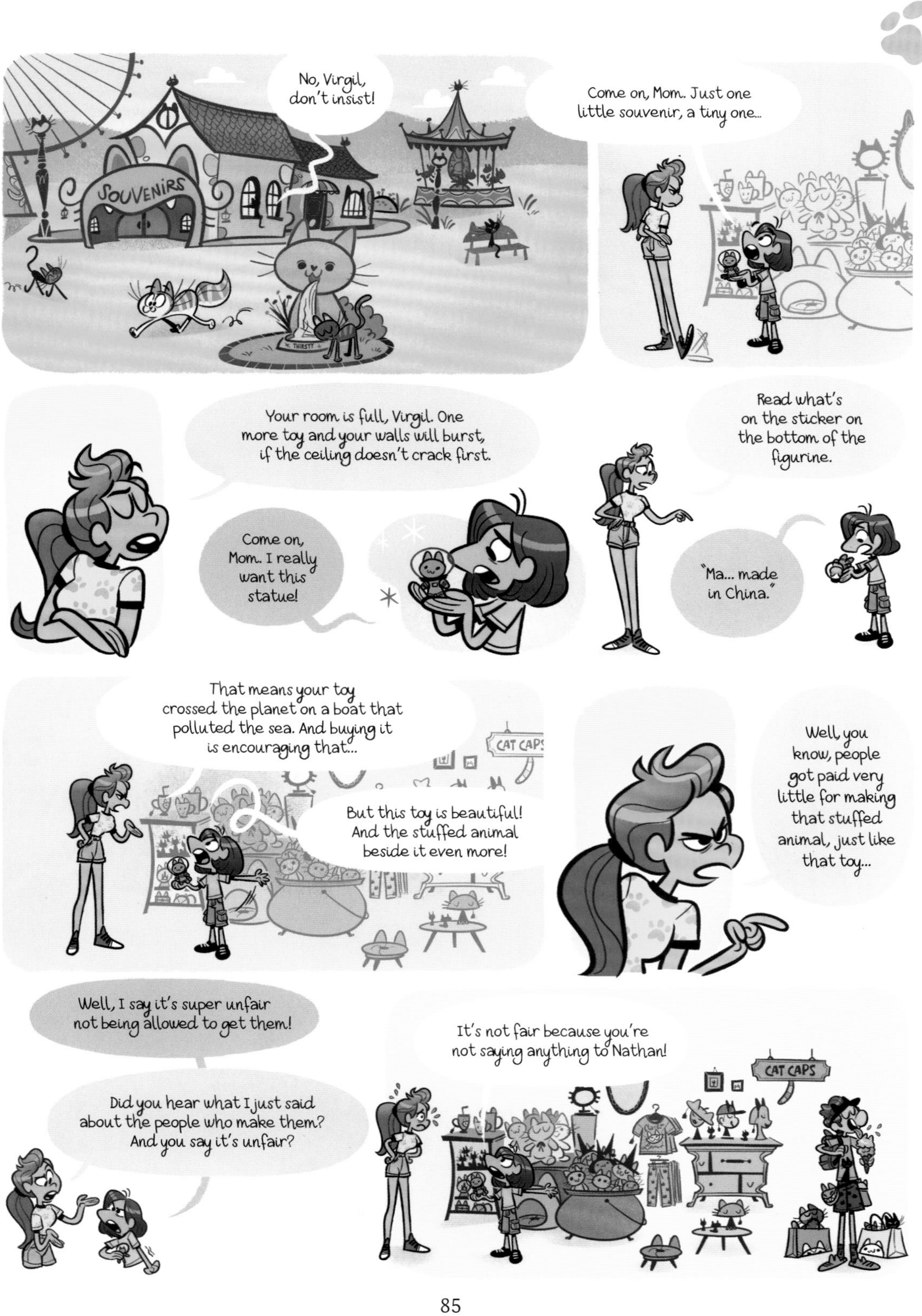

No, Virgil, don't insist!
SOUVENIRS
THIRSTY
Come on, Mom. Just one little souvenir, a tiny one...
Your room is full, Virgil. One more toy and your walls will burst, if the ceiling doesn't crack first.
Come on, Mom. I really want this statue!
Read what's on the sticker on the bottom of the figurine.
"Ma... made in China."
That means your toy crossed the planet on a boat that polluted the sea. And buying it is encouraging that...
CAT CAPS
But this toy is beautiful! And the stuffed animal beside it even more!
Well, you know, people got paid very little for making that stuffed animal, just like that toy...
Well, I say it's super unfair not being allowed to get them!
Did you hear what I just said about the people who make them? And you say it's unfair?
It's not fair because you're not saying anything to Nathan!
CAT CAPS

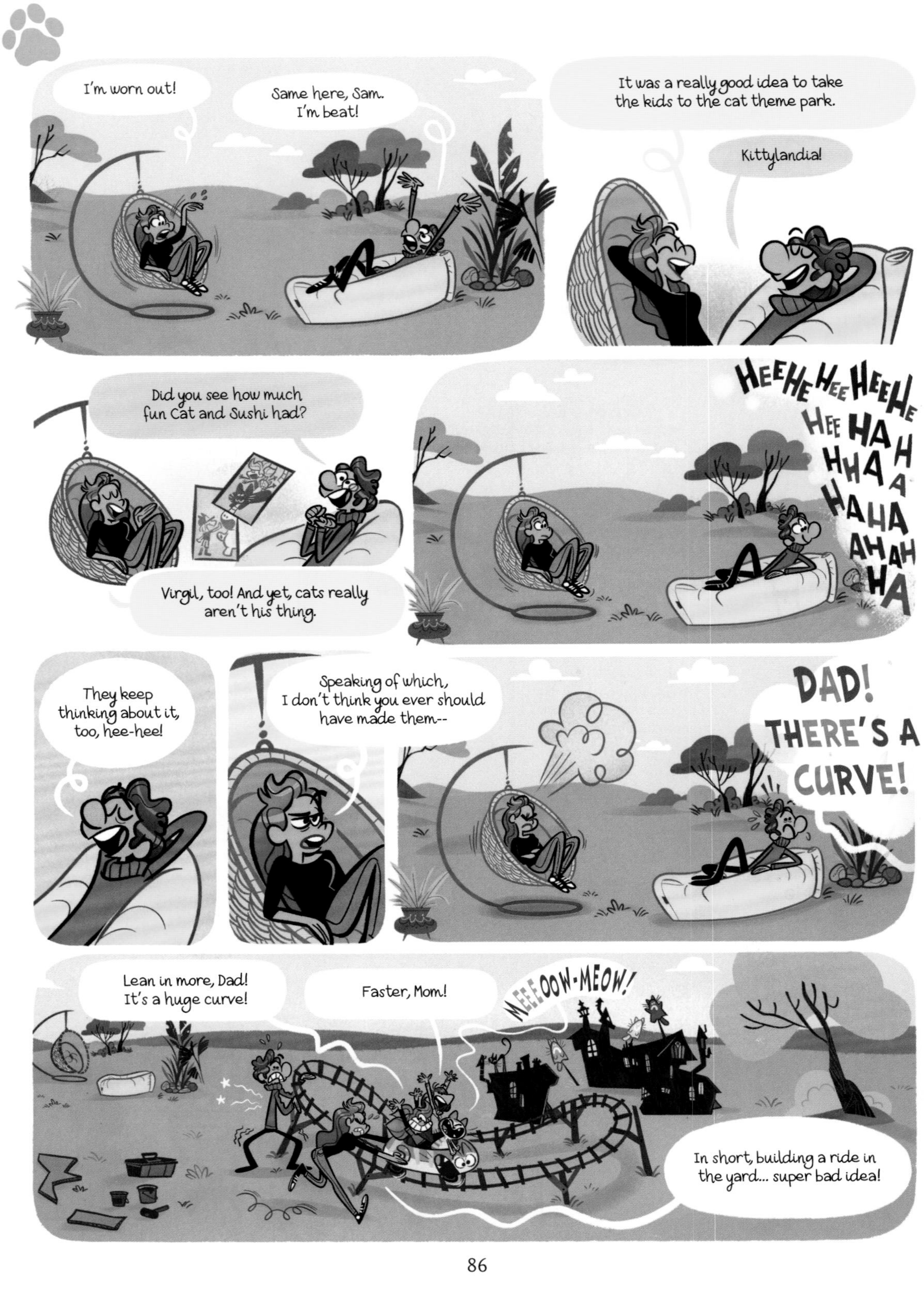
I'm worn out!
Same here, Sam. I'm beat!
It was a really good idea to take the kids to the cat theme park.
Kittylandia!
Did you see how much fun Cat and Sushi had?
Virgil, too! And yet, cats really aren't his thing.
HEEHE HEE HEEHE HEE HAH HHAA HAHA AHAH HA
They keep thinking about it, too, hee-hee!
Speaking of which, I don't think you ever should have made them--
DAD! THERE'S A CURVE!
Lean in more, Dad! It's a huge curve!
Faster, Mom!
MEEEOOW-MEOW!
In short, building a ride in the yard... super bad idea!

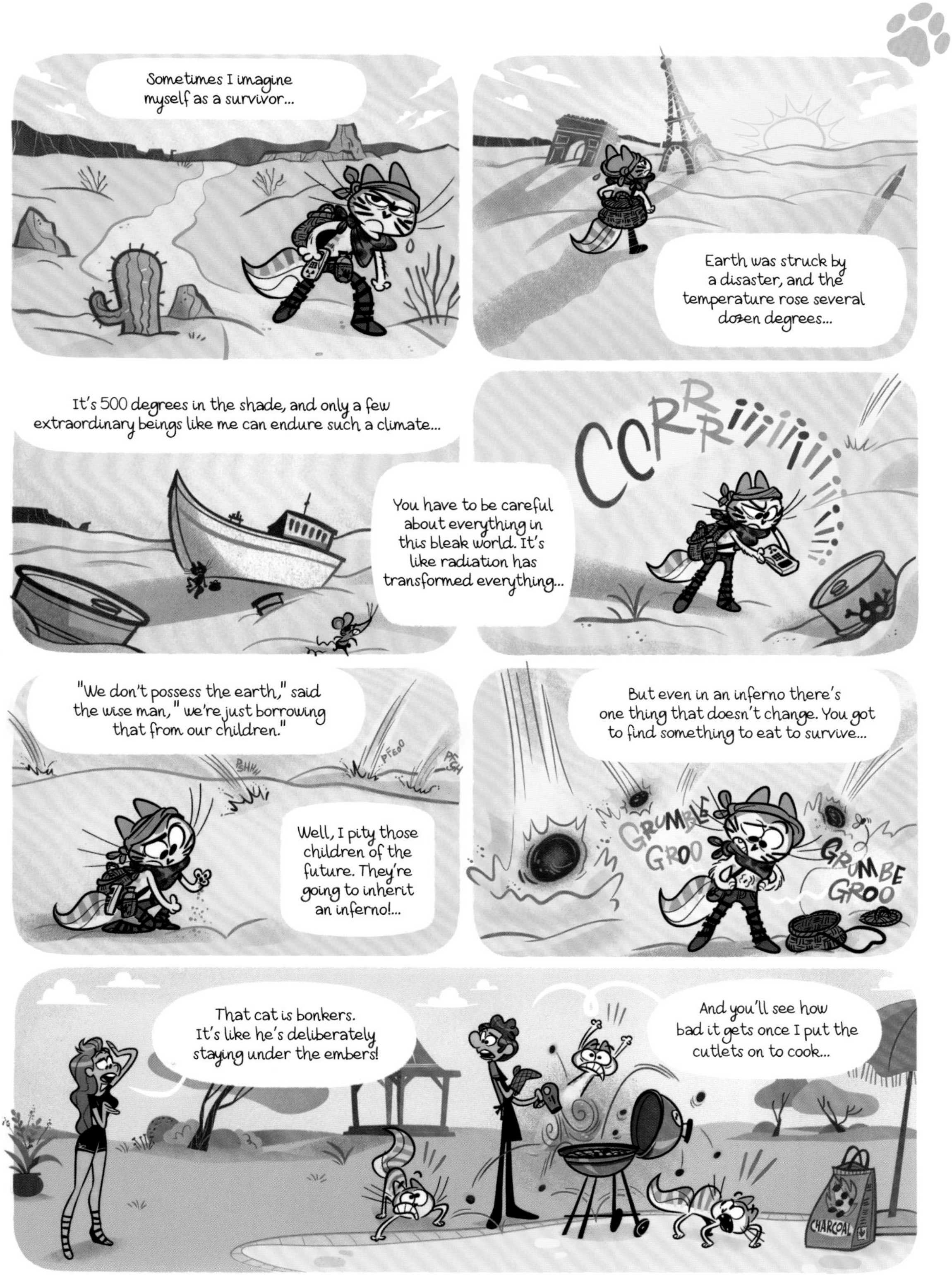

Sometimes I imagine myself as a survivor...
Earth was struck by a disaster, and the temperature rose several dozen degrees...
It's 500 degrees in the shade, and only a few extraordinary beings like me can endure such a climate...
You have to be careful about everything in this bleak world. It's like radiation has transformed everything...
CCRRRiiiiiiiiii
"We don't possess the earth," said the wise man, " we're just borrowing that from our children."
PSHH
PFEOO
PFSH
Well, I pity those children of the future. They're going to inherit an inferno!...
But even in an inferno there's one thing that doesn't change. You got to find something to eat to survive...
GRUMBLE GROO
GRUMBE GROO
That cat is bonkers. It's like he's deliberately staying under the embers!
And you'll see how bad it gets once I put the cutlets on to cook...
CHARCOAL

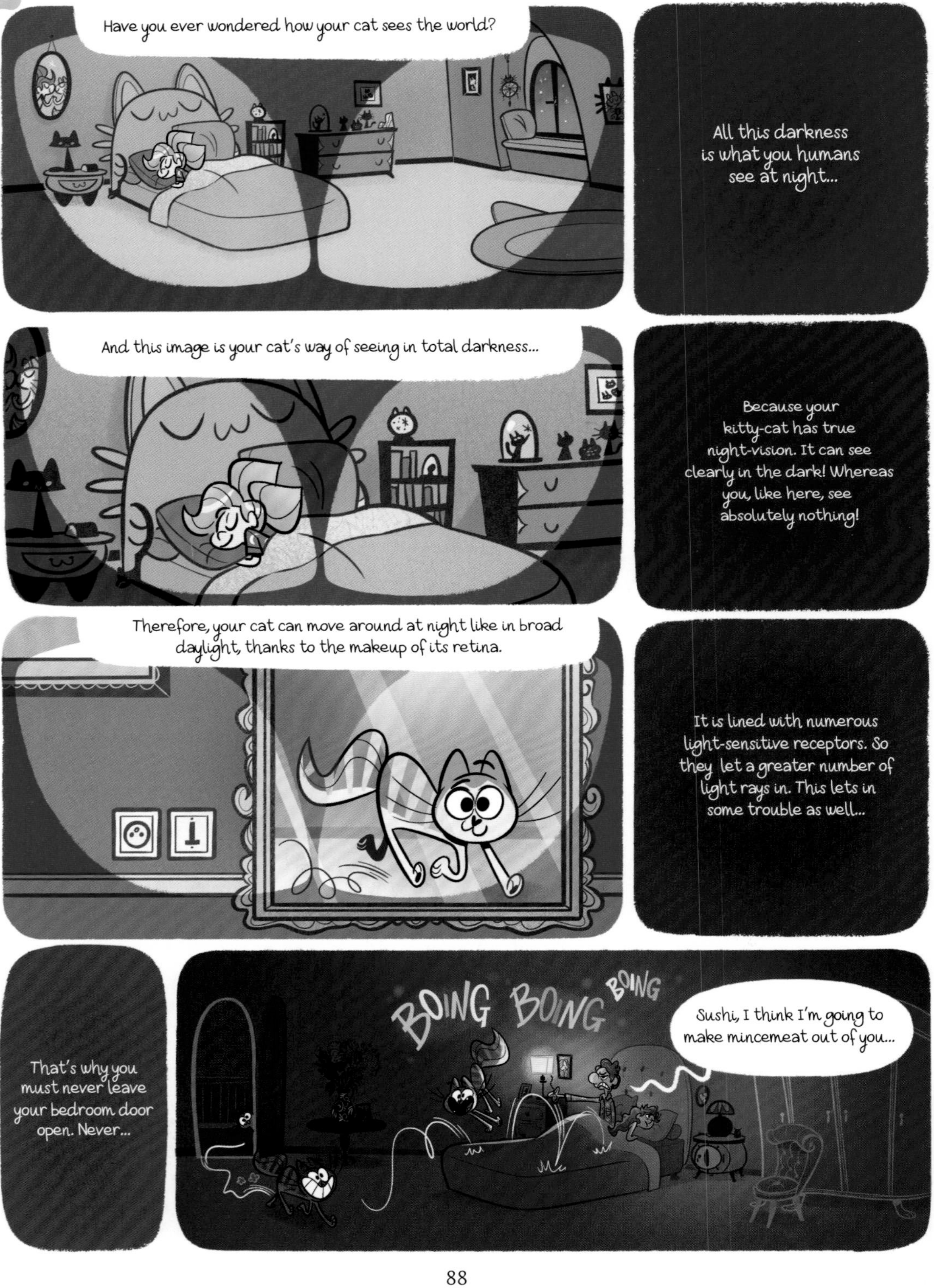
Have you ever wondered how your cat sees the world?
All this darkness is what you humans see at night...
And this image is your cat's way of seeing in total darkness...
Because your kitty-cat has true night-vision. It can see clearly in the dark! Whereas you, like here, see absolutely nothing!
Therefore, your cat can move around at night like in broad daylight, thanks to the makeup of its retina.
It is lined with numerous light-sensitive receptors. So they let a greater number of light rays in. This lets in some trouble as well...
That's why you must never leave your bedroom door open. Never...
BOING BOING BOING
Sushi, I think I'm going to make mincemeat out of you...

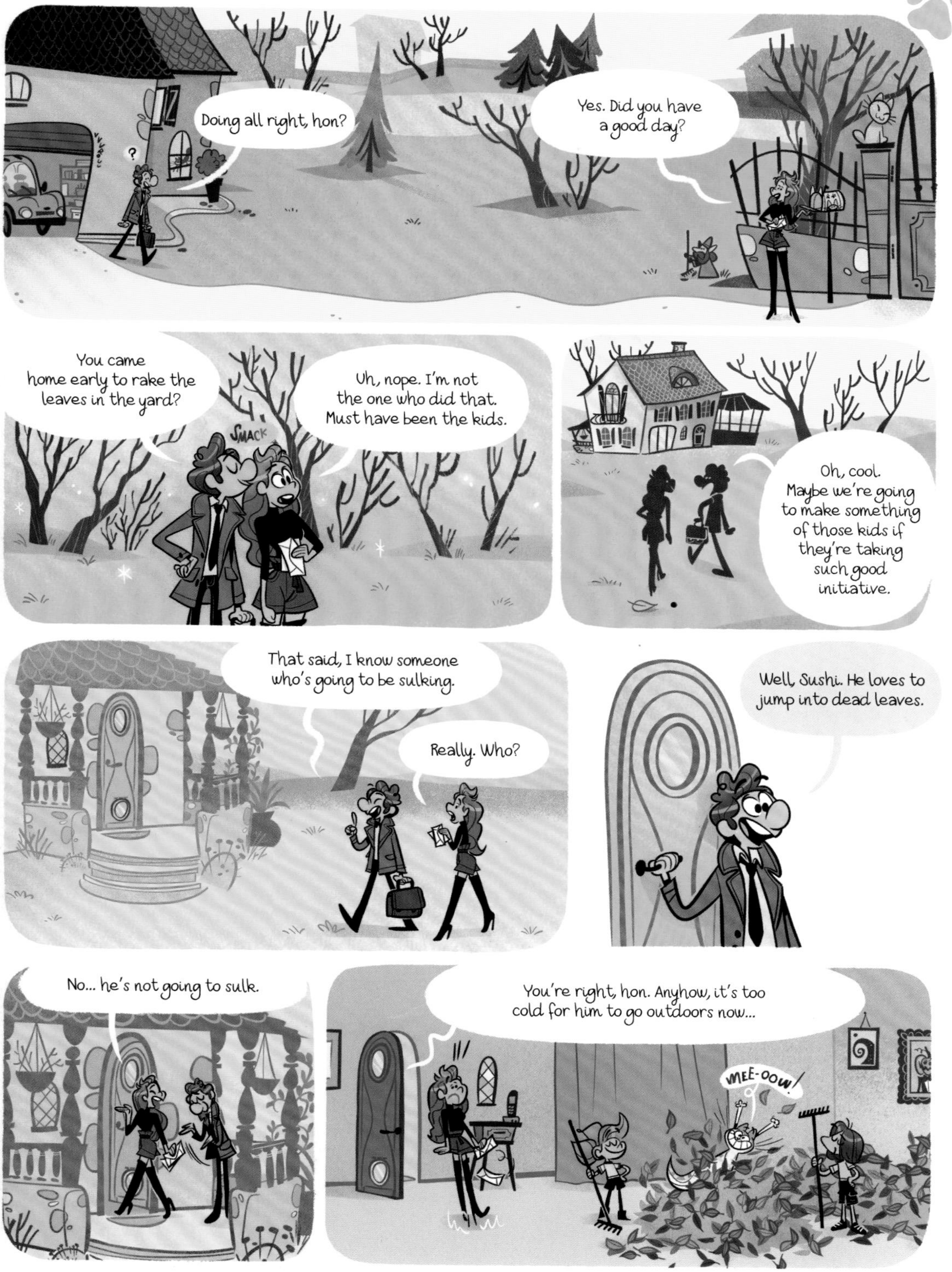
Doing all right, hon?
Yes. Did you have a good day?
You came home early to rake the leaves in the yard?
SMACK
Uh, nope. I'm not the one who did that. Must have been the kids.
Oh, cool. Maybe we're going to make something of those kids if they're taking such good initiative.
That said, I know someone who's going to be sulking.
Really. Who?
Well, Sushi. He loves to jump into dead leaves.
No... he's not going to sulk.
You're right, hon. Anyhow, it's too cold for him to go outdoors now...
MEE-OOW!

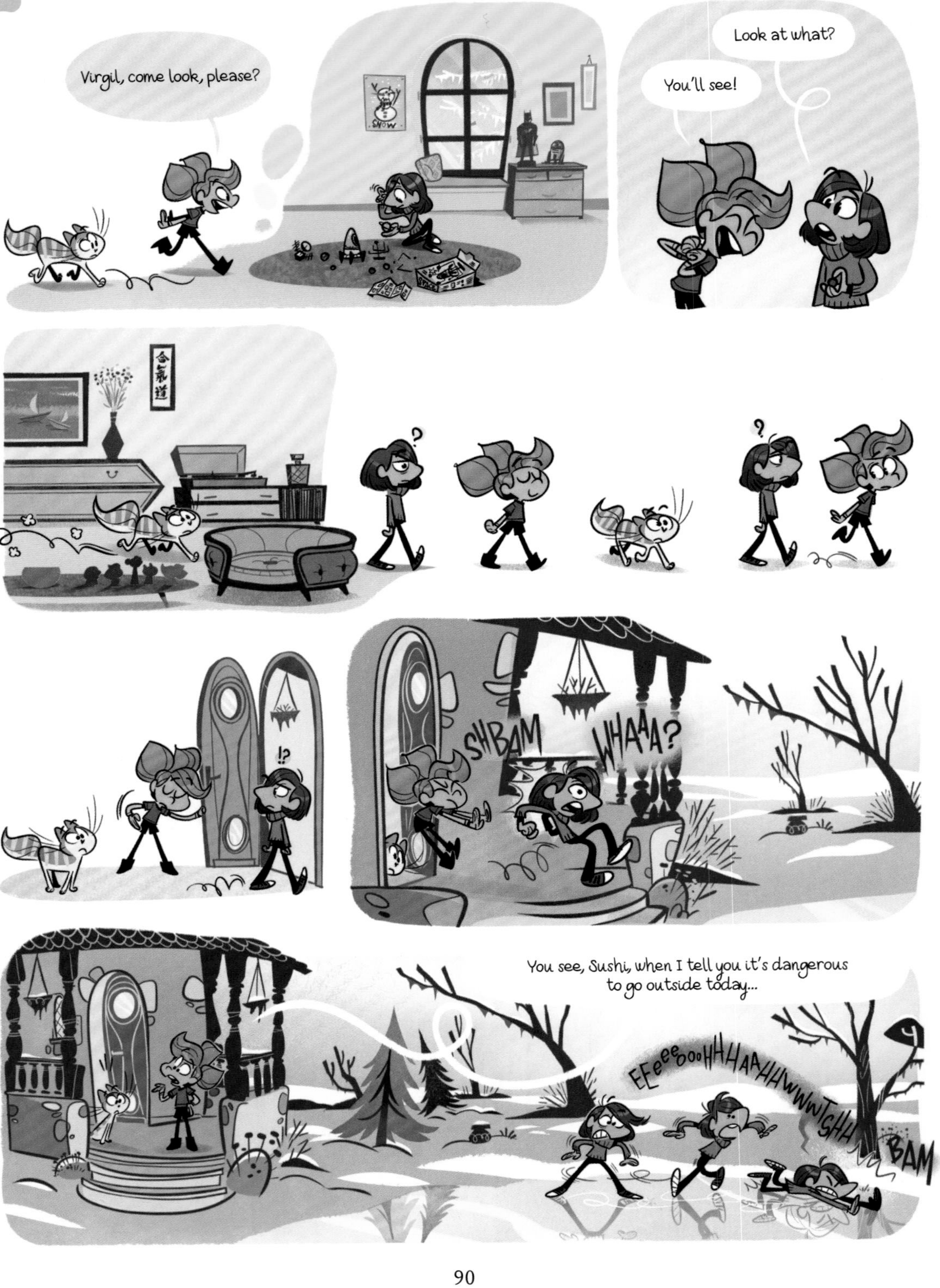
Virgil, come look, please?
Look at what?
You'll see!
?
?
!?
SHBAM
WHAAA?
You see, Sushi, when I tell you it's dangerous to go outside today...
EEeeeoooHHHAAHHWWWTGHH
BAM

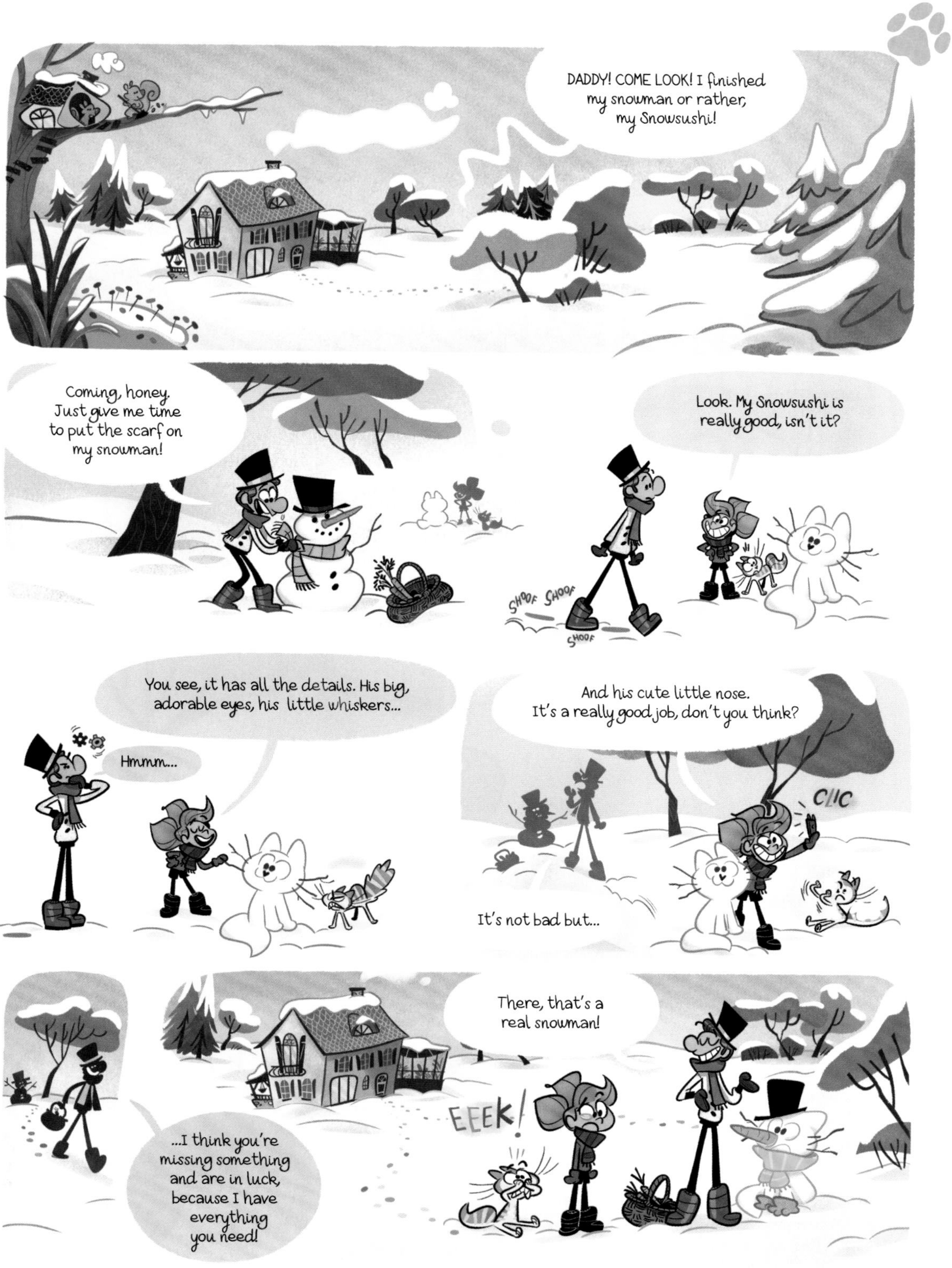
DADDY! COME LOOK! I finished my snowman or rather, my Snowsushi!
Coming, honey. Just give me time to put the scarf on my snowman!
Look. My Snowsushi is really good, isn't it?
SHOOF SHOOF
SHOOF
You see, it has all the details. His big, adorable eyes, his little whiskers...
Hmmm...
And his cute little nose. It's a really good job, don't you think?
CLIC
It's not bad but...
...I think you're missing something and are in luck, because I have everything you need!
There, that's a real snowman!
EEEK!

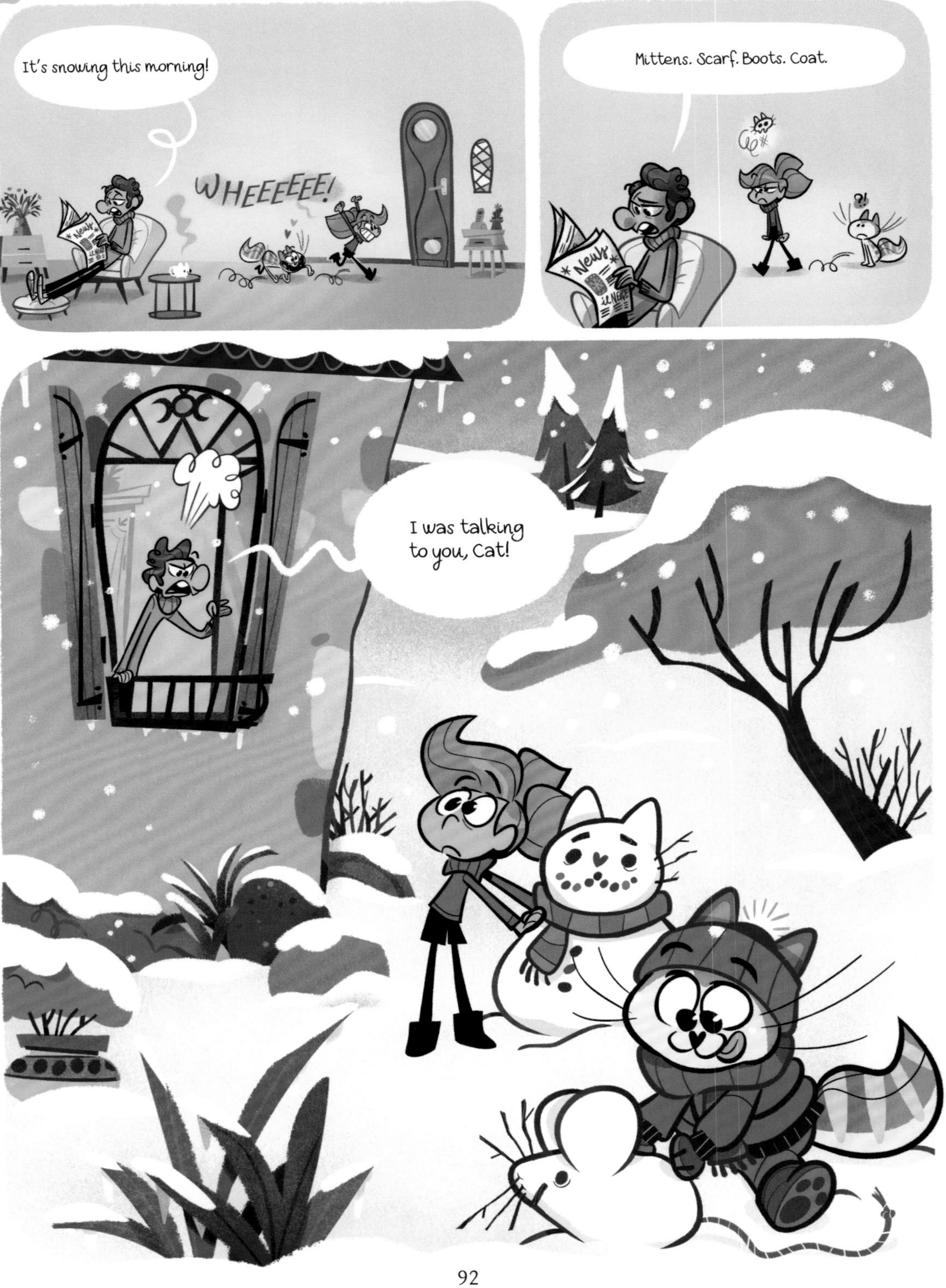
It's snowing this morning!
WHEEEEEE!
Mittens. Scarf. Boots. Coat.
I was talking to you, Cat!

# WATCH OUT FOR PAPERCUTZ

Welcome to the fear-fraught fourth CAT & CAT graphic novel by Christophe Cazenove and Hervé Richez, writers, and Yrgane Ramon, artist, from Papercutz, those fearless folks dedicated to publishing great graphic novels for all ages. I'm Jim Salicrup, Editor-in-Chief and a big fraidy cat, too!

Not long ago I rode the Wonder Wheel at Coney Island, and made the mistake of choosing the cars that swing while the big wheel goes round and round. Let me tell you—they should rename that ride the Terror Wheel, as far as I'm concerned. I'm not kidding. I was really scared as I rode what I thought was a "baby ride" because it seemed very likely I'd fall out of that ride, as it seemed very flimsy to me. It should be noted I left the ride totally safe and unharmed despite my fears.

That frightening experience came back to me when I recently read "What Goes Up" in THE LOUD HOUSE Summer Special #1 graphic novel from Papercutz, based on the hit Nickelodeon animated series. Lincoln Loud's friend Ronnie Anne Santiago goes to an amusement park with her dad, and even though he's terrified of many of the rides, he agrees to go on the Ferris wheel with her, and here's a peek at some of what happens...

BREATHE IN. BREATHE OUT.
THIS WAS MY FAVORITE RIDE WHEN I WAS LITTLE! I LOVE SEEING EVERYTHING FROM SO HIGH UP!
WE'RE HIGH UP, ALRIGHT.
SURE ARE! SEE THE ANIMAL BARN?

nickelodeon
THE LOUD HOUSE
SUMMER SPECIAL
PAPERCUTZ

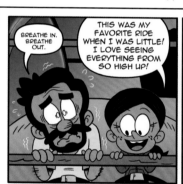

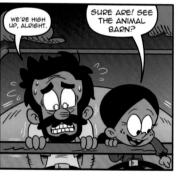

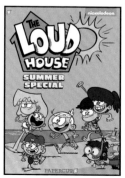

Be sure to get the full story in THE LOUD HOUSE Summer Special #1, available now at booksellers and libraries everywhere.

When Cat, her dad Nat, Sam, Virgil, and Sushi visit Kittylandia it doesn't really seem that scary, although note the only one scared on the cover is Nathan... Gee, do you suppose the title of this graphic novel is referring to him and not Sushi?

Kittylandia isn't the first crazy theme park to appear in a Papercutz graphic novel. Do you remember when Stephen Cling built Kakieland right next door to the HOTEL TRANSYLVANIA to drive them out, so that he could make it his own hotel for the theme park's guests? If not, just pick up either HOTEL TRANSYLVANIA #1 or HOTEL TRANSYLVANIA 3 IN 1 #1 for the full story. It features all your favorite monstrous characters from the hit film series in all-new stories that we're sure you'll enjoy.

Believe it or not there actually are several theme parks based on characters published by Papercutz. There are three (count 'em) Smurfs theme parks scattered around the world. And there's an Asterix theme park just north of Paris, France. There are Nickelodeon theme parks too, in the Mall of America and in New Jersey. But in a crazy way, I see Papercutz as a sort of theme park and each of our graphic novels is a fantastic ride. Whether it's the rollercoaster thrills of titles with larger-than-life characters such as DINOSAUR EXPLORERS and THE MYTHICS or the fun of such lovable characters such as THE FUZZY BASEBALL team (the Fernwood Valley Fuzzies) or THE GEEKY F@B 5, there's always lots of thrilling fun and excitement to be found in your favorite Papercutz graphic novels. Just check out the preview of the totally strange ATTACK OF THE STUFF "The Life and Times of Bill Waddler," preview on the following pages. This graphic novel, created by best-selling author Jim Benton, is guaranteed to be unlike any graphic novel you ever read before.

Thanks,
Jim

**STAY IN TOUCH!**

EMAIL: salicrup@papercutz.com
WEB: www.papercutz.com
TWITTER: @papercutzgn
INSTAGRAM: @papercutzgn
FACEBOOK: PAPERCUTZGRAPHICNOVELS
FANMAIL: Papercutz, 160 Broadway, Suite 700, East Wing, New York, NY 10038
Go to papercutz.com and sign up for the free Papercutz e-newsletter!

SPECIAL PREVIEW OF

# ATTACK OF THE STUFF

"The Life and Times of Bill Waddler"

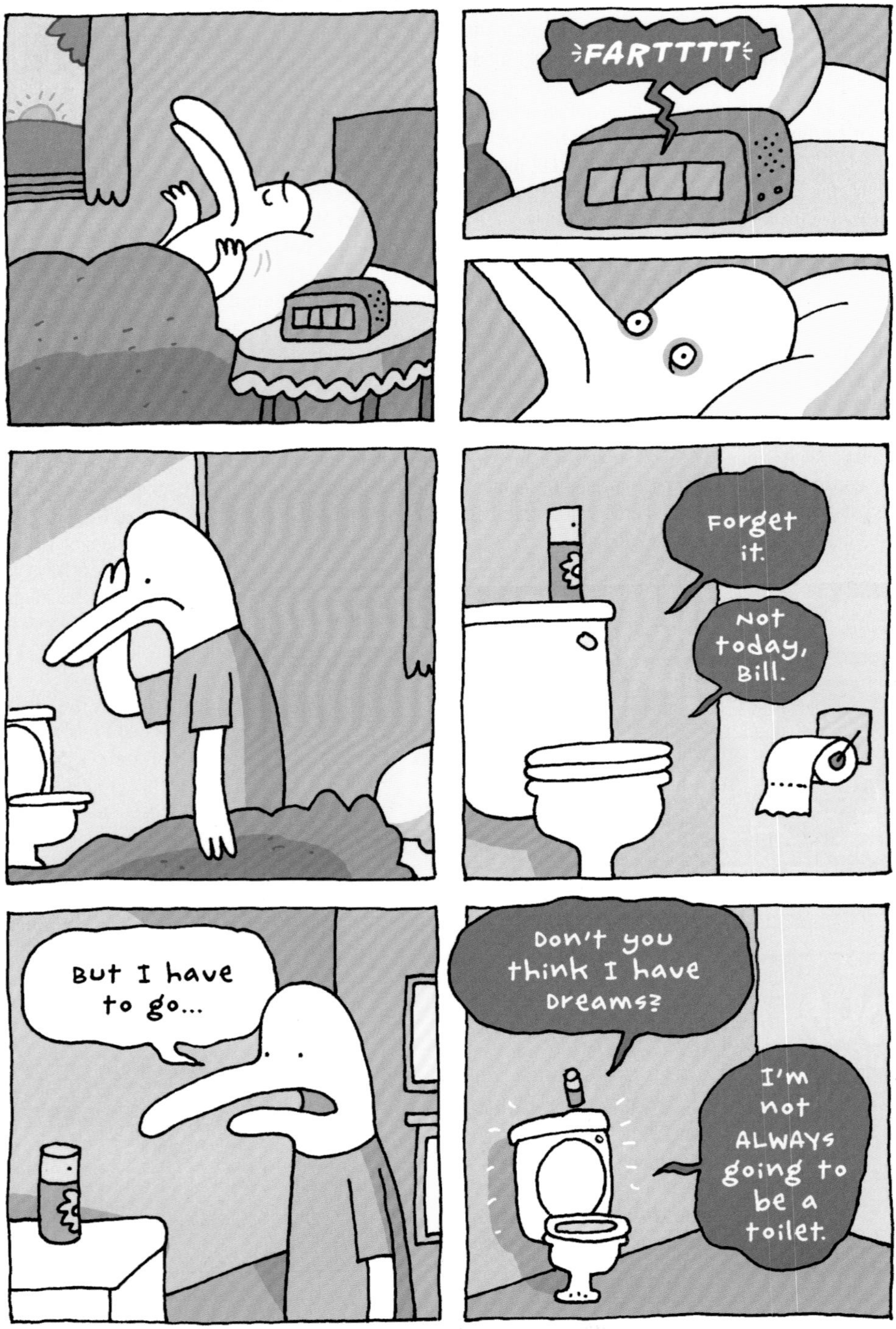

FARTTTT
Forget it.
Not today, Bill.
But I have to go...
Don't you think I have dreams?
I'm not ALWAYS going to be a toilet.

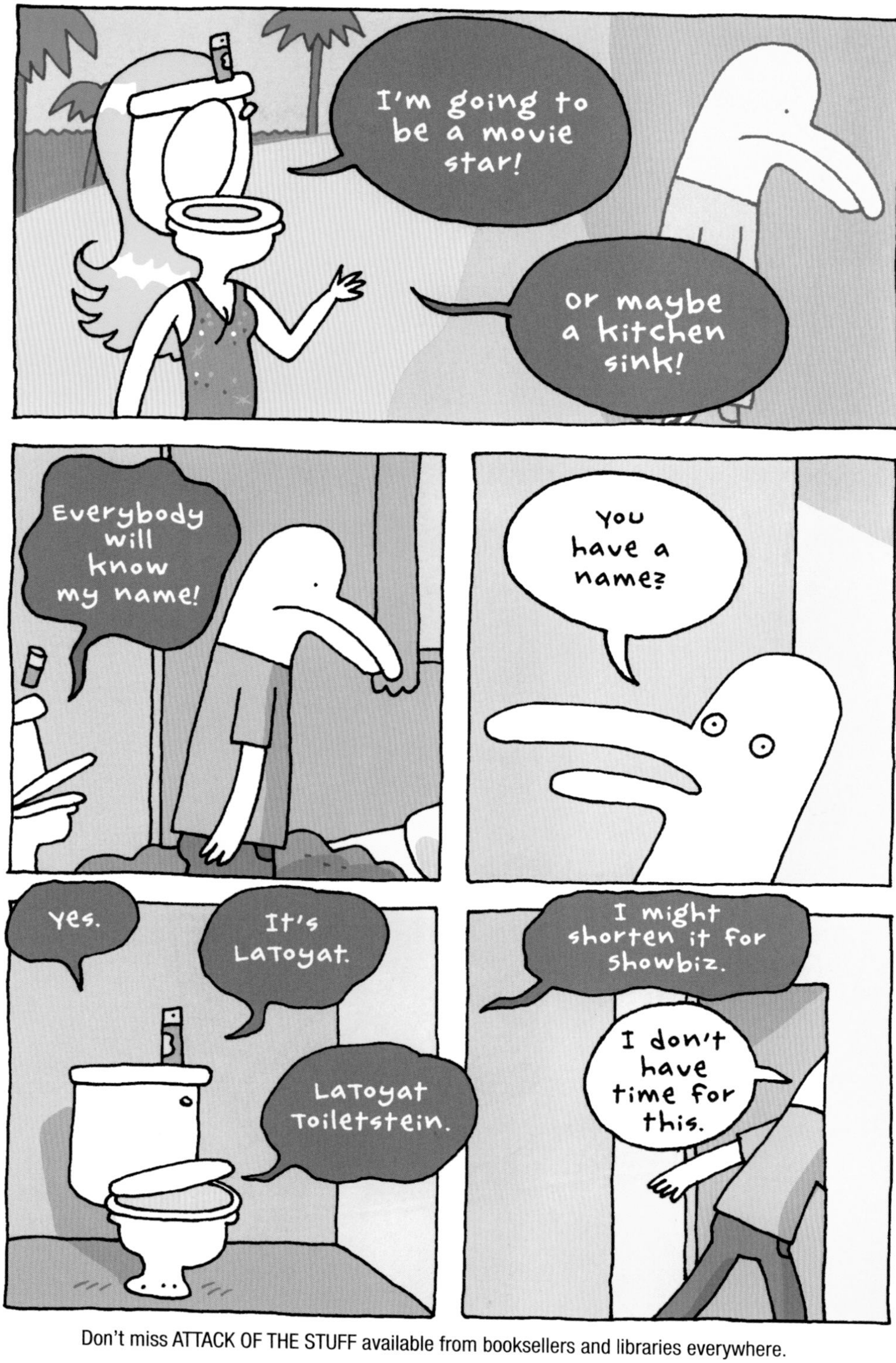
I'm going to be a movie star!
Or maybe a kitchen sink!
Everybody will know my name!
You have a name?
Yes.
It's LaToyat.
LaToyat Toiletstein.
I might shorten it for showbiz.
I don't have time for this.

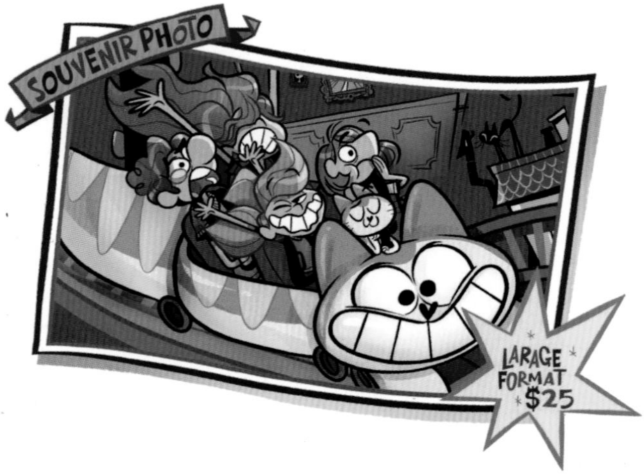
SOUVENIR PHOTO
LARAGE FORMAT $25